J. J. TABASCO'S DO-IT-YOURSELF DETECTIVE AGENCY

J. J. TABASCO'S DO-IT-YOURSELF DETECTIVE AGENCY

CARL MARTIN JOHNSON

SPARKPRESS

Published in 2026 by
SparkPress, an imprint of The Stable Book Group

32 Court Street, Suite 2109
Brooklyn, NY 11201
https://gosparkpress.com
The Library of Congress Control Number is available upon request.
ISBN: 978-1-68463-346-3
eISBN: 978-1-68463-347-0

Interior Designer: Tabitha Lahr

Printed in the United States

For Patricia Johnson and Celia Blue Johnson

PROLOGUE

Of course, I didn't know the body I found was the first victim because I didn't know there would be any more victims. Serial killings are not normal in Cancún, and I had no idea this poor fellow was the first of many. But that's not right either, since a medical examiner had already determined that he died of a self-ingested fentanyl overdose, and he had even been embalmed. His lifeless body was propped upright against the fence on the major road turning into downtown Cancún. In front of him was a cardboard and papier-mâché model of some sort of castle. He was posed to convey a kind of message, but it took us a long time to figure it out.

I'd been playing poker with some friends and it was well into the small night hours when my headlights swept over the corpse. The sight shocked the hell out of me. It took me a while to work up the nerve to approach the man. I mean, he looked dead, all right. All made up for a funeral. I called my police buddy, Chief of Police Octavio "Tavi" Fuentes. He'd been playing cards with me, so he was still awake.

Tavi pulled up at the head of a three-car procession, lights flashing, but no sirens. A Puccini opera was blasting from his sound system when he opened his door. He was an opera fan of the worst kind. He drove me and his police force crazy with the constant devotion to all the most famous tenors, from Caruso to Pavarotti to Domingo. The only vacation he ever treated his long-suffering wife to was to the great opera houses of the world, and he made her endure abject penury while he saved for these sacred musical pilgrimages.

He turned off his sound and stepped out of his car. He waved at me and stuck oversized plugs in each of his ears. I shouted at him as he approached.

"Tavi! Would you please take those damned plugs out of your ears?!"

He bent toward me and shook his head uncomprehendingly. I reached out and pulled the plug out of his left ear.

"Tavi, how can I talk to you with those things in!"

He snatched the stopper I'd retrieved but didn't reinsert it. "I must protect my ears in case I have to shoot somebody. My eardrums are delicate instruments of operatic appreciation. I can't risk their injury."

"You've never shot anyone, OK."

"Oh, yes, my friend. But there is always a first time." He walked carefully up to the corpse.

I followed closely. "I didn't touch anything. He was very dead when I caught him in my headlights."

Tavi yelled to his cops to canvass the area for clues and set up security tape. He turned to me. "Jaime Meyer."

"From the Jewish Meyer family?"

"Yes. Very important people in Cancún." He leaned forward to touch the white cotton dressing gown that covered the body. "Dry." He looked back at me. "Put here after last night's rain."

"But why?"

"I don't know. He only died yesterday. Drug overdose according to the medical report. His family is heartbroken."

"Maybe you should call the morgue and see how he was stolen."

"I agree."

The Chief called me the next day to let me know the corpse theft looked to have been an act of vandalism, perhaps even anti-Semitism. The Meyer family received solemn assurances from the mayor and police that they would get to the bottom of the matter and punish the perpetrators. But we all knew that wasn't likely. After a few days, the case rarely crossed my mind, in spite of the fact that it was the most unusual criminal occurrence I had ever seen.

A week later, my agency was hired for a lucrative and interesting case that put the dead Meyer case out of my mind completely, for a while.

CHAPTER 1

The fat man wasn't dead, at least as far as I knew. I should have killed him, but I didn't. The Indians didn't either. That surprised me.

I didn't like getting shot at. It wasn't the first time, but that doesn't mean I was used to it. I don't think of myself as a coward, just a person with a keen desire for self-preservation. So getting myself into a situation where someone was trying to kill me was cause for serious self-examination. A quote popped into my mind: "The human race is a race of cowards, and I am not only marching in that procession but carrying a banner." I have an extensive memory of useless and often irrelevant quotes, but I'm not great when it comes to remembering the sources. I think that one belongs to Mark Twain, though. Years ago, a girlfriend told me, "You couldn't conceive an original thought if you emerged from the womb of the goddess of wisdom herself." Hurtful, but on the mark, I guess.

Jayde was good-looking. OK, she was a knockout. One smile and I was on her leash. You know, beauty is an outward gift, which is seldom despised, except by those to whom it has been refused. Don't know who said that, but you can see what I mean about the quote thing.

I'd better start from the beginning.

❋ ❋ ❋

I have a small but not thriving business on the Mexican coast. Cancún. I chose a place outside my native country because "friends" in the FBI let me know my recent activities in Central America could lead to an enforced stay in federal housing of the less pleasant kind. I think that would be wholly unjustified, but I never underestimate the stupidity of the federal bureaucracy. Anyway, I accepted the recommendation that I stay outside my homeland's borders until there is a change in administration or the powers that be simply forget about me. I hate to admit it, but I'm a very little fish.

I came up with an ingenious—if I do say so myself—way of making a living, albeit a bare living, without violating Mexican private investigator licensing laws, thus enabling me (with a little bribery) to stay in the country and avoid starvation. I set up a "Do-It-Yourself" detective agency. You may wonder how a guy who speaks only passing Spanish finds clients in Mexico. Well, like they say about real estate, it's all about location. Cancún has lots of people passing through, and many of them are American or at least speak English. I have all the cabbies in town on "finder's fee." If they hear a fare complain about a situation that calls for investigation, the cabbie hands over my card.

I get a lot of requests to recover stolen property—jewelry and the like. And a fair amount of matrimonial indiscretion—guys down here with their secretaries, women with their personal trainers. And I tell them how to use their computer to find out what they want to know. Most of what investigators do, I've learned, can be done on a computer. So I sit with my clients and we search the internet. Through a friend in the US who can bust any conceivable security system, I can get my hands on any hotel registration and room information in Cancún or anywhere, really. I can find out who checked in with whom and whether those names check out with Mexican immigration records. Of course, the good old cash incentive to hotel staff works well, too.

Stolen jewelry, credit cards, and so on are a little different. On those cases, I work with the local fences. Sometimes the goods are redeemed by the owners, sometimes not. I leave that bargaining up to the clients if they're contacted by the thieves. But I don't give them my contacts, or I'd have no deals. They just need to decide whether it's worth paying ransom or better to leave it to their insurance.

But in all cases, I only instruct the client. I don't handle the deal myself. This keeps me clean. (Although I may stretch this requirement from time to time, if I feel like taking a chance.) One time an undercover cop busted me for actually searching the net myself, and he hit me for a big mordida. So I just sit beside clients and let them use their own laptop, notepad, or smartphone or whatever. Thus the name "J.J. Tabasco's Do-It-Yourself Detective Agency." Catchy, right?

My junior partner is a handsome guy by the name of Jesús "Jesse" María Obregón, who, despite his namesakes, is almost completely amoral. That's OK with me. Morals can be a handicap in my line of work. But Jesse is on a constant quest for self-improvement.

Despite the fact that it's hotter than hell, Jesse wears cowboy boots. And he usually wears short-sleeved shirts and loose slacks. I wear sandals and polo shirts, mainly, and cargo pants because the side pockets are handy for carrying my phone and notebook.

Okay, no more stalling. I'll tell you about the woman, an explanation I've been avoiding because it's going to expose me for the sucker I am.

From what I could tell, she was a natural blonde, with shoulder-length hair that looked wildly groomed, for lack of a better description. In fact "wildly groomed" described nearly everything about her. She managed to be regal and erotic just sitting in a chair across from me.

She got my name and address from one of my commissioned cabbies. I couldn't imagine why a woman of her obvious class needed a low-life investigator, but I don't look gift horses in the mouth, and this filly was a gift for the eyes.

"Mr. Tabasco . . ."

"JJ is fine, ma'am."

"Jayde. With a *y* after the *a*. Jayde Olivia Blackwood."

I had a reddish-brown caterpillar crawling across my upper lip. I was trying to cultivate a "Latin lover" look. Jesse had that look without a moustache. But I wasn't Jesse. I tore myself away from the mirror framed on the back of my office door, resigned to the fact that I was no more than ruggedly handsome . . . and that might be stretching it.

I turned sideways, trying to find something in my appearance that would build my confidence. I'm five ten, not tall. I wasn't fat yet, but I was a year short of thirty, so at that point, who knew what the future held. I worked out occasionally, but I wasn't Olympic material. So I knew if I didn't win a woman like Jayde with my razor wit and gentle charm, I didn't stand a chance. But I was happy to take her on as a client because I really needed the money, although I felt a little guilty (not very) for taking her money. I had a standard fee of $300 a day US, and she plunked down a week's worth in cash, then started telling me what she wanted. I muttered a lame protest about not needing so much money up front but let it wither away as I shoveled the cash into my desk drawer, trying to hide my enthusiasm for getting a customer who could actually pay. Then I tried to appear to listen respectfully while silently deciding which of my overdue bills to pay first.

"I'm being followed," she whispered.

"I see," I replied, feigning interest.

"I'm frightened."

"I see."

"I don't know what to do."

"I see." This is my standard reply to clients. Lets them feel understood when I don't have a clue.

"That's why I came to see you, Mr. Tabasco. I mean JJ."

"Sure, go on."

"Someone is following me, and I want you to find out who it is."

Any man with a libido would follow her. But I figured I'd better narrow it down by asking the reason.

"I don't know," she answered. "I want you to find that out too."

She had a kind of sexy innocence I was sure would make any man slay dragons for her. A teasing golden lock fell over her eye and she brushed it away with a casual sweep of her hand. I must have been caught staring.

"Oh," she said, covering her left hand with her right. "An accident, years ago."

I nodded without comment. The little finger was gone, almost. Down to the knuckle. Well, as the saying goes, a bit of imperfection only accentuates true beauty. Something like that. I tore my eyes away and tried hard to give her my full attention.

"It will prey on your mind until your curiosity is satisfied, so I will tell you now and be done with it." She smiled indulgently. "I shot it off."

Wow! I wasn't expecting that.

"I reached into my purse for a small nine-millimeter I used to carry, safety off, and pulled it out by the trigger. It got stuck and I was panicking, so I clawed it out with both hands. *Bam!* Finger gone."

"I . . . I . . ."

"I stopped the fellow coming at me, though. That was years ago."

I was sure I looked like an idiot, but she just grinned at my discomfiture. I wondered if she was just having me on.

"Well, I . . . I . . ." I stammered again. "Let's see where we can . . ." I took hold of my pen and made ready to note-take. "First of all, what does this person look like?"

"I don't know. I haven't exactly seen him."

"I see." My fallback again. I waited for her to continue. When she didn't, I said, "Can you give my any information about this man at all? Or woman?"

"No."

I tapped my pad nervously with my pen. "Aha. Then, can you tell me what makes you think you're being followed."

"I just have a feeling."

"A feeling?"

"You know, a kind of creepiness that makes the little hairs on your arm stand up, not always, just sometimes."

I nodded. Neither of us spoke for a long minute.

"I see." Yes, that again.

"I knew you would understand, JJ. You have a sympathetic face."

Her smile melted me. But I had to say it. "Miss, I mean, Jayde. I don't know how to put this exactly." I rubbed my nose. I always do that when I'm nervous. "Have you ever thought about maybe, ah, well, some medical advice?"

Her face went from angry to hurt. "I am not imagining things! You must believe me. I really need help!" I felt small.

My cell phone rang. "Texas Fight." My alma mater's fight song. I was pretty sure it was the only cell tune like that in this part of the world. Maybe not. It was a client, and I'd have time to think. I answered, "JJ."

"Señor Tabasco, you promised to call me every Monday."

Señora Lupita Alvarez. Her husband left town almost thirty years ago, and she wanted me to get him back. Oh, God.

"I'm so sorry, Señora Alvarez," I lied. "But I have nothing new to report." That part was true.

"That disappoints me, Señor Tabasco. Disappoints me greatly. You know I am an abandoned woman. I want him brought back to his responsibility, to me."

"Yes, Señora, you have been terribly wronged. I agree."

"Please treat my case with urgency, Señor Tabasco!"

"Yes, ma'am. Remember, I can only show you what to do."

"I will come in tomorrow. Please be available."

"Yes, I will . . ." She hung up. I smiled sheepishly at Jayde. "A client." (Señora Alvarez did come in the next day, but only to fire me.)

Jayde picked up where I'd interrupted her. "So, will you help me? Please."

What could I do? I was smitten. I paused a minute for effect. "I'll try." I tapped my pen against the writing pad, trying to look professional. "First, I'll go over how I operate. It's probably not what you're used to."

"I'm not used to anything. Nobody else has agreed to help me." She rose briefly then sat back down. It looked like she was going to kiss me in gratitude but second-guessed herself.

Jesse barged in without knocking, as usual. Jayde gave him a quick but appreciative once-over. He returned the look. "Oh, I am so sorry." No he wasn't. "I did not know you had a client."

I introduced them, then felt a little sick as he took her hand and kissed it like a silent movie star. But I was still glad he came in. I didn't know if this beautiful woman was crazy, and he could help me figure it out.

"Jesse, this lady suspects someone is following her."

"Of course. Any man who would not—"

"No, Jesse." I sighed. "We need to find out if what she suspects is true or not."

"I see," Jesse said. He was learning.

I told the lovely Jayde that Jesse would shadow her for a few days, and I urged her to just go about her business as if she were a typical tourist. I should have made clear what I meant by "typical tourist."

CHAPTER 2

I don't think I have much of a command presence. My clients regularly ignore what I tell them to do. Not only did Jayde not act like an ordinary, well-behaved tourist, she slunk around her hotel like a woman who was sure she was being followed. Jesse told me that she looked over her shoulder every few steps and on her single trip to the hotel restaurant. For the rest of the next two days she stayed in her room alone and ordered room service. That is definitely not what a normal tourist in Cancún would do. Who flies to a beach resort and isolates herself? That reminded me I didn't know enough of her background. I decided I should give her a visit.

I waited too long.

The room was trashed. I expected to find blood spatters on the wall. But I didn't. The clothes and makeup from her drawers were dumped onto the floor. I didn't close the door behind me in case I had to run. I reached for a gun, which I didn't have. Carrying in Mexico puts you behind bars with people who may not love gringos like me.

I backed into the hallway and ran to the elevator. I didn't know what was happening, but I knew it wasn't good. I was worried about my client but even more worried about myself. While I banged on the elevator door, I called my partner.

"Jesse, what the hell happened?!"

He answered with his "you just woke me up" voice. "Qué pasa, jefe?"

"Where's our client?"

"Which one?"

"*Jayde*, the blonde who says she's being followed."

"I don't know."

"You were supposed to tail her."

"Don't worry, JJ. I'll keep an eye on her. She's probably just crazy."

"You *didn't* keep an eye on her. And now she's gone!"

"Híjole, well . . ."

"Never mind. Get back here to her hotel and do some digging."

"OK. But I have a bit of gossip for you."

"What?"

"Have you heard of Aureliano Buendía?

"Rings a bell, maybe. Why?"

"He is jefe of the Río Seco cartel."

"Mexico has more cartels than stars in the sky. What the hell does it have to do with us?"

"My sources tell me he will be making a move to set up an operation in Cancún."

"Well, we'll stay out of his way. Now get over here, please."

"I'll be there in five."

I hung up. I'd be lucky if he showed up before midnight. I called Jayde. No answer. I didn't leave a message. I'd keep calling until I got her.

I sprinted through the hotel lobby in a hurry to get to my car. I don't know where I thought I was rushing. Just nervous, I guess. Then it crossed my mind that I'd already been paid, so I slowed up.

That was the first time I saw the fat man. He was wearing a white linen suit, white shirt with a thin black tie, white shoes and socks, and a white panama hat with a black hat band, continuously wiping the sweat from his face with a handkerchief the size of a small bath towel. He walked into the lobby leading a huge iguana on a red leash. I paused only briefly at the sight, though it was a truly bizarre scene. Fat men leading lizards is not something I had much experience with. The man looked like a jolly Santa Claus in tropical drag. How he got the iguana to keep up with his hurried pace was a phenomenon I would have paused to consider in other circumstances. But for now I had to find my client.

I waited at the entry to the hotel's circular drive until Jesse pulled up. His sheepish grin told me he knew he'd screwed up. This was a guy used to getting a pass on screwups because people, particularly women, were hypnotized by his handsomeness. Men were jealous sometimes, and luckily for Jesse, he was also big, strong, and a quick-reflexed fighter. But he avoided altercations, which made those who didn't know him suspect he might be a bit . . . cowardly, which he wasn't.

But he was a screwup. And he'd lost our client. Even though I didn't know if she was in danger, I felt a responsibility, which I sometimes do. Maybe it was because she was a looker, or maybe I just had an uncharacteristic twinge of conscience. Whatever the reason, I resolved to find her.

As I walked down the hotel steps, I passed an elderly woman holding a tiny Chihuahua. She was crowned by a flame-red hairdo, stacked stiff and high. She looked directly at me and nodded with a knowing smile. She seemed to know me, but I was almost certain I'd never seen her before. She would surely have stuck in my mind. I was left with an odd feeling, but I "what the helled" it and carried on.

❋ ❋ ❋

I asked Jesse to take us to a café that catered to locals, meaning they charged what non-tourists could afford. I ordered a kind of Mexican hamburger, loaded with jalapeños and sauce that'd eat out your stomach if you weren't careful. Jesse just had a coffee. While we sat there, I tried to lay out a plan of action.

"Maybe she is just out shopping," he said.

"Jesse, her room was ransacked, really trashed. Even I wouldn't leave the room like that."

"Maybe somebody was looking for something she had, not looking for her."

"Maybe, and if that's the case, maybe she's okay."

"There are more things in heaven and earth, Horatio, than are dreamed of in your philosophy," Jesse said.

My mouth hung open before I collected myself. "What the hell?" I sputtered.

Jesse grinned. "*Hamlet*?"

"How . . ."

"Book club. We are reading famous plays."

Sometimes the world just needs to bowl me over. Jesse in a book club did that. "Since when are you in a book club?"

"Since Inez invited me last month. I intend to improve myself in order to make myself acceptable to a lady of quality's family in marriage."

"What lady are you talking about?"

"The one I will find when I have improved myself."

After the shock of Jesse's announcement subsided, I asked, "Is this lady in your book club?"

"Oh, no. Only Inez, myself, and Tavi."

"Tavi?!"

"Yes. The three of us are just the beginning. It was Inez's idea, but we all agree that we must improve the intellectual atmosphere of Cancún."

"Well, you have your work cut out for you. Cancún is all about boobs and beaches."

Jesse smiled. "Yes, but you know the saying: Rome wasn't built in an afternoon."

"A day, Jesse. Rome wasn't built in *a day*."

He nodded wisely. "You see, it took more than an afternoon."

I dialed Jayde again. She still wasn't answering, so I left my number.

Jesse dropped me off at my office, also known as my home, then I asked him to hunt for Jayde through his taxi friends. She'd said she hadn't rented a car yet, so she'd either taken a cab somewhere or maybe a bus. She didn't seem like the bus type.

There was a light tap on my door, and in walked my friend, Octavio Fuentes.

"Hey, Tavi," I greeted him.

"Buenas tardes, JJ." He tossed his hat onto my desk and flopped into my client chair. The hat flew toward the edge, knocking a cheap souvenir crocodile into the air and sending it smashing to the floor. Tavi reached out in a futile attempt to save the plaster reptile and shot his chair onto the floor as well. I wasn't surprised. Tavi had a kind temperament but was the clumsiest person I'd ever met.

He picked up the various pieces of the statuette and set them on my desk with an apologetic grin.

"Forget it, Tavi. It was just junk."

He righted the chair and sat down gingerly while straightening his freshly ironed uniform shirt. "I've come to ask a favor, if you have a moment to spare."

"Sure. What do you need?"

"We found another body. Much like the one you found on the side of the road a few weeks ago. It was posed."

"What kind of pose do you mean?"

"It's hard for me to describe. I'll take you to it before we move it to the morgue. You can compare it to the way the Meyer boy's body was set up. Perhaps something will come to your mind that has not occurred to me."

"You think the Buendía guy, the cartel?"

He let a noncommittal shrug pass for an answer.

I got up. "OK. Let's go."

By the time we got to the scene, there was a canvas-covered frame shielding the body from the view of passing traffic. Tavi said a hotel employee on his way to work had spotted it and called it in early that morning. Tavi and his crew had shown up quickly and started working the area but had come up with nothing helpful.

The body was dressed in a kind of Roman toga, lying sprawled on a mattress, the right hand holding an empty wine bottle and left arm wrapped around a scantily clad mannequin, one of whose plastic breasts was pressed against the corpse's lips. Another mannequin, topless but wearing a bikini bottom, lay pressed to his other side, and a third bent over in front of him with his feet resting on her naked rump.

"Anything?" asked Tavi.

I shook my head. "Not really. Other than it looks like the same person or people did both. It's too strange not to be. But why?"

I took a close look at the body. This one hadn't been embalmed. It had gone beyond rigor mortis, and the rotting smell of putrefaction slapped me in the face.

"I guess you don't know how he died," I said.

"No. And we don't know who this one is. Doesn't look familiar to me or my police. Not to you, either, right?"

"No. Sorry."

"I'll take you back to your office, then. I forgot to tell you that Inez wants you to contact her. No hurry. She just said if you were in the neighborhood to stop in. She says something funny is going on in Cancún, and she wants to ask you about it."

"Something funny about these bodies?"

"No. She doesn't know about all this. Must be something else."

On the way back to my office I asked Tavi if he'd heard anything about a cartel coming to Cancún. He said he'd heard rumors.

"What will you do about it?"

"What all the police across this country do, my friend. Pretend they do not exist."

Inez Jones wasn't clumsy, and sometimes not friendly, but she was very easy on the eyes and usually had me wrapped around her finger. I had sort of flirted with Inez, on and off, but she never responded. She wasn't cold, exactly, just proper. Inez didn't have a love interest as far as I knew. I hadn't given up, but when I pushed, it was softly. So I knocked and waited for her "*entra*" before turning the knob and walking into her spartan office.

An engraved plate on her door read, *Inez Jones, Agente de Bienes Raíces* and below that *Inez Jones, Licensed Real Estate Agent.*

"Afternoon, Inez. Do you have a minute?"

"Yes, my friend. How can I help you?" She motioned to a chair and I sat.

I was mesmerized by her beauty, as usual, and for a moment I just stared. When her brow wrinkled uneasily, I came to my senses. "To be honest, I'm not really sure. Tavi said you wanted to discuss something strange going on in Cancún." I focused on a curl of shiny black hair she pushed back from one of her deep brown eyes. "Tavi said you thought something strange was going on around here, and I thought it might be pertinent to a case I'm working."

She rose slowly, like she was thinking pretty hard, then moved over to her window and looked out as she talked to me.

"I have lived here all my life. When the . . . harmony . . . of things is disrupted, I can feel it."

I waited for a minute, but she didn't say anything more, just looked out into the tropical afternoon like she was expecting someone, or something, she was afraid would show up. I decided to prime the pump.

"Are you talking about people?" I asked. "Because I've seen a couple of oddballs today."

She turned back to me and rested her marvelous posterior against the windowsill.

"Not people, really. I haven't noticed that. Just a feeling." She waved her hand dismissively. "And little things. We had rain yesterday for a few minutes. We never have rain this time of year. And it was not much more than a sprinkle. When is the last time you experienced a sprinkle in Cancún?"

"Well, I get your point, but . . ."

She started back toward her desk, then appeared to change her mind and turned back to the window. "I saw a crocodile yesterday when I was driving home. On the road."

"Well, Inez, there are crocodiles all over Quintana Roo, all over the Yucatán."

"Have you seen one in town? On the road?"

"No, but—"

"It's true it may have happened before. A rarity still, no?"

One of those huge black spiders that scares me to death edged onto the window glass. I debated telling her, but I decided it might creep her out even more. "Oh, yeah, rare. That's true." How was she not seeing that spider? "Uh, well, I hope you wouldn't mind letting me know if you get anything more, you know, concrete."

She laughed at herself. "It's probably nothing. But yes, I will let you know."

"Maybe you've heard that the Río Seco cartel is sniffing around Cancún."

"That is not what is giving me this weird feeling, but, yes, I have heard this. In fact, a lawyer from Mexico City called and asked me to look for an estate for a client he would not name. The price range he quoted was in the millions. Who but a narcotraficante has such a budget? These kinds of men will corrupt my beloved city."

"Will you find something for them?"

She shrugged her defeat. "Probably. Yes. If I do not, someone else will."

I kept my eyes open for wandering crocs on the way home but didn't see any.

CHAPTER 3

The doll left outside my door wasn't the kind you give to your kid sister. It looked like a miniature scarecrow and had a chicken's wishbone stabbed through where I assumed the heart should be. The round rag face was white with a crimson smile slashed on. Meant to be me, I suppose. If the voodoo doll was left there to terrorize me, it didn't work, at least not much. It did make me think hard, though, about what the hell was going on. Maybe this kind of thing was what Inez meant about mysterious stuff in Cancún. What any of it had to do with me I couldn't guess. But it did occur to me that things had started getting weird only after the blonde bombshell client paid me a visit.

Tavi called to let me know this morning's posed corpse's cause of death was almost certainly fentanyl, according to the medical examiner. So both the posed dead men likely died from the drug. It would take a day or two to confirm. Meanwhile, they were running the new dead guy's fingerprints.

I called Jesse. I don't know why I wanted Jesse to come over. Could be I thought two minds are better than one. In truth, I probably just wanted the company. Inez's creepy feeling had begun to infect me. Also Jesse had promised to bring coffee. I needed it.

He took his time. When he finally showed up, the coffee was barely warm. I microwaved it back to drinkable. Jesse finished his and looked through my kitchen cabinet for donuts or other sweets without luck. He sat across from me with a pout. Then he picked up the doll and studied it. "It's just a doll. Some kid probably left it as a trick."

"Come on, Jesse. It's not just a doll. It's a *voodoo* kind of doll. But who? Why? Why would somebody have a problem with me?"

"Could be an old client. You know, you have screwed up some cases."

"What? I . . . I have not. I've never . . . I mean, I don't . . ." I rubbed my nose. "Not for a very long time!"

"I think we should take the doll to Mama Juana. She'll know."

"Who the hell is Mama Juana?"

"She is a kind of priestess."

"Priestess of what?"

"Santa Muerte. The Indios puros mix indigenous and Catholic stuff. They make things like your doll."

"It's not my doll! I hope." I grabbed the keys to my truck. "Let's go."

I could hear Mama Juana's high-pitched laughter as we walked up to the door of her ramshackle casita. She was a happy-natured, ultra-skinny woman of indeterminate years over ninety. As we neared, I could see she was tickled by some game show on an enormous television screen. Her walnut-hued skin and dyed black hair were in stark contrast to irises of such a pale amber shade they were almost invisible. She wore a heavy necklace of various shells and claws mixed with some silver trinkets. The door was open, but Jesse knocked and waited respectfully for the old woman to acknowledge us.

"Jesús María, mi amor! Adelante!" she sang out, her eyes still fixed on the TV screen. "Espera un momentito. Tengo que ver este." She must have seen me from the corner of her eye. "Quién es el gringo?"

Jesse stood aside to better expose me. "Un amigo, Abuelita."

She punched the remote to still the TV and stood slowly. "Hello, young man." She smiled. "You are not as pretty as my Jesús María, but you will do. Sientense." She motioned to a couple of rickety chairs near her own threadbare lounger before noticing the raggedy figure in my hand and reaching out for it. I let it go.

"Qué es esta?" She held it close to her eyes to examine. "Ahhh . . . hermosa."

The doll was no more than six inches tall, and now I could see clearly it was a female, wearing a long skirt and blouse that, to my surprise, seemed to be made from an old plaid shirt I'd recently thrown out. A medallion on a tiny chain hung around its neck. I would have said a saint medal, except the face on the medal was a death's head. The doll's facial features had been painted with some delicacy, and the hair, which was the same color as my own, was affixed by a thin red ribbon band. Two gray-and-white-striped feathers dangled from the headband on strands of yellow yarn.

"La Santa Muerte," the old woman breathed softly. She looked at me hard. "Where did you find this, señor?"

"Leaning against my door. Can you tell me what it is? Please? Ma'am?"

Instead of responding, she reached into the drawer of the small table beside her and brought forth a thin, short-bladed knife. With the touch of a surgeon, she sliced open the back of the figure. Then she laid the knife down and poked inside the doll with tweezer-like fingers. She pulled out, bit by bit, tissue paper, a small shell, a dead scorpion—and a photo of me from the neck up. She stopped and held the picture out for me to see.

"That's me!" I said.

The old woman nodded and handed the doll back to me. I accepted it as I would have a dead rat, pinched grudgingly between finger and thumb. I looked over at Jesse. His expression told me he wanted nothing to do with it.

"This is a special doll," she confided. "It is a charm to keep a lover faithful, but it has something extra, something dangerous. I don't want to alarm you, señor."

"Go ahead. Tell me, please." Want to or not, she was alarming me.

"The danger only comes if the person the doll is for . . . you, young man . . . disturbs that which was sleeping."

"Sleeping?"

She looked at me with sympathy. "Sleeping could mean hidden. Something that should remain hidden."

I stood and paced the room. Then I stopped and laughed. "Here I am getting worked up over a damned silly doll. Excuse the language." I tossed the figure to Jesse, who welcomed it as he would a stinging scorpion. "Get rid of that for me, partner."

I offered the bruja my hand, which she took with a smile. "Call me, señor, if you need my help."

"Thanks, ma'am. I'll be fine. Just wanted some information."

I dropped some pesos on the table, bowed like a gentleman, and led Jesse out the door.

I have to admit that in spite of my bravado with the old woman, I was a little worried. Still, I had more important things to concern me, like the whereabouts of my pretty client. I had professional ethics after all. (OK, not many, but losing a client was something that just hit me wrong.) I didn't know exactly what to do about it. Maybe a shot or two of mescal would help.

Jesse dropped me off and went looking for Jayde. I hoped he'd keep at it until he found her, but I was tired and looking forward to a drink. So, for the moment I thought, to hell with it. But luck was with me. My door was open, and there she was.

CHAPTER 4

Sitting in my office like a queen on her throne was the lovely Jayde. I walked in open-mouthed.

"How did you get in here?"

She gave an innocent shrug. "I told your landlord I was your fiancée."

"What? Never mind." I held back my annoyance. After all, she was my client. "How can . . ." I took a breath. "How can I find out who's following you if I can't even find you?"

"Oh, yes." She shook a gentle finger in my direction. "You probably need to do a little better there."

Flabbergasted, I leaned forward, elbows on my desk. Even pretty women can irritate me if they try hard enough. "I could do better if you cooperated with me. Like telling me if you're going to disappear for a day or two."

"Not a day or two. Well, maybe a day, not two."

I sighed my exasperation. "To know if you're being followed, I have to follow you myself."

She smiled like a kid used to getting her way. "OK. I'll be good."

"Have you been to your room?"

"Yes, someone tore it up pretty well. That's why I came here."

"I saw it. I thought you might have been harmed."

"How did you get into my hotel room?"

"I . . . never mind."

She grinned and wagged her finger again. "So you were bad too. Did you tell them you were my fiancé?"

"No, let's stick to the subject." I stood and opened the door. "Starting now, let me know your movements in advance. And answer your cell. Put me on speed dial."

"OK." She stood up slowly and began to slink toward the door. "You make me feel safe already."

I turned to let her pass. "Say, did you by any chance leave a doll at my door earlier?"

"A doll?" She looked at me like I was off my rocker. "You're kidding, right?"

"OK. Yeah. Never mind." I waved her on her way.

I would have sworn she purred as she slid by me on her way out.

I slept well. The mescal helped. But I woke up with worries on my mind, and first thing I called Jayde. She answered, which surprised me. Still in bed but awake. She asked me to meet her for coffee, and I told her if I was going to find her stalker we shouldn't be seen together. So, I arranged to tail her from the hotel's al fresco café in an hour. Told her not to watch for me. Best if it didn't look like she knew I was around.

She was just getting up from her table when I arrived.

I got into a cab and followed her to the shopping mall, then hopped out and tailed her twenty yards behind on foot as she wandered from store to store, buying nothing and constantly looking back to find me. I nearly gave up in frustration, but she finally stopped looking over her shoulder and acted like a normal shopper, even picking up a souvenir or two.

My job isn't the easiest way to make a living. I take that back. It's probably one of the easiest but also most nerve-racking ways to put food on the table. It is what I do, though, because of the cards fate has dealt me. So I had to get on with it.

All that day and the next I didn't spot anyone following her as I trailed her from shop to café and back to her hotel again. Nobody seemed to give her more notice than any woman who looked like her was bound to get. And the routine continued. I talked to her every night by phone to see where she'd be going the next day but made no face-to-face contact. Day after day of seeing no one following her, I decided she was crazy, albeit hot.

Then, something happened when I wasn't really paying attention. Tavi ran the second corpse's prints and ID'd him as Reynaldo Oscar Lopez, a sicario with the Río Seco cartel. Probably a scout for the cartel's planned move. That took my mind off Jayde, I'm not proud to say. Jayde had paid me for a week's work, and my ethics, tepid though they might have been, forced me to exhibit at least a semblance of performing my duties. And it was a good thing. (Well, that's debatable, I guess, seeing how things turned out.) Who was it who said, "A watched pot never boils"? It sure did in this case.

There were two people following her late one morning along the tourist walk. I could swear to it. Not a team of two. Two separate stalkers. I took pics with my phone to email Jayde later. Hopefully she could identify them. Both stalkers were nondescript, medium-height males. Both light-skinned, could have been Mexican or any other European derivative. Hard to distinguish between them, except one was wearing a shirt with blue flowers on it and the other a shirt with red flowers on it. I was wondering if either of them realized they had competition, when the one in the blue flowered shirt seemed to be brushed by the stalker in the red flowered shirt and collapsed on the sidewalk in front of a crowded coffee house. He didn't get up.

Jayde kept walking, too far ahead to notice. I decided to risk getting closer to the man to see what had happened. Didn't take much to figure it out. From about ten feet away, I could see a pool of bright red arterial blood flooding from beneath his body. I didn't want to get too close. People were beginning to notice. Soon there would be screams and cops. Best I could figure, he'd been stabbed and by someone who knew where and how to stab quick and clean. Knew how to kill without giving the victim a chance to make noise.

I don't like becoming involved with people who are capable of this kind of damage. This was more than I'd bargained for. I was going to have a real heart-to-heart with my client and not over the phone. It was too late to follow the fellow in the red flowered shirt. He had dissolved into the crowd. I took a quick photo of the victim with my cell and raced away.

Then the screams started. Only a minute or so later, I looked back over my shoulder and saw emergency vehicles screeching to a halt.

I pulled out my phone and punched in Jayde's number with my trembling fingers.

When she answered, I said, "I need you to meet me right away."

She replied, "Where?"

I told her to meet me at my favorite little watering hole. Not fancy but clean. Didn't show up on any tourist maps. I couldn't be sure she wouldn't be followed, but I could set Jesse up to keep an eye out. He did. Took it seriously this time.

She was there when I arrived. I should have gotten there before her to scope out the scene, I guess, just in case anyone else was following her. I took a seat beside her at the bar. Julio was the bartender and a good friend. I'd ask him later if she'd talked to anyone while she was waiting for me. For now, I just nodded to him and pointed to Jayde's glass and the empty space in front of me. He nodded back and got busy.

"Sorry I'm late."

"You're not. I'm early."

She took her margarita from Julio without comment. I sipped my mescal gently. I needed a sober night for a change.

"Anything of interest happen today?" I led in.

"No. I shopped a lot. Didn't really buy much."

"No problems at all?"

"None. I looked for you, but I didn't see you."

"You weren't supposed to see me." She didn't reply, only looked down at her drink. "You didn't notice anything out of the ordinary?"

"Why are you asking me this?"

"A man, who I think was following you, was killed on the sidewalk seconds after you passed that very spot."

If she was faking her shock, she deserved a good Hollywood agent. She wheezed, "Nooooo . . ."

"He was only half a block behind you when it happened."

"But I didn't hear—"

"It took a few seconds before the screaming started in the crowd. The dead guy didn't make a sound." I held my phone up to show her the picture I'd taken of him. She pushed it away.

"Don't know him?"

"No."

"Never seen him around?"

"I don't think so. He was following me?"

"Yes. I'm pretty sure of that."

"So now you believe me."

"I . . ."

She shook her head. "I know you didn't. But I knew I was being followed."

"Do you know why he was following you?"

"No, as I told you."

I couldn't tell if that was the truth. I didn't see anything in her expression that would contradict what she'd said, yet I had a strong feeling she was keeping something back.

"I'm scared now. I mean more than before."

I couldn't blame her. I didn't know for sure it was a murder I'd witnessed, but I knew there was far more blood spread across the sidewalk than a human being is meant to lose. For a moment she just sat there silently.

I ordered another round. We poured them down our throats to try to dull the horror of what had just happened. It didn't work, so I told her I'd take her back to her hotel.

I called Jesse to pick us up, and we drove past the site of the presumed murder. The crowd had largely dispersed, but the crimson stain still covered the sidewalk. Luckily, Jayde didn't notice.

At the hotel, Jayde wouldn't let me leave until I checked out her room.

My house was a small casita set off to the side on my landlord's much larger place. I used the front room as an office. The rent was a little high, but I liked having an address in the better part of town. Made me seem more reputable. There were private guards for the neighborhood, so not much burglary or other crime. And my landlord, who was more than slightly eccentric, had organized his own special system for deterring thieves. He called it Demetrius. Demetrius was a rooster. Not just an ordinary rooster, but a gamecock. A huge fighting bird my landlord had bought from a breeder at a pelea de gallos (cockfight) the year before. It's a "sport" that's still legal in Mexico. My dueño made a pile of cash gambling on the fights, then decided to start a business in "guard cocks." So far, Demetrius was his only investment, to the best of my knowledge. My landlord kept the razor-sharp steel fighting spurs on the homicidal bird at all times. The damned bird was so arrogant, he thought the sun rose just to hear him crow. I think that's a quote, but I don't know from where.

And Demetrius hated me.

Demetrius was always vigilant. I usually kept an eye out for him, but so much had happened that day, I completely forgot about him. That was unfortunate, because Demetrius, for reasons I could not fathom, was more effective against me than against trespassers. He was silent, striking hard before a person had a chance to save himself. I usually heard the rustling of his feathers, kind of like autumn leaves stirring in the wind, the instant before he attacked.

This night I heard his wings flapping and felt the sting of his blades on my calf at the same moment. I kicked back hard and set a new speed record for the fifty-yard dash. The average human can run 8.6 miles per hour. The average chicken can run 9 mph. And Demetrius is not average. I jammed my key into the lock just as the sadistic chicken regrouped for another charge. I kicked at him again and slammed the door shut. Safely inside, I looked down and checked the damage. My jeans were slit, but the cuts to my ankle weren't deep. I swore I'd get a twelve gauge. To hell with Mexican gun laws.

I took a quick shower, scrambled eggs, and hit the sack.

I'm not much of a dreamer, the nighttime variety that is. Come to think of it, I'm not much of a daytime dreamer, as in "don't give up on your dreams," either. Don't ask me about my dreams. They're always useless. I hear about people who have their real-life problems solved by their unconscious sleeping minds. Not me. My dreams are boring even when I understand them. I sleep to sleep. But guess what? I dreamt something worthwhile for a change. Good for me.

CHAPTER 5

I woke with an idea. It was more of a suspicion, really. In my dream, a hot blonde was tempting me and tempting me until I just fell into her arms, except her arms were octopus tentacles that wrapped around me until I couldn't breathe.

Jayde was playing me. I was almost certain.

I called Jesse and asked him to meet me at María Elena's dump of a café. The walls needed a fresh coat of paint, and the floor was cracking and begging for new wood. But the prices were low, and the place was known by Cancún natives for serving great breakfasts. I always ordered huevos rancheros and saw no reason to change.

Jesse was seated and eating by the time I got there. I was late because I'd taken a few minutes to scrape Demetrius' shit off my shoes. I'd believed in doggy heaven since my puppy died when I was five. That damn rooster made me pray for a chicken hell.

María Elena owned the place and was a truly fine hostess. She had my coffee to me by the time my butt hit the chair. I didn't need to tell her what I wanted—she'd put it in front of me within ten minutes. Never failed. I smiled at her and took a sip from my cup.

Jesse said, "I googled her last night. Nothing. Tried every variation of her name I could think of."

It didn't surprise me. "I bet she's not traveling under her real name. If she's using a false passport, she's doing some serious US lawbreaking."

He swallowed and took a sip of his jugo de naranja. "Maybe we should question her more, before we get involved in something that's way out of our league."

"I agree," I said as my breakfast plate was set in front of me. "After I eat."

I didn't call to tell her we were coming. So I guess it served me right that she wasn't there. Not answering her phone either. I turned Jesse loose to see if he could run across her at one of the shopping areas. The concierge said she'd told him she was going to look for a gift for somebody.

I went back to my office and hit the computer. Every half hour or so I'd try Jayde's cell again. Finally, I stopped leaving messages, then just gave up.

Considering the limitations on what I was allowed to do as a PI operating without a license, I knew I shouldn't be doing anything but showing her what to do. But the risk of being called out for doing more was small. Most likely, it meant passing out a mordida or two if I got caught. It might have been my curiosity that induced me to stay on the case. But I needed the money, and I'd take a few risks for that too.

While it's a big no-no for a Mexican to own a firearm in Mexico without a special permit, it's an even bigger no-no for a foreigner. That's one reason the cartels have such power. Unlike the average citizen, narcotraficantes don't give a damn about the law. I kept my little snub-nose .38 tightly wrapped and secured taped to the top of my toilet tank. My only box of bullets was hidden under a potted plant on the bathroom windowsill. A tingle of warning pushed me to check the revolver and make sure it was loaded. I did and it was. I deliberated whether to carry it but decided to leave it where it was for the time being. Even though, as fellow Texas intellectual Coach Darrell Royal said, "If worms carried pistols, birds wouldn't eat 'em."

I spent a couple of hours going over the same internet ground Jesse had, to see if I could find what he hadn't. I thought, not to blow my own horn, I'm kind of an expert in the field. A second sweep sometimes yields rewards. This time it didn't. So I decided to hit the pavement, to make the rounds of my contacts. As Woody Allen said, "Eighty percent of success is showing up." Couldn't do worse than slapping impotently at the computer keyboard.

My old Toyota pickup was waiting faithfully in the drive. Even with 120,000 miles logged on the odometer, she ran fine. The air conditioner was putting out a fair amount of cool air, so it was bearable to be in the truck. I had no specific destination in mind. I just hoped I might get lucky.

And I did.

One of the main priorities of Cancún's tourism board is to maintain the look of the streets most frequented by tourists. Just about the whole of the economy depends on visitors being comfortable as they stroll around with cash to spend. This means homeless people and those begging for money are kept away. Even the sale of souvenirs is restricted to places regulated by the tourist bureau. The locals are naturally friendly, and crime, at least against tourists, is rare.

My pickpocket friend, Lizardo Gómez, was an exception. He prided himself on selecting his victims from those who seemed able to afford the loss of their cash, never credit cards, which he left in the wallets and purses and dropped them off at hotel lobbies, where they were certain to find their way back to their owners. On a few occasions I'd hired him to retrieve information that required his nimble fingers to obtain. But now I just wanted to ask if he'd seen my client, whom I was certain he would have targeted as a prime candidate for his talents.

"I'm sure that was the woman I saw just a few minutes ago," he said. "Hard to miss her."

"Yeah," I responded. "Real looker."

"Sure, but the car."

"What about the car? What car?"

"Yellow convertible, man. Beautiful kind of light yellow, very shiny, must be expensive. A Mercedes."

I slipped him twenty dollars. "Which way?"

"Toward the market."

I called Jesse and told him to catch up with me and then slipped off in pursuit. There's not much traffic in Cancún, not compared to Los Angeles or Mexico City, anyway. It wasn't long before I saw the lemon-colored Merc up ahead. It stood out like a Christmas tree ornament on a cactus. If she was worried about being followed, why the hell had she rented such a flashy car? She drove way over the speed limit, which was nothing new for me. After all, this was Mexico. But I don't know if she was pushing my buttons or just reckless by nature. I had to nearly run her off the road to get her to stop for me. After I slid to a stop on the side of the road, she greeted me like we were on our way to a party and motioned me to the passenger seat.

"Where are we going?"

"To see a man with some information I need," she answered. "In a town called Puerto Morelos. Do you know it?"

I said I did. It's a small town down the coastal highway. She sped us off without elaborating.

I hoped Jesse would hang back and keep out of sight behind us. His old Nissan was beige and the absolute opposite of Jayde's sexy ride, so he'd have no trouble keeping a low profile.

After an hour's driving, Jayde had to slow for traffic as we neared Puerto Morelos. That's when she dropped the bombshell.

"You're a what!?"

"I'm an insurance investigator."

"What are you investigating? And why hire me?"

"One of our policyholders owns a very special painting, which he claims was stolen. We don't believe him. But if it *was* stolen, we want it back."

She honked mercilessly at a poor delivery truck holding us back.

"What kind of money are we talking about?"

"In the neighborhood of twenty-five million."

I digested that for a moment. "That's, well, that's . . ."

"Yes," she continued for me. "It's a lot. That's why I'm here."

"Who was the artist? Must be dead if his work is so expensive."

"A famous man, but not as an artist."

"Then why is it worth so much?"

"It's been held in a private collection. Only rumors about its existence. It's the person who painted it that makes it worth so much, and maybe the subject."

"Who? And what, then?"

She turned briefly to me with a teasing smile. "The painter was *Hernán Cortés*. The subject of the missing artwork was the beautiful Aztec woman who helped Cortés in his conquest of Montezuma's empire."

"*Cortés, the Spanish conquistador*?"

"That's the man."

"Where has it been hiding all these years?"

"One private collection after another at first. Then it just disappeared. Until we got an insurance claim. Our associate who wrote the policy must have been bribed to keep it confidential, even from us."

"Was the claim robbery?"

"Yes."

"Who was the owner?"

"A fellow named Juaquín Guzmán."

I stared at her for a second. "Not . . ."

She laughed. "Yep. *El Chapo.* Shorty. None other."

I sat in silence for a long time. I certainly hadn't seen any of that coming. Funny thing was, I believed her, improbable as the story was. Another drug king in my life, for God's sake! "Then why did you hire me?"

"As I said, I think people are following me."

"Why?"

"Why do I think that, or why are they following me?"

"Well, both."

"I think that because, just like you've seen, they are. I don't know who they are, and I want to find out. And as to why they are following me, I think they want to be there if I find the painting. I think they'd like to take it from me."

"Damn." That was my witty response. "I'm not a bodyguard, you know."

"Can you find one for me?"

"Probably my partner, but I'd better have a conversation with him first."

We didn't talk a lot after that until we got to Puerto Morelos. Lots of stuff running through my mind, though.

She surprised me by pulling up in front of the Puerto Morelos Municipal Police building. It was a single-story modest affair, but it had a large sign. She saw the question on my face.

"Come on," she said. "I have an appointment with Chief Ignacio Gómez. Seems like a nice guy. On the phone, anyway. You might as well tag along."

I followed like a pet dog, wondering why she'd brought me along.

Chief Gómez was a short, stocky man with a friendly smile. But when I shook his hand, I felt enough strength to crush my puny mitt if he wanted. I decided to stay on his good side. Jayde, though, did not seem fazed. She had him eating out of her hand right away. "Chief . . ."

He waved her formality off with a grin. "Nacho, señorita."

"Thank you. I'm Jayde."

"And I . . ." I began, but neither of them paid any attention, so I shut up.

"Where is he?" Jayde asked.

"In the interrogation room. I will take you. It will be more conducive to questioning him there."

"Thank you."

He got up and led us to a bare, windowless room with gray cinderblock walls where a plywood table and metal folding chairs were the only furniture. A meek, thin fellow in a worn T-shirt and jeans sat with his legs under his chair, nervously rubbing one sneaker-clad foot against the other. His stringy black hair was badly in need of a brush and a wash. He looked like a whipped puppy dog. I felt sorry for him.

"You have some information you want to share with me, Ruben?" Jayde asked as she sat.

The chief and I remained standing. I'd been sitting on the long drive, and the metal chairs looked about as comfortable as a death row jail cell. I could tell Gómez stood just to make clear he was el jefe.

The prisoner's mouth widened to reveal a crooked set of tobacco-stained teeth. "Sí, señora."

"OK. Go ahead."

"I am a poor man, señora. And, as you can see, I am imprisoned here with no money for un abogado to help me."

"I see," Jayde said coldly. "How much is your information worth, do you think, Ruben?"

"I am a simple man. I want only to return to my family," he smiled winsomely, and I thought I caught a glimpse of a conniving soul behind the humble facade.

Jayde sat stony-faced. She was used to bargain-making.

Ruben shifted uneasily on his chair. Jayde didn't buy into his act. "I know you understand, señora," he finally continued. "You have a family, no?"

"No."

"Surely you have children or brothers or sisters. You know how they need their father."

"My nieces and nephews are pains in the butt. My brother-in-law is a fellow criminal. You'd get along well." She let her kind face harden. "Now cut the crap and tell me what you have and what you want for it."

By the time we left the station, they'd made a deal. Ruben walked out with us. I wondered if what he'd offered that was worth as much as Jayde paid the chief to have him released, not to mention the thousand bucks Ruben now had in his pocket.

As the three of us got into Jayde's Merc, I glanced down the block and saw what looked like a pile of bright red hair in the back seat of a taxi pulling away from the curb. It rang a muted bell in my mind, but I dismissed it.

We dropped Ruben at the bus station after buying him lunch. At the restaurant he'd told us about a conversation he'd had in a Laredo jail (he was a multi-country criminal of no significant achievement). His cellmate had heard of an art object of great value that El Chapo had entrusted to an unknown associate in Cancún. (This info was the inducement for Jayde to bite on the invitation from Chief Nacho.) When Ruben was arrested for burglary in Puerto Morelos, he tried to use the knowledge to get a break. Successfully, it turned out. But really, all we had learned was that there was a map to the location where the art was supposedly stored. And that the person who probably had the map was a fat European man.

Jayde kept the top down on the drive back to Cancún. There was no moon, so the stars had no competition. They sparkled like bright jewels in the deep black sky. I looked up and swallowed their beauty until they soothed me into a deep sleep. For a while anyway, I forgot about the growing dangers of this case. I dreamt of finding a great treasure, but of course, my dreams didn't usually add up to much.

⁂

That night, my dreams continued to be inconsequential fantasies, so the buzzing of my cell didn't interrupt anything important. I scrambled around my bedside table, knocked the phone to the floor, and was surprised to hear Tavi on the other end. "Tavi?" I mumbled. "Pretty early for you."

"Another one."

"Another what?" I was still sleep-fuzzy.

"Body. Posed like the other two."

"Damn. Where?"

"The turnoff from the highway to your place. Get down here if you want to look."

I did want to look. I wanted to look nice and close. These murders probably didn't have anything to do with me, but they were getting close to home, literally.

When I arrived, the body was still in full view. The dawn light was just enough to see by and not yet enough to distract morning traffic. The cab driver who had called it in had been picking up a couple of fishermen.

Tavi shone his flashlight on the body so I could get a good look. "Like the other two, verdad?"

"Yes." It was. All three of them were like dead clowns staged in a horrific carnival. But this lifeless body was grossly obese. His lips were painted with cheap lipstick and his face powdered white. In one hand, he held a huge turkey drumstick dripping gravy on a bedsheet that was tied around his neck as a napkin and covered his chest and bulging stomach. The other hand grasped a large goblet that had spilled red wine over his sheet-napkin. The body leaned against a wooden table overflowing with loaves of bread, desserts, a large ham, and bowls of fruit.

"This is truly weird" was my keen, dark-of-morning observation.

"I wanted your opinion before we photograph the scene and take the body back to the morgue," he said. "If I say what I think, my superiors will perhaps not believe me."

"I don't think they would doubt your—"

He held up his hand. "My friend, you and I are aware of my skills and judgment in detecting and other law enforcement matters, but the men I report to are not blessed with such insight."

"Cause of death?" I asked. "From what you can tell so far?"

"Almost surely the same as the other two."

"Fentanyl."

"Yes. The medical examiner will verify."

For a moment we looked at the dead man in silence. Then we looked at each other, neither of us wanting to voice what we were both thinking. Then I decided to say what I knew he was reluctant to.

"Serial killer?"

Tavi nodded.

CHAPTER 6

"You were followed, all right," Jesse said. "Not very professionally, either."

I looked at Jayde, who was sitting across from me at the table in the courtyard of her hotel. She was concentrating on the mild surf breaking in front of us, or so it seemed.

I tore my thoughts away from the previous night's comic carnage. "Yes, you were followed, and I think we can agree why."

She pulled her gaze from the ocean and back to me. "Yes." She sipped her margarita. "Now the question is by how many."

"I agree," Jesse said. "I've spotted three. The man who was killed, the man who killed him, and the little old redheaded lady I told you about."

"I think I saw her when we were leaving the police station. Back of a cab. That red hair stands out like a polar bear on a Cancún beach. What about the guy who stabbed the stalker in the flowered shirt?"

"I haven't seen him since the killing. Either he's quit following you, or he's good at it," Jesse answered.

Jayde stood. "I'm tired. Think I'll go to my room."

"Jesse will see you up, just in case."

I stayed after they'd gone. I like sitting in the courtyards of hotels I can't afford, especially if I have a view of a beautiful beach and lovely ladies in small bikinis. I should have been thinking about the case and helping my client, but I was just engaging in sweet lazy voyeurism.

I closed my eyes and drifted into a pleasant doze. When I opened them, the fat man was standing in front of me and staring at my face.

"Mr. Tabasco?" The accent was posh Brit.

I straightened uneasily. "Uh . . . yes, I am Tabasco."

He was wearing that same white shirt and coat with a thin black tie, white pants and shoes, and white panama hat with a black hat band. I thought it must be a kind of uniform. And again he was leading his huge iguana on a red leash. I scooted my feet under my chair and away from the dinosaur remnant.

"Does that thing bite?"

The fat man's belly jiggled as he laughed. Sadistic enjoyment of my discomfort.

"Rarely, Mr. Tabasco. Rarely, I assure you."

"That does not *assure* me at all. *Rarely* means it happens. Has he been fed?"

"He is primarily an herbivore, which is why I call him Herbert. He will not eat you."

The fat man wiped his face with a huge white handkerchief and took a seat across from me, considerately tying the creature to his chair leg, a safe distance from my throat. "I will join you, if I may." He handed me a card. "I am Kaspar R. Gutman, dealer in fine art and antiquities." This was verified by his card, along with its New York address and phone numbers. "I believe we may have coinciding interests, and I would like to see if perhaps some sort of . . ." he searched for the word, "*arrangement* might be negotiated."

He hadn't offered to shake hands but was otherwise cordial, if a little formal. I realized he must be the fat man that Ruben, the fellow we got out of jail, had been talking about. This situation was making me feel kind of rattled. I mean, what kind of person walks around Mexico with an iguana on a leash? But I decided to hear him out. "OK. Talk."

"Haha . . . direct, to the point. I like your style, Mr. Tabasco."

"I'm listening."

He leaned forward conspiratorially. "I am aware that you have taken on a certain Miss Jayde Blackwood as a client."

"My dealings with clients are confidential."

"Of course."

Red flags were going up all over the place. Whoever this man was, he'd bring trouble, of that I was certain. "Just hold on, Mr. . . ." I read from his card, "Gutman. I'm not comfortable with this conversation already, and we're not even having the conversation yet."

"I will approach the matter more delicately, then." The fat man took a huge cigar from his shirt pocket and lit it with the grace of an aficionado. He puffed twice before continuing. "Your client is pursuing an object, a painting, to be precise, that I am eager to acquire."

"Then why not talk to her?"

He chuckled as if I were naive, which I am. "Miss Blackwood would be reluctant to deal with me, as our interests in the painting are mutually exclusive." He chuckled again.

"Okay. So what do you want from me?"

"I would like to suggest an agreement for . . ." He searched for words again. "Let us say, transfer of information."

"What does that mean?"

"In simple terms, it means that you advise me on the progress she is making toward her goal of finding the artwork. With a substantial financial incentive for your cooperation in this regard. And an attractive bonus should this information lead to my successfully obtaining the object."

"You're trying to buy me, Mr. Gutman."

"I prefer to think I am bidding for your services."

I had to know. I hoped I wouldn't be tempted, but I had to know. "What kind of incentive are we talking about?"

Gutman smiled and nodded his acknowledgment of my weakness. "A retainer of twenty-five thousand dollars and a bonus of twice that should I end up with the painting."

I confess, my knee-jerk reaction was to say yes. But something held me back. I'd like to say ethics. Maybe that was part of it. Truly, though, it was mostly fear that reined me in. One of the three stalkers following Jayde just the day before had been killed, and whether it had been at the fat man's orders, I didn't know. At any rate, it was too much too fast. In the words of the great Mark Twain, *there are several good protections against temptation, but the surest is cowardice.* "I better think about it," I answered at last.

A quick look of disappointment flashed across Gutman's face, and I saw something really evil behind the joviality. "Certainly," he said, rising from his chair. "You have my number on the card. Call me when you have decided."

Once again, he didn't offer his hand. He untied his pet, then stopped after a few steps and turned back to me. "But don't take too long." He tipped his hat and shuffled away.

My cell vibrated in my pocket. "Hey, Tavi. What have you got?"

"It was fentanyl, all right. He was from the Luna Nueva cartel. So we have two bodies from two rival cartels looking at coming to Cancún. Maybe this is some kind of gang war."

"OK. Thanks for keeping me in the loop. Talk later."

I sat there awhile and collected my thoughts. I decided I should pay another visit to Inez Jones.

When I got to her office, she was reluctant to open up.

"I don't know what else to tell you," she said, but the way she shifted her eyes away told me she *did* know what else to tell me. For some reason, she was not . . . well, forthcoming is the word.

"You told me that you felt the 'harmony' of things in Cancún was being messed up, remember?"

"Yes."

"Well, I agree with you. I saw a guy killed, at least I think he was, and—"

She held up her hand. "I don't want to know. I am occupied with my own problems."

"Didn't you offer to help me . . . before?"

"I didn't offer to help you. I simply told you something was wrong."

"And that's it? Nothing else you can tell me?"

"No."

I gave up. I rose to go and she walked me to the door. Before she opened it, she stopped for a moment. "I will give you my opinion, if you want it."

"Sure."

"You are becoming involved in something that could result in great danger to you. It is not like the cases you are used to."

I frowned at her casting aspersions on my abilities. Probably because I wanted her to see me as a tough guy. "You think I can't handle myself?"

She gave me a sweet smile, like a big sister to her baby brother, and patted my arm. "Of course you can, JJ. Just take care. I am used to having you around."

I shook my head. "I think you're not telling me something you'd intended to tell me. Did something happen to change your mind?"

She held my arm and guided me to the hallway door. "I know you have heard some very dangerous people are coming to our town. That is the evil I felt before, I suppose. But I think there is more."

She opened the door and let me through. I had very mixed feelings. She hadn't exactly expressed confidence in me. On the other hand, she'd kind of said she liked me. Oh, well. I wished I could talk to her about the serial killer, but I'd made a promise to Tavi. And meanwhile, I had a case to solve.

CHAPTER 7

I suppose there have been serial killers since before humans evolved from whatever we were before. Or least we've been killing each other since Cain and Abel. But without newspapers and television, only the very worst of them got much attention. Just kept chopping and slashing away until the Devil took them home. So I guess it was only a matter of time until Cancún got our own.

Serial killers and voodoo dolls were a potent mix to keep me up at night. Really, the posed corpses we were being gifted weren't the first such victims in modern times. Back in 2019, we had a twenty-two-year-old kid named Cruz who committed a multi-homicide. But since then, it had been fairly quiet. Cancún residents weren't looking for signs of lethal danger in their neighbors' eyes or peeking out their doors before leaving their homes to make sure unfamiliar persons were not slinking around their streets. But that was about to change.

Tavi had managed so far to keep a lid on publicity. A miracle, really, given that *Cancún Post* and *Cancún Sun*, to say nothing about the national television networks and wire services, would gladly pay any cop willing to leak the story. But the cops were loyal to Tavi. The tourists, however, were not.

A film crew from Hollywood was on the way to set up for a pre-dawn shoot when they spotted another posed cadaver at an intersection where it was sure to be noticed. Naturally, with an Oscar-winning cinematographer and an ambitious young director, the crime scene was recorded extensively and to a frightening perfection that would have eluded even the major networks' camera crews. By evening it would be out over every major news outlet in the world.

The Hollywood studio financing the movie ordered the director to find a way to work the killing into the script. The fact that the film was a romantic comedy made no difference to them.

When Tavi called me this time, I was surprised at how calmly he was taking this new development. In fact, he'd asked the American film people to share a copy of their recording of the crime scene to augment his own video and still photos. When I got to the scene, he was listening with great interest to the cinematographer. He reluctantly pulled himself away when he saw me approach. I was shocked at the happy expression on his face. "What good luck!" he said.

I was truly bewildered. "Luck? The *murder*?"

"Oh, no, no, no. The murder I will tell you about. But that man I was talking to is a famous cinematographer. He was actually contracted to film Luciano Pavarotti's last tour of the United States! What good fortune that he is right here in my backyard, so to speak."

"Sure, I guess. Now, what about this killing? Just like the others?"

"Similar, amigo. And, once again, I would like you to take a look and see what you think connects it to the others."

This time, the body was leaning back in a luxurious leather chair positioned in front of a mahogany desk. The guy was dressed in a fashionable gray three-piece suit, white shirt, and maroon tie. In his lap and spread across the desk were cloth bags spilling gold coins in rivers onto the surrounding dirt. I bent down for closer inspection and saw the "gold coins" were poker chips that had been sprayed with gold paint.

I looked over my shoulder to find Tavi right behind me. "Sure looks like the work of the same artist," I said. I straightened up and shook my head. "What the hell is going on?"

Tavi took my arm and led me away from the forensic folks near the body. He spoke as softly as he could and still have me hear him. "I don't even need to wait for the autopsy to tell me *fentanyl*."

"Have you identified the most recent ones?"

He pulled me farther from the small crowd that now milled around the body. "You know the first, the young man from the Cancún Jewish community. The rest, those two . . ." He bent so close to my ear I thought he might kiss me. "Cartel sicarios, both of them."

I must have flinched because he grabbed me close and put his finger to his lips. "Shhhh! Even my own men don't know yet. But they will after the media gets the gringo film crew's stuff today."

"Can't you stop them from releasing it?"

"Ha, ha! It is sometimes possible with our local media. But never with the Americans. They would just get a good laugh."

"Damn! What will you do?"

Tavi shook his head sadly. "The first body, the Jewish fellow. The second from the Río Seco cartel. The third from La Luna Nueva group." He waved his hand back toward the posed corpse in disgust. "And this piece of garbage from Río Seco, otra vez."

I was beginning to see the problem. "So, a tit for tat. Maybe the next one, if there is a next one, will be Luna Nueva again."

"Sí. A titty tatty . . . the thing you said. And I am sure there will be a next one, compa."

"Wow. I wish I could help. But I don't . . ."

He took my arm and guided me slowly back toward my car, confiding in me as we walked. "You and your associates speak to people who will not talk to police. Find out what you can."

"But Tavi, they won't trust me again if they find out I'm giving their information to you."

"JJ, amigo, you will admit I have helped you in the past, no?"

I could see where he was going with this, so I gave him a grudging "Yes."

"Then please allow me to call in this as a favor in return."

I nodded without enthusiasm. He gave me a friendly pat on the shoulder. "Bueno, muy bueno."

Tavi opened my driver's side door and held it for a minute, his other hand still on my shoulder. I couldn't tell if he was angry or sad. Maybe both. "You know, JJ, I love Cancún. We live on tourism here. I don't know which will be worse for that industry, a serial killer on the loose or cartels moving in."

"We'll find the serial killer. I have faith in you."

"Yes. And the tourists' fear of the serial killer will fade away after he is caught. But the horror of the cartels' violencia will endure longer." He closed my door and stepped back from the car. Then he bent toward me again. "You know what is the worst thing, compadre?"

I shook my head.

"This shit will make my plan to bring opera to Cancún very hard. And that is my life's ambition." He turned and moved disconsolately back to the made-up cartel gunman. I felt sad for him.

CHAPTER 8

I like my little truck. It doesn't use much gas, the tires are cheap to replace, and I can use it to haul things. You may be wondering what I haul. (OK, probably you don't care.) Well, I haul lots of stuff from time to time. Not every day, maybe not every week. But when I have something to take from one place to another and need a little space, it comes in handy. This particular day, I was carrying a big wooden desk I'd picked up for a few bucks from a fellow gringo who was going back to the States. And it saved my life.

The bullet hit the thick wood with a *whop*. I had the window down since the night was fairly cool, so I heard the shot. Of course, it took me a while to assess what the hell was happening. I stomped on the brakes, but then the fear bit me and I sped up. I wasn't armed, and, even if I had been, I wasn't keen to get out in the night and chase somebody who was trying to kill me. I decided to take a backstreet route to the police station, and I hoped Tavi would be there. Meanwhile, I called Jesse.

"Let's meet at the office," he suggested. "If we go to the cops, we will have a lot of explaining to do. Also, I am not sure any of those cops can be trusted. Except Tavi, of course."

I took his advice and headed home.

* * *

Inez was right. Jesse and I were in way over our heads. We were good at sneaky divorce-related pics and the occasional child support scofflaw, but we fell pretty short on cases where people were killing each other.

When I pulled up, Jesse was already waiting by his old bomb of a car. He went around to the bed of my pickup and used his pocketknife to dig the bullet out of the desk.

"From an AR15." He held it out for me to see, then pointed to the hole in the wood. "Looks like an inch or so to the left would have caused you some grief."

That was a pretty accurate assessment. And it scared me more than a little. I put on a brave, stern expression which, in hindsight, I'm sure looked forced and stupid. "Maybe," I shrugged. "Let's go inside and figure out how to work this case." I walked a few steps past my gate, keeping a wary eye out for the damned rooster, before I remembered the desk. "Might as well take the desk in. How about a hand?"

"Sure, jefe," he smiled. "If you don't think it's bad luck."

We didn't reach any worthwhile conclusions that night, other than I needed some wood filler for my new furniture. (It is a fine desk, really. Walnut. And I got it for a song.) Actually, we did reach one conclusion: Someone had tried to kill me and probably would try again. I didn't have the money to leave town, so I decided to carry the .38 I had hidden. Yes, I knew it was illegal and no match for an AR15, and I couldn't hit anything with it anyway. But having it would make me feel better. Kind of a lucky charm.

We also determined the only reason I would be important enough to kill was someone must have thought I had some information about Jayde or her case. I didn't. Maybe I should have put up a big sign in front of my office: I KNOW NOTHING ABOUT THE THING JAYDE OLIVIA BLACKWOOD IS LOOKING FOR. I didn't do that because it wouldn't have done any good, not because of professional ethics. My survival is more important to me than my ethics.

The next morning I awoke to an insistent banging on my door. I'd slept poorly, so I was bleary-eyed and cranky when I threw on my robe. "Who is it?" I looked through my spyhole and saw a flaming red stack of hair and heard a high-pitched yapping. A heavily made-up woman of at least eighty years looked back at me with the lively green eyes of a twenty-year-old.

"My name is Hermione Gingold. I wish to speak with you, Mr. Tabasco." Her tone was pleasant but firm. Her name rang a bell way in the back of my mind, but I dismissed that thought and opened the door an inch.

"What can I—?" I flinched as the tiny dog she was holding lunged at me murderously. "Hey! Is that thing—?"

She grinned at my chagrin. "Mustn't worry. Napoleon rarely bites."

"That's twice in two days I've been told not to worry. I need people to stop saying that." I looked around hopefully for Demetrius. Maybe he could take on this mini wolf. "Say, did you happen to see a big chicken in the yard?"

"Yes, there was a rather intimidating bird that rushed toward us, but Napoleon scared him off."

Great. Not afraid to attack a grown man but scared off by a mouse dog. What a fine fighting cock! I opened the door a little wider. She shoved past me and walked into the room.

"Thank you, Mr. Tabasco. If you're offering coffee, I accept."

"I . . . uh, sure." She was a pushy one, but I couldn't help envying her self-confidence.

"Maybe I should get dressed."

"No need. You're fine as you are." She set her scrawny pet on the floor, and he proceeded to pee on my sofa.

"Hey! Could you please—"

She held up her hand to silence me. "Not to worry. Napoleon just needed to mark his new territory. He's finished."

"Wait a minute! This is not his territory."

"Best not to worry. Make the coffee and you will feel better, Mr. Tabasco."

Some days I feel inadequate for life. This was one of those days. I did as I was instructed. I went into the kitchen and came back carrying a cup of coffee.

"Ah, thank you, Mr. Tabasco. You are a fine host."

"I'm not a host . . . I . . ." I was just waking up. "Could you please tell me why you're here, Miss . . . uh?"

"Gingold. Hermione Gingold."

"Yes." I sat across from her. "Why do I think I know that name?"

"I couldn't possibly know, Mr. Tabasco. It isn't a common name. Neither is yours, may I suggest."

People sometimes ask me about my name. It's also the name of a Mexican state and a very hot sauce made in Louisiana. I've told people it's an old Spanish name, which is a lie. "Tabasco" is derived from a Mexican Indian word for a hot pepper. My original family name was "Dillard." My great-grandfather and his brother got into a fight with some men over a card game in New Orleans. People got shot, so the story goes. My great-uncle was caught by the law, but my great-grandfather escaped into Texas where the Texas Rangers corralled him outside Corpus Cristi. He got away by bribing a jailer, they say, and made it into Mexico where he hid out at a brothel in the state of Tabasco. Thus the name. He eventually crossed back into Texas under his new identity of Tabasco and settled in Ft. Worth, where he set up a successful dry goods store. "Never mind. How can I help you, Mrs.—"

"Ms."

"OK, Ms. Gin . . ." I gave up. "What are you here for?"

"I want to hire you, Mr. Tabasco."

"Hire me for what, ma'am?"

"To find a piece of art."

"What sort of art?"

"No need to be coy, Mr. Tabasco. I've seen you with at least one other interested party."

I tied the belt on my robe, realizing I was wearing only my Superman pajama pants beneath. "I'm sure you know I can't have more than one client in the matter, Ms. Gingold."

"Call me Hermione." She smiled coquettishly. "And I'll call you JJ."

"OK. But you know I can't take you on as a client, at least one pursuing the same end."

"I sympathize with your ethical dilemma, Mr. . . . eh, JJ. So I am willing to significantly increase your fee as a balm to your conscience." She produced a checkbook in a gold-embossed holder and flipped it open to a blank check. Then she poised an expensive-looking pen over the paper.

"You think you can buy my honor, Ms. . . ." I sputtered. "Is that what you think?"

"Yes, JJ. I do."

She knew me, all right. And yet something was holding me back from my natural greed. "Well, ma'am. You've been misinformed!" My indignation sounded false even to me. "I come from the honorable family of Tabasco, known for our—"

She waved me off and chuckled indulgently. "JJ, my dear. I know all about your illustrious ancestry."

I huffed for a second or two. Then I couldn't help myself. "What sort of fee are we talking about here?"

"Fifty thousand dollars, US. And another fifty after you get me the painting."

I tried not to look eager. Then I thought about how good Jayde looked walking away from our last meeting. I was torn between lust and greed. They compete for first place among my favorite vices. I covered my unease by taking a sip of my coffee. Rather, it would have covered my unease had I not spilled it down the open front of my robe. It took all my self-control not to scream like a baby. I took a couple of deep breaths and hoped she didn't notice the tears rolling from my eyes. "I'll have to take this matter under consideration, Hermione. I'm sure you understand."

She chuckled again. "Of course, JJ." She returned her check-book to her purse and drew forth a card and handed it to me. It read "Hermione P. Gingold" followed by a phone number. "Call me. I'll be around."

She rose, waking her angry little pet, who snarled viciously at me again. What had I ever done to him? I wondered. Also, how could I get him alone to throw him to the local crocs?

I opened the door for her and found Demetrius waiting for me. Hermione brushed past me and put her animal down. The rooster, coward that he was, streaked away like feathered light-ning. Hermione whistled sharply, and Napoleon, after a few threatening farewell yaps, jumped back into her arms. "You should get a dog, JJ." were her parting words.

After my red-headed temptress left me alone, I recalled that someone had tried to kill me the night before. Along with an increasingly strange cast of characters, I seemed to be attracting at least one person who wished me ill. I could only wonder why. Somebody was overestimating my abilities.

CHAPTER 9

I thought I should call or see Tavi, but I couldn't tell him anything about Jayde's case. My would-be assassin was wasting a bullet. I wasn't "hot on the trail" of the missing painting. In fact, I didn't have a clue about its whereabouts. So, what the hell was going on? One thing for sure, if Jayde didn't want to be followed, she should have stopped wearing that tiny red bikini. Every pair of male eyes was trailing us (her) as we walked along the beach. That's where I found her, and she wasn't hard to spot.

"You know you're not exactly keeping a low profile. With that car you're renting, and . . ." I tried hard to look at her face when I spoke, and I caught a glimpse of her grin as I failed. ". . . that bathing suit."

"I know, but it's intentional. I've changed my tactics. Now I think we should try to flush them out."

I shook my head in disbelief. "I'd say we've flushed something out. Last night somebody shot at me."

She stopped. "Oh, no! Were you hit?"

"No, but it was just luck that I wasn't."

"What should we do about that? Did you go to the police?"

"No. I have a friend there, but if I wanted help, I'd have to tell him about your case."

"So what now?"

"I don't know. Probably the best thing is to get the thing done, to get the whatever it is found and you on a plane back to the States."

Just then, we passed a man in a flowered shirt reclining in a beach chair shadowed by a huge hotel umbrella. I kept us walking but gasped, "Oh, hell!" as I nearly stumbled over my own feet.

Jayde caught me. "What's wrong?"

"See that man under the umbrella, the blue one with the hotel logo?

"Where?" She turned.

"Don't look!"

"If I don't look then how can I see? What am I supposed to—"

"Just keep walking. Act like nothing is wrong."

"Well, nothing is wrong. Is it?"

I snuck a look back over my shoulder. "My God! The son of a bitch is grinning at me."

"I really don't understand what's going on right now."

"That's the man I saw kill the man who was following you two days ago."

"Should you go arrest him or something?"

"What?" I was about to reveal myself as the coward I am at times. "I don't have a gun. And that guy is a killer."

"Let's go find a cop, then."

"Just keep walking."

I pulled her along until we reached the walkway to her hotel. The man was wearing the same red flowered shirt I saw him with when he took down his competitor. At least I guess the fellow was his competitor. Otherwise, why kill him? This was really getting to be too much for me. We had to "fish or cut bait," like my grandpa used to say.

I left her at the elevator, but she called me before I could even leave the hotel lobby.

"Something wrong?" I asked.

"I just wanted to remind you that the fat man probably has a map. We should get that."

"How?"

"I'll leave that up to you. I think members of your profession likely have contacts among people on both sides of the law. People with special skills that might be useful for us."

"Now you want me to arrange a burglary? I should show you the inside of a Mexican prison sometime."

"The sooner we get the map, the sooner your problems will be over."

"*My* problems?" I had to keep myself from shouting. People in the lobby were looking at me. "I think you wanted me to steal that map all along."

"Once I knew what a brave man you are," she purred. "It did cross my mind."

"I'll call you later."

I was disgusted with myself. This was a job I should never have taken on. It was going to get me killed. If Jayde had been ugly or even just plain, I wouldn't have done it. I'm just a weak-willed sucker when it comes to a pretty woman. And that brought a quote from the long dead Egyptian Akhenaton to mind: "When virtue and modesty enlighten her charms, the luster of a beautiful woman is brighter than the stars of heaven, and the influence of her power it is in vain to resist." That said, I don't know about the virtue and modesty bit.

Jayde was right about one thing. I did have friends who, for a price, would be happy to do a little breaking and entering. Jesse would do it, but I didn't want him at risk. Someone else came to mind. Someone with more criminal cunning.

❋ ❋ ❋

Lizardo was in his usual hunting ground on the tourist promenade when I caught up with him. It appeared he'd had a productive morning because he was counting the bills in a pile of cash when I touched his shoulder.

"Híjole!" He jumped.

"Sorry, buddy. Didn't mean to startle you."

He relaxed quickly when he saw it was me. "JJ snuck up on me, compadre." He grinned.

I marveled for the thousandth time how a street crook could look so innocent. You would almost apologize to him if his hand got hung up when he was relieving you of your wallet. "I have a job for you, if you want it. But it might get you in trouble."

"Aha!" he laughed. "So it must be a crime, hehe."

"Well . . ."

He patted my arm. "It's OK, amigo. I'm your man. As long as I don't have to kill anybody."

"Does your cousin still work at La Hacienda?"

"Sí."

"Could she get you a room key?"

"For a few pesos, of course. She trusts me, so it cannot be for a very bad thing."

"No. I just need to find a paper. A map, actually."

"And you want me to search someone's room for it?"

"Yes."

"That should not be a problem, my friend."

Lizardo was a good guy. I didn't want to get him in any trouble, but I needed the damn map.

CHAPTER 10

Lizardo found me back on the promenade. His hand was bleeding and wrapped in a handkerchief. "Nothing there, JJ. Not a damn thing. I searched thoroughly and restored everything to good order, then moved to the closet on my way out. When I slid the door back, a little green dragon struck me."

"We better get you to the hospital."

Nothing was going to be easy in this case. I could feel it. Something as simple as searching a hotel room almost turned into a catastrophe. The fat man had left his lizard to guard things. Turns out that reptile was a hell of a lot more effective, and surely more vicious, than a pit bull.

The emergency room doctor only half believed our story that Lizardo had been attacked while playing with his neighbor's mutt. He insisted on rabies shots, which Lizardo suffered through while cursing me and whispering through clenched teeth that I was going to pay twice what we'd agreed upon.

This was in spite of the fact that the search yielded nothing at all. "I'm really sorry about the bite, Lizardo. Damn, what a freaky thing."

"Yes. Very few people can say they were bitten by a dragon."

"Technically, it's an iguana."

He held up his stitched hand. "I say dragon."

Fair enough. "Hey, about the map. If it's not in his room, that means it has to be on him, right?"

"Do you want me to check?" he asked. "Added fee, of course."

"Of course. How could you do that?"

"I search him."

"All his pockets at once?"

"No, but close. I make two or three passes."

"Without getting caught?"

My friend feigned hurt. "Do you forget who I am?"

"Right. Sorry."

"I will take all he has in his pockets. And," he waved his hand in artistic flourish, "for a small additional fee, I will return each object to its original place."

I smiled and shook my head in honest admiration. Then a new thought struck me. "If he has the map, could you take it to a hotel or someplace, copy it, and put it back where you got it? Without the fat man knowing?"

My fleet-fingered friend took a theatrical bow and rose with his open palm held toward me. I reached into my pocket. It was worth every peso.

It took less than an hour for him to come back with a copy of the map. When I showed it to Jayde, I expected her to be ecstatic. She nodded appreciatively, that's all.

"Isn't this what you wanted?" I complained.

She patted my hand maternally. "It's part of it."

I must admit I was exasperated. The woman was dragging me further and further into a scheme that was becoming very dangerous, and I didn't feel I was getting the kudos I deserved.

"What does that mean? I went to a hell of a lot of trouble to get this damn map. I can't even tell what it's a map of."

"Of course you can't tell. You have to have the code. Two codes, actually. I have one. That's what the fat man is after."

"He has the other code?"

"Maybe. But I don't think so. He would have had it with the map."

"So who has it?"

"I think I know," she nodded. "I was certain he had the map, but there is someone else. Someone else who has been following me. Probably so I would lead her to the map. She wouldn't be after me unless she either had the key or knew about it. Oh, well, I'm confused and tired." She got up from the table and looked around the lobby. Then she folded the map into a small square and passed it to me in a handshake. "You keep this. Do you have someplace safe?"

"Yes. I'll make a couple of copies and hide them all. What about your code?"

"Not that I don't trust you, but I'll keep that."

I picked up Jesse on my way to see Tavi. I wanted to let him know about the killer in red and the shot taken at me. Of course, he knew there had been a murder in the tourist area, but understaffed as he was, he wasn't likely to ever find out who the perpetrator was. I thought if I gave him a hand, he might assign me some protection.

He leaned way back in his chair. "The man murdered on the walkway was a known criminal from Mexico City. He is no loss to the world. I don't really care who did it. And I've already had to assign more of my police to patrol duty. We have to find the serial killer. That is my priority."

"What about the shot someone took at me? Can you give me some protection?"

"Can you tell me about the case you are working on?" He quickly held up his hand to stop the interruption I was about to make. “Please don’t insult me by saying you are not on a case, amigo.”

“You know I can’t do that, Tavi.”

He nodded toward Jesse, who had been sitting quietly on my left. “Then make use of Jesús María as your guardaespaldas. He is strong and competent.”

Jesse followed my lead as we rose to go. “You’ll miss me if I get killed,” I parted.

Tavi chuckled. “True. But I’ll get over it.”

As Jesse and I walked to our vehicles, I spoke quietly. “Still have that nine-millimeter?”

“Cómo no.”

“Better start carrying it, I think. I’ve got the .38.”

“We could very well go to jail if la policia, other than Tavi, finds us with them.”

“At least keep it in your car. If I have to choose between jail and the cemetery, I’ll take the little room with steel bars on the window.”

CHAPTER 11

"I googled Hermione Gingold," I told Jayde as she sipped her coffee. "Now I know where I heard her name before. Old movies."

"Oh," she seemed unsurprised. "Maybe she's just using the name. Although, parents name their kids lots of weird things. Or she could be a descendant or something."

"The *something* is a fake," I answered. "How about you?" I had to ask. "I couldn't find you on the internet at all. Pretty unusual."

She laughed, or made a sound that approximated a laugh. "I've been very careful to keep a nearly invisible internet footprint. In my business, it's practically a requirement."

I looked around paranoically. She smiled. That kind of made me angry. Why was I scared and not her?

"We have to finish this thing, Jayde. I don't go for heavy deals like this much."

"All we have to do is find the missing piece of the puzzle. If the fat man doesn't have it, then Hermione, or whoever she is, must have it." She patted my hand like a big sister calming her baby brother, which I hated. Then she shivered.

"Don't tell me you're cold," I said.

"No. I just get these feelings when the weather changes."

I pointed at the clear blue sky. "Look up there. No changes. Just blue skies."

"Maybe. Who knows? But I get these feelings when—"

This time it was me interrupting. "We can talk about the weather after we get this deal done, if we ever do. I don't want to drag this out forever. You hired me for a week."

Once again, she flashed her knowing smile. But this time she accompanied it with an envelope which she took carefully from her bag and passed to me. "Here is an extended retainer, JJ. Tell me if it is not enough."

The envelope was thick with hundred-dollar bills. I controlled myself and didn't take it out and count it. It was enough to hire me for a year I was sure. I cleared my throat.

"That is in addition to the agreement we have already, of course," she said. "Just an incentive to make up for the trouble of the moment."

My greed usually overcomes my cowardice. And this time was no exception. I slid the envelope into my pocket.

"OK. What's our next step? Since we don't have both the codes to the map, are we at a stalemate?"

"Hermione is lurking around somewhere," she answered. "We just have to lure her in and grab her."

"Lure her in? Why can't I just call her?"

Another laugh. "That is better, I think. If your *ethics* will allow, tell her you will take her case."

"My reputation—" I began.

She shook her head a bit, amused. "Yes, I know. Well, work it out with your conscience. Just remember someone tried to kill you. It was likely her, or someone hired by her."

She was right. My ethics took a back seat to my health.

CHAPTER 12

The turnoff from the main road to the winding lane toward my house that curves a quarter of a mile through lush tropical vegetation is hard to see if you don't know where to look. I like that because it keeps most uninvited visitors away. This day it didn't.

Around the first bend, a large new SUV was spread across the graveled parkway, blocking me from moving forward. I thought about turning around, but that would have been difficult because of the thick jungle growth on both sides. Instead, I got out to see what the problem was. Stupid move. I should have just backed up.

Doors opened on the SUV, and three burly men slowly emerged and headed steadily for me. I didn't know who they were, but I knew they weren't there to wish me Merry Christmas.

"J.J. Tabasco?" asked the largest one, who looked like he'd been through a war and lost.

"Yes," I stammered, "Can I help you gentlemen?"

The large man stopped just in front of me and smiled the kind of smile a sadistic torturer smiles when he's going to boil you in oil. I thought about running, but just then a cloth bag was dropped over my head and my hands were zip-tied behind me.

"Llaves?" the big man asked one of the others.

"Sí, aquí están," one of them answered.

"Muévelo." I could hear my little truck driven mercilessly into the growth.

"Hey, careful with my truck," I said and was rewarded with a slap on the side of my head.

"Shut your mouth, cabrón! Don't talk unless I tell you." The big ugly one again. (I know it was Dorothy Parker who said, "Beauty is only skin deep, but ugly goes clean to the bone.")

I decided I should take his advice, so I let them lead me without protest to sit between two of them in the SUV. I tried to think of something that'd better my chances of getting out of my predicament, but since I really didn't know what my predicament was, I couldn't come up with any ideas. I just sat there listening to a Mexican ranchero station and trying to figure out what the hell had been putrefying in the bag my head was wearing.

It didn't seem long before we stopped and I was hustled out of the SUV and up what felt like a flagstone path. I could hear a door opening, and I was shoved through before it closed behind me.

A male voice that had the ring of authority boomed. "Idiotas! Qué es este estupidez! Sueltenlo!"

The bag was snatched off my head, and the zip ties were quickly cut to free my hands. The man who had apparently given the orders stood in front of me with an apologetic expression on his face. He was tall, thin, and dignified-looking. He wore a white linen tropical suit, cream shirt, and black tie. There was just enough gray at his temples to give him a sophisticated look. He looked like somebody had plucked him out of central casting to play a billionaire CEO of some international oil conglomerate.

"I apologize for my men, Señor Tabasco. They were not meant to abuse you."

I just nodded. I really had no idea what the hell was going on, but I cooperated as the man took my arm and guided me into what must have been his study. The furniture was wood and leather but light enough to fit into the décor of the mansion

I'd seen in a TV fan magazine spread about a famous Mexican telenovela star who had recently relocated to Hollywood.

He motioned me to a wingback chair across a low table of mahogany inlaid with silver geometric designs, then signaled to an attendant.

"I hope you will take coffee with me, Mr. Tabasco."

I nodded again. Some great vocabulary, huh?

"Forgive me. I have not introduced myself." He reached across the table to shake my hand. "I am Aureliano Buendía."

I froze mid-shake. It was the first time I'd ever met a real cartel jefe. I knew I should say something. But "pleased to meet you" seemed inadequate. I said it anyway.

"I know you are wondering why you are here. It is because . . ." He paused while an attractive young woman in a modest cotton dress brought in a coffee tray and poured two cups.

I refused sugar and cream with a shake of my head, rather than a nod for a change. For the first time I noticed a pearl-handled pistol peeking out of the drug lord's suit jacket.

Buendía sipped his coffee and continued. "It is because I want to retain you for a special project."

My coffee cup was shaking so hard I had to set it down before I made a real mess. "Sir . . . Mr. Buendía . . . I . . . I don't . . . I don't even own a gun." I find lying the best strategy if it advances my self-protection.

The three lovelies who had abducted me nearly killed themselves laughing. Even the aristocratic jefe cracked a smile.

He held up his hand placatingly. "No, no, my friend. Although, I see by your reaction that you are aware of my line of business. Is that not so?"

I paused to gather my voice. "Yes, sir. I mean, Jefe. I mean, I do know who you are . . . Mr. Buendía."

He swept his arm in the direction of his soldiers. "No, Mr. Tabasco. I am Jefe to my soldiers. You and I are on a different relationship level. To you, I am Aureliano or Mr. Buendía. I think ‘Mr. Buendía.’ And I will call you ‘Mr. Tabasco.’ We are two professionals dealing in a business matter.”

“Yes, sir, I mean, Mr. Buendía. But I don’t believe I have any skills you would find useful.”

“You are too modest, my new friend.” His smile turned cold for a moment. “Yes, I have decided we will be friends.” He smiled, then lowered his voice. “But you must still call me Mr. Buendía.”

I nodded and began to speak when he interrupted.

“Now, to the matter at hand.” He rose from his chair and walked to the French doors that led out to a patio. He looked at the sky. “I think rain is coming.”

Oh, God. Not him, too.

He turned back to me. “You have been recommended to me by trustworthy sources as a competent investigator.”

“Who . . .?”

He raised his hand palm outward to silence me. I zipped up.

“It is enough to say that I am satisfied with their recommendation. They may confide in you if they wish.” He walked back to his chair and sat, leaning forward just enough to intimidate a timid fellow like me. “I want you to find out who is killing my men.”

There it was. “Mr. Buendía, I investigate unfaithful spouses, runaways, stolen property. Things like that. I wouldn’t be much help in . . .” My voice trailed off as I waited for him to respond.

He stared at me in silence long enough for me to badly need a trip to the bathroom.

“Before I decide to begin operations in a new location, I do extensive research. I have found, through my network, that your network is excellent. You are able to bring information to bear from more sources than the police, who extort me for huge amounts and do not have your access to petty criminals and community gossip.”

“Yes, but I have clients at the moment. I wouldn’t be able to give your . . . um . . . situation the attention it deserves.”

Buendía laughed knowingly. "I am sure you will find a way to place my case as your top priority." He waved his finger in the direction of his heavies. "If any of your other clients complain, I will have my associates speak to them."

The big one gave me another evil grin. I could just imagine him "speaking" to Jayde.

Buendía held out his hand, and the smallest of the three associates placed an envelope in it. I could see it was stuffed with greenbacks. Buendía held it out to me. When I hesitated for a second, he shot me a hard look that melted to his former graciousness as soon as I took the money. "Good. We have a deal," he said, getting up and moving past me toward his front door.

I took my cue and followed him. He stopped and shook my hand.

"You must understand, Mr. Tabasco. My men are brave and loyal, but they are mostly uneducated and superstitious." He tapped the big ugly fellow on his shoulder. "For example, Ernesto here is perhaps my most courageous sicario. I treasure him for that quality, yet he is of little value in matters of planning and strategy. Ernesto will forgive me if I recount an incident that illustrates my concern."

Buendía pulled Ernesto and me a few feet away from the other two and spoke softly. "A few weeks ago, Ernesto drove me and my wife to a small restaurant, a favorite of my wife, in a little village with only one single streetlight. When I escorted my wife from the restaurant, we could not see Ernesto by our car, which he'd parked in a dark lane beside the café. Then my wife spotted him under the streetlamp and called him over. I asked him what he was doing. 'Looking for the keys, Jefe,' he said. 'How did you lose them way over there, Ernesto?' I asked him. 'Oh, no, Jefe,' he said, 'I lost them by the car, but it is too dark to find them over there. Here the light is much better, under the streetlamp.'"

Buendía gave an avuncular chuckle. My smile was tempered by a threatening look from Ernesto.

"So you see, Mr. Tabasco, if a serial killer is murdering my men, some will believe it is some sort of demon, while some others will be unwilling to work because they fear there is a madman lurking in every shadow. In either case, these men will be unwilling to work. If it is only an ordinary, everyday competitor from one of my rivals, we can handle that easily. Find out which it is. And quickly." The tall, dignified cartel boss leaned toward me as if imparting a great confidence. "This expansion of my enterprise is important to me, Mr. Tabasco. I need the cash flow. You see, my wife wants me to transition into legitimate property development in the Houston area. She wants to join the Junior League and a country club. Do you understand?"

Don't mess up now, I said to myself. You're close to getting out of here alive. I said, "Oh, yes, Mr. Buendía. Like Honoré de Balzac said, 'Behind every great fortune lies a great crime.'"

The jefe smiled. "I like that. Whoever this Balzac is, he is wise. I imagine he does well on the self-development circuit. If you hear he is coming to Mexico, let me know."

Inez called as I was on my way back to my casita after retrieving my truck from the jungle growth it was stuck in. Buendía's people just dropped me off where they had picked me up. No offer of help. I didn't press it. I was just glad to see them go.

"I can tell someone has been looking for something in my office," Inez said. She sounded concerned but not panicky. "I left early, but I may have disturbed them when I returned for my glasses."

"Do you want me to come by?" I asked.

"I would appreciate that, JJ. I want you to look and see if you, I don't know, have any ideas. I locked up when I left. I am sure of that. But the door was unlocked when I returned."

I called Jesse and asked him to meet me at her office.

He was sitting in his car when I pulled up behind him at Inez's place. The radio was on and he was popping pills into his mouth as he hummed along with the music.

"What the hell are you doing?"

He snapped the top on the pill bottle and shoved it quickly into the glove box. "Vitamins," he stammered. He couldn't look me in the eye.

"Are you on drugs?"

"No, no," he blushed. "That is, yes, but—"

"I can't believe it. You, of all people."

"They are drugs for my health, JJ. Not illegal stuff."

"Your health? What's wrong with you?"

He mumbled something I couldn't make out. "What?" I pressed.

"Manhood," he shot out in an embarrassed whisper.

"Manhood?"

He looked at me, exasperated. "Testosterone."

I laughed. "Jesse, you're younger than I am. Don't tell me you're having trouble—"

"No. I am a manly man. But I want to stay that way."

I barely smothered my laugh. Poor Jesse opened the door without looking at me. "Inez is waiting for us."

I followed him in, trying to control my giggling before we got to her office door.

She met us before we had a chance to knock. Even in her harried state, she looked beautiful.

I draped my arm over her shoulder. "Are you okay?"

She didn't recoil, but she didn't exactly warm into me. She walked to her desk and sat down. "Thank you for coming. I could have called the police, at least Tavi, but I don't have anything concrete to tell them."

"You told JJ someone had broken into your office, didn't you?" Jesse asked.

"Not exactly *broke in*. I just know someone has been here. Looking for something."

I was confused, but Inez wasn't a woman to panic. "Why do you think that, Inez?"

She spread her arms to take in the room. "Look around. What do you see?"

"Uh, nothing special. All very neat. Doesn't seem anyone was searching for anything."

"Exactly. When have you ever seen my desk this orderly?"

Jesse nodded. "She has a point. Inez is sort of messy."

Inez glared at him but then softened and said, "Let's just say I am not obsessively neat."

"Oh, I didn't mean—" But she dismissed his apology with a raised hand.

I nodded. "I take your point, Inez. Somebody had a look and, instead of putting things back the way they were, kind of overdid it and put things back the way he thought they should be, not taking into account your, uh, more casual way of doing things."

"OK, no need to patronize. Yes, that is what I mean. And it makes it far more sinister. More worrisome than some burglar. Obviously professional."

"You know, you were right about odd things happening, at least dangerous things," I said. "It's because of me. Well, maybe not *because* of me but because of what I'm doing, because of a case I'm working on. There is an object of pretty high value involved and some hard people are looking for it. Somebody must have seen me coming into your office and now thinks you're involved. Did you check your files?"

She frowned and went to her file cabinet. She opened the drawers one by one and checked the files briefly. She slammed the last one shut. "They have been through them. I know exactly how they are organized. They put them back fairly close to how I had them, but not perfectly." She walked back to her desk but didn't sit. "I suppose I would never have noticed, though, if you had not mentioned it."

"OK," I said. "I don't think you're really in any danger, but we should tell Tavi about this. I'm sure he'll get a patrol car to pass by here and your home every so often, just in case."

She nodded. I stood to go. "Jesse will follow you home tonight and park out front for a while. Just so you'll feel more secure."

"Thank you." She walked us to the door. As we went out she touched my arm. "Another thing. I feel a storm coming, I think."

"A storm?"

"Yes. I sense them."

"I haven't heard any weather reports that say anything's brewing."

"Even so."

"You're the second woman today to tell me that."

"Then you should take notice."

I smiled at her. "I will. Thanks, Inez." Then I stopped. "I want to caution you about something else. It may not affect you, but I think you should know all the same. Have you heard of a man named Aureliano Buendía?"

"The cartel boss?"

"He's in town, looking to set up an operation."

"I know. I sold him the house that belonged to the telenovela star."

My jaw hit the floor. I looked at Jesse, who just shrugged.

"Inez!" I shouted. "I can't believe you would help someone like that move into Cancún?"

"Oh, don't be so sanctimonious, JJ. If not me, another realtor would have sold him a house. Besides, I did you a favor in the process."

"What?! What kind of favor?"

"I recommended you as the best private investigator in Cancún. He would not say what he wanted investigated, but I'm sure he will contact you."

I just shook my head. "I'm sure he will. God help me."

"You should be grateful, JJ. I know he'll pay well."

I looked up at the sky when Jesse and I got outside. Clear as blue glass. So much for women's intuition.

CHAPTER 13

The sun rose in a clear sky the next morning, too. I had half expected at least a shower after Jayde and Inez both predicted a tempest. I was pleased they were wrong. (As some wise person said: "Prediction is difficult, especially about the future.") I had slept in until after 9:00 a.m. because I had let my cell phone battery run down. I had so much on my mind the night before that I forgot to plug it in. When it powered up enough to see my messages, I found I had a stack of them. Messages from Tavi were interspersed with two from Jayde and a couple from Jesse after 6:00 a.m. I was about to begin answering them when Jesse knocked on my door.

"Our client is in jail," he reported.

We made it to the carcel in light speed. I was on the phone with Tavi when we pulled up. "Come on, Tavi! She's not a criminal."

"She ran into a police car. I had to arrest her. She was so drunk she could not stand without help."

"I'm just outside. I want to get her out of there," I said.

"Come right to my office."

And I did. Tavi was apologetic, but I could see his point after I read the arrest report. Thing was, it just didn't sound like Jayde. He let me take her after I posted bail. She was still messed up. I couldn't believe how disheveled she looked. "Windblown" would have been an understatement.

"Jayde. Are you OK? I mean I know you're not OK, but can you talk about it?" I asked as I helped her into Jesse's car. I wanted to know what the hell was going on, but she was still drunk, or something, and I couldn't press it.

I told Jesse to drive Jayde to her hotel. We took her to her room and watched her fall onto the bed. With no hope of any kind of conversation leading to real information, we left and let her sleep.

The damage to the cop car was minor. The busted headlight would be easily replaced. I told Tavi Jayde would pay for that, as well as the fine for drunken driving, a charge that could have gotten her deported, but Tavi didn't press it.

Something about the whole drunk driving thing didn't add up. Jayde may not have been a teetotaler, but she was no drunk. She had far too much class to get herself into this kind of situation. I knew I wasn't going to get any answers out of her until the next day, but for some reason, the whole thing seemed so odd, I got to worrying about Inez. I called her office but got no answer. I drove by her office, but she wasn't there. There was no reason for anyone to target her. So why? I felt guilty. I was the only reason anyone would be after her. I was going to find her and keep her safe if I could.

"Where could Inez be, if she's not at her office?" I asked, leaving a message on Jesse's cell. "We need to find her and put her someplace where she's safe. Call me back as soon as you get this."

I felt bad for Jayde. I knew the drinking bust wasn't her fault. Still, I was feeling less and less qualified to deal with this situation I'd gotten involved in. Jayde told Tavi she'd only had one margarita at the Dos Gatos café, a little place I knew well. I was too nervous to sit and think, which I probably needed to do, so I headed there to talk to Felipe Rivera, the manager. I had done a little work for him when his wife ran off with a Canadian tourist. It was early for the lunch crowd. Felipe brought me coffee and asked how he could help me.

"I have a client, a norteamericana, who was in here last night."

"There were a number of turistas here last night."

"This one is very attractive, una rubia, probably dining alone."

"Yes, I think I know the rubia. I recommended to her the carne asada."

"Did she have much to drink?"

"No. Mineral water, and I believe one margarita while she waited for her meal."

"Do you remember who served her?"

"Esmeralda. She is new. I remember well because there were two beauties, one fair and one dark," he smiled. "Tonic to my old heart."

"Could I talk to Esmeralda?"

"She did not come in today. Maybe she is sick. I will call you if she arrives later."

I thanked him, but I didn't think Esmeralda was going to come in.

I called Jesse and filled him in as I walked back to my truck. "I'm pretty sure Jayde's drink was spiked. To get her out of the way. At least charged with DUI and deported or maybe even killed in a wreck. I don't think they cared either way."

"I picked up her car like you asked."

Jesse had retrieved her rental car from the police compound after paying an exorbitant fee so the police wouldn't report the accident to the car rental company.

"Good, but we need to keep looking for Inez. I'm worried about her. Check with her friends. She's still living with her mother, isn't she?"

"I think so," he answered. "Last I heard. Her father has been dead a long time. She kind of nurses her mother. Alzheimer's coming on."

"Drop by and see if her mother can tell you anything."

"OK, but the old lady is not always . . . lucid, I think is the word."

"Jesse, just turn on your gentlemanly charm. Who knows?"

Now I really had to sit somewhere quiet—not my office, with people knocking on the door—and think about what to do next. There was a place I visited less often than I should. In fact, I hadn't been to Mass in months. Basilica Santa María del Mar was where I was sure to have peace and quiet this time of day, other than a devout rosary-praying abuelita or two.

Sure enough, when I entered there was just me and the sweet grandmother I nodded to. She gave me a toothless smile. That alone was worth the visit. I said a quick Hail Mary and Our Father, then asked God to forgive me while I concentrated on my earthly problems.

When I was a kid, I used to ask my guardian angel to help me out of tight spots. So I figured, what the heck, it couldn't hurt to try it. Didn't hurt, but I guess he was busy, because after fifteen minutes, I found it wasn't going to help.

I crossed myself, genuflected, and walked down the aisle to the exit. The old lady smiled and spoke in a voice that was smoother than I would have expected.

"Cuídate, joven. Viene tormenta." Take care, young man. Storm is coming. I smiled back at her. All these women telling me about a storm. I hoped it wasn't an omen.

I checked the sky when I left the church. Clear. I checked the Weather Channel app on my cell. Nothing coming that I could see. Even so, it worried me. As if I didn't have enough to worry about. I headed to Jayde's hotel to see if she was awake.

⁂ ⁂ ⁂

She was. With a dynamite hangover.

"Do you want me to get some aspirin for you?" I offered.

She lay sprawled on the gold-toned bedcover, but nothing short of a nuclear holocaust could make her look anything but desirable.

"Yes. In a minute. First I want you to tell me what happened to me."

"I think you were drugged."

"*Drugged*?"

"Well, you only had one drink. Isn't that right?"

"Oh, yes. Just one, I'm sure of that."

"So something in that drink got you."

"Yes. I'm surprised I couldn't taste it, though."

"Are you feeling better now?"

"Still groggy. How much trouble am I in? I remember hitting a police car."

"It's all smoothed over. You'll get the price when I give you your bill."

She moved to the window and looked out at the beach. "I can't believe someone tried to kill me. That's never happened before."

"Not kill you. I mean not necessarily kill you. Just get you out of the way. But didn't mind if they killed you in doing that, seems like."

She turned to me. "Can you keep me safe? No offense, but you don't seem like the bodyguard type."

I tried not to show the hit to my masculinity. But she was right. "Maybe not so much. Jesse is, though. He looks mild, but he can hold his own. And I can pull a trigger if I have to."

"Have you ever done that? Aiming at a bad guy, I'm talking about."

I blushed. "I would be capable of that if I had to."

"After last night, I suppose police protection is out of the question."

"I can get some help from my friend there in a pinch. No regular protection. I'm already using that up, anyway, for another friend who may have run into trouble because of this case."

"Who?"

"A friend here. She has nothing at all to do with what we're working on. I'm not sure exactly why she's being targeted. Whoever is going after you must think she is involved. Probably because I went to see her right after you hired me. She said she had a bad feeling about things, but she wasn't certain about why."

"I'm sorry she's caught up in our problems."

"Yeah, well, I'll take care of her too. I hope."

"Maybe you should contact the fat man. He has part of the puzzle we need. I'm sure of that. See if we could work out a deal."

"We've got his part. A copy of it."

"Remember, there is that other missing part. And we need it. I bet he knows where it is, if he doesn't already have it."

"OK, I'll see what I can do."

Not much, as it turned out.

"What?" The fat man chuckled as he sipped his tequila sunrise. "You are offering me a finder's fee?"

"A deal. You and my client both win."

"I cannot see how."

"If we pool our information, we can find the painting, probably. My client gets the painting. Her employer, the insurance company, anyway. Or at least they don't have to pay. You get a big chunk of money."

His jolly expression took a lustful turn as his eyes followed two young lovelies in tiny bikinis walking by. He slipped back into mercenary mode as he spoke to me. "There is more involved here than money. More important than money."

"Don't tell me you aren't in this for the money."

"Oh, yes, indeed I am in it for the money. I fully admit to being a greedy man. I also want to be alive to enjoy that money."

"What are you talking about, Mr. Gutman?"

"Don't be so formal, JJ. Call me Kaspar."

"OK, Kaspar. What?"

"It would undoubtedly cost my life if I were to betray the owner of this painting. The work of art is his security for a new start when he's released from his incarceration. I would need sufficient funds to finance a foolproof new identity."

"I thought he was in for life."

"Ha! That was his sentence. He has other ideas. But in prison or out, he could find me. You see, we both have ethics. My ethics are reinforced by certain death should I not live up to them, no pun intended. You, on the other hand, could make a great deal of money and be under no such penalty should you put your own interests slightly ahead of your client's."

"I don't—"

"Let me caution you, young friend. The matter is becoming more urgent and volatile. I am not a man of violence; however, there are those who labor under no scruples in that area. It would be prudent of you to cooperate with me. If, for some reason, you feel you cannot, then at least end your relationship with your current client."

"Are you threatening me?"

"Goodness, no. I would never threaten. Just a friendly caution."

I rose to go without extending my hand. He accepted the slight with a nod. "Another caution, if you will pardon me."

I stopped and waited for him to continue.

"I've been informed there is an elderly woman poking around. Bright red hair. My sources tell me she has visited with you. She is more dangerous than she seems. If I were you, I would avoid her."

"Any more friendly advice?"

"No. But I hope you will think over what I said. I assure you my advice is offered with the best of intentions."

"I'm sure. By the way, where's your lizard?"

I think he was actually insulted, yet he recovered quickly. "Iguana, JJ. Herbert is an iguana. He is resting after a large meal."

I didn't want to picture the mini-dragon mid-feast. I left.

I'm not particularly brave, but I am stubborn. I didn't like the fat man telling me what to do. I made up my mind to call Hermione or whoever she was. I was pretty sure she had the last piece of the puzzle. She might be more open to a deal than Gutman. I needed to clear it with Jayde first. But I was going to do it anyway.

CHAPTER 14

How the serial killer got the corpse of a man as beefy as the one he had posed down to the edge of the surf was anyone's guess. We, at least Tavi and I, were starting to believe there might be two killers involved.

This one was set up in one of the beach chairs facing the Hotel Esmeralda's balconies so that, along with the sunrise, the guests would be greeted by the mysterious killer's creation. Or killers'? The cadaver was dressed in a simple track suit, holding a wooden baseball bat in his right hand and a beaten store mannequin by his left. (I wondered where the killer was getting the mannequins.) The bat was raised mid-swing, as if about to inflict harsh punishment on the poor doll, and the killer had used some kind of makeup to paint an angry scowl on the cadaver's face.

Tavi's cops were trying to hold the TV reporters and their cameras back, but they were leaking closer and closer to the scene. The newspaper people had arrived earlier. The story would be all over Mexico by the next day.

Tavi sipped from a cup of coffee as we walked carefully around the body, trying to keep from disturbing potential clues. "You can imagine some rich tourist waking up to a beautiful dawn and this monstrosity slaps his groggy vision," he said.

"A tourist called it in?"

"Yes, a hotel guest, actually several hotel guests, called the hotel front desk, and they sent a security guard to see what was up. He called us."

"Usual cause of death?"

"I believe so.'"

I looked around the beach. In addition to the newspeople and cops, there were dozens of hotel guests from Hotel Esmeralda, and more pouring steadily over from neighboring hotels.

"The Chamber of Commerce is going to have a heart attack when this hits the press. It was bad enough before," I said.

"They have already been here," Tavi exhaled in exasperation. "I think they will have my job if I do not find the killer soon."

"Or killers," I said.

"Yes. Or killers," he agreed.

I hesitated nervously before continuing. "Tavi, I want to tell you something. I hope it doesn't make you mad."

"OK. Go ahead."

"I, well, I've been hired by somebody to find out who's doing these murders."

"Good. I, too, will pay you if you can find him. Ha ha."

"I better just come out with it. The client is Aureliano Buendía."

I watched Tavi closely, waiting for the explosion, which didn't come. I added, "You know, the cartel chief, *that* Aureliano Buendía." Still no reaction from my Chief of Police friend.

"Yes, I know. He called to ask about you. I gave you a good reference."

For a moment, I was too stunned to speak. "You know he's trying to set up in Cancún, in your town?"

"Yes."

"You don't care?"

"My friend, this is Mexico. The best I can do is to convince him to avoid bloodshed in the tourist areas and keep his drugs safe."

CHAPTER 15

I drove straight back to my office. Jesse was going to meet me there to help plan our next move with Jayde, so, when I heard a knock, I thought Jesse must have forgotten his key. I opened the door to a very strange sight.

Standing on my doorstep was a man who couldn't have been more than five feet, two or three inches tall, wearing a white guayabera and cargo shorts with sandals. He wore wraparound sunglasses. Around his neck hung a fortune in gold chains of varying thicknesses, and on his wrist he wore what I was sure must be one of the most expensive Rolexes ever made. He had twin .357 Magnum revolvers holstered for convenient cross drawing on his thick leather belt. Arrayed a yard or so behind him stood three near giants of at least six and a half to seven feet dressed much like the little man, except for the gold accoutrements.

Behind them was a black SUV with darkened windows. What was most incredible about the sight, though, was what the short guy had cuddled in his arms: Demetrius, the man-killing fighting cock. The little guy kissed the murderous raptor and set him gently on the ground. "I love these fighting cocks. I have several myself." Then he looked up at me and entered without invitation. "You are Tabasco."

It wasn't a question. He looked around my office and chose the chair in front of my desk before waving me to my chair behind it. "Take a seat. Get comfortable."

I took a seat, but I wasn't close to comfortable. "Sir . . . I . . . I don't . . ." I stammered.

The little man chuckled. "Of course. You were not expecting me. Your friend did not call you?"

"No, I mean . . . what friend, Mr. . . .?"

He reached across the desk without standing. I had to lean over to get hold of his hand that was so large I couldn't believe it was attached to the rest of him.

"I am Sammy Delgado. Some people call me 'Little Sammy,' but they only do it once." He chuckled at his joke. "Inez is your friend, no?"

I should have known. Inez's business referrals were going to get me killed. "Yes, she is a friend."

"And an excellent real estate agent. It took her only a few days to find a perfect estate for me and my associates. Modern architecture. Lots of glass for letting in light. It was designed and built by an artist who died recently, I believe. Only a kilometer past your turnoff. Do you know it?"

I did. It is a garish piece of garbage. "Oh, yes. Beautiful place."

"Yes. I am well-known for my good taste in architecture, as well as fashion." He slapped his knees decisively. "Now to business. Inez said you are just the man for a job I need done."

Not again. "Inez overestimates my abilities, Li . . . Mr. Sammy. I don't even own a gun."

"Ha ha. No, no, no, Tabasco. Not that kind of job." He pointed over his shoulder at the three heavies standing just past the open door. "I have skilled people for that."

He stood up and walked to a window to take in the view of my landlord's house a couple of hundred yards away.

"I like that big house." He turned back to me. "Not for me, though. Too old-fashioned."

"Then . . ."

"Yes," he went on, "I understand you're working with the police here to find the serial killer. Is that right?"

"I am only—"

"Don't be modest. My contacts in the Cancún police say good things about you."

Before I could deny, he continued. "Two of my men have been killed by this monster, including the most recent. I want you to find out who is doing the murders and report it to me. Mexico has no capital punishment. I do."

"I don't know . . ."

"I have a competitor trying to keep me from operating in Cancún. It is possible it could be him trying to scare my people. Most of my men are Santa Muerte and very superstitious. He reached behind him without turning. "Horatio." A thick stack of hundred-dollar bills was placed in his hand, and he tossed it unceremoniously in front of me. "You are hired. I expect to be your top priority."

The dark giant who had delivered the money stepped back as his cell phone rang. He answered softly and handed the phone to his boss. "Isabela."

I thought I saw a look of fear cross Sammy's face. He fumbled for the phone and walked to a corner of the office. "Sí, querida," he answered in a meek tone. "Sí, querida. Por supuesto, querida. Pero . . . pero . . . pero . . ." He held up a finger and smiled in embarrassment at my seeing him so whipped as he hurried outside for privacy.

The guardaespaldas Sammy had called "Horatio" was the tallest of the three. He had mahogany-dark skin and eyes that matched. His hair was long, straight, and jet black, and it was pulled back and tied in a ponytail. His clothing looked like it came from the same tailor his two colleagues and his boss patronized. He stood like a statue of a Spartan warrior in front of the door, and I was shocked to see he was wearing thick, heavy mascara. He noticed my stare, and he winked.

I jerked back in my chair as if I'd been struck by a wasp. The giant laughed, then spoke in perfect American English, with a soft feminine bent. "Little Sammy is afraid of nothing in the world except his wives. The one he is talking to now is Isabela in Laredo. She is shorter than Sammy and broad as she is tall. His other one lives in Juárez. That is Victoria. She and I share fashion tips almost every day on our smartphones. She is a real beauty because of my suggestions. She is very stubborn about her eye shadow, though. I keep telling her mauve is much sexier than peacock blue on girls with our complexion. I am really talented in that area. I should have become a cosmetician instead of a sicario. It is a much more fulfilling profession."

I overcame my shock enough to speak just as there were sounds of a scuffle outside. I jumped up but froze when Horatio tapped the huge .44 Magnum on his belt.

"Best to sit," he said. "Little Sammy gets nervous."

I sat. "No problem."

One of the bodyguards who had remained posted outside shoved Jesse through the door and said, "Este cabrón dice que es tu socio."

"Yes, he is my associate. He's—"

He pushed Jesse toward me and returned to his post.

Horatio smiled and winked at Jesse. "Well, hello handsome."

Jesse looked at me.

I said, "Jesse, this is Horatio. He works for Little Sammy Delgado."

Jesse's eyes widened. "The Little Sammy who—"

"Yes, that one, sweetie," Horatio offered. "He has hired your services."

Jesse nodded. "OK. Your English is excellent, Mr. Horatio, for a sicario, I mean no accent or—"

"No, dearest, I am an Okie. University of Oklahoma, School of Drama. I should be a star by now, but there are few roles for a mixed African Choctaw giant, it seems. Oh well, we all have our crosses to bear."

Little Sammy called from outside. "Horatio! Vamos."

Horatio turned his flirty smile into a serious scowl and growled.

"Bye, guys. Back into my tough guy character."

I followed him to the door.

Little Sammy called out, "My wife wants me home in Laredo tonight, Tabasco. I have to get to the airport. I'll call you tomorrow."

Jesse was waiting for an explanation when I closed the door. I just shook my head. "Do me a favor and go have a talk with Inez."

CHAPTER 16

Jesse held the doll toward me as if he wanted me to take it. "Inez wasn't there, but I found this."

I didn't want to touch it, so I backed away a step. "Where was it?"

"Leaning against her door. Just like yours."

"It's different, a little."

"Not much. Smaller, I guess." He set it on my desk. "We could check with Mama Juana again. See if she can see any difference that means anything."

I picked it up and tossed it to him. "Good call, run it by her. I don't know what's going on, but this doll business creeps me out."

"I bet the skirt is made from something Inez wore," he said as he studied the figure. "The hair is dark, probably from Inez, but it could be from any one of millions of people." He stuck his finger under the medallion hanging from the doll's neck. "Same kind of medal. See, death's head, like the one on yours."

I shivered. "OK. You made your point. Whatever it is, it's creepy. See if Mama can tell us something useful."

❋ ❋ ❋

Jayde had given me permission to approach the redheaded woman with a deal. More or less the same one I'd offered the fat man, ten percent of approved valuation finder's fee *if* she had the remaining part of the code. I called and left a message. That morning, I'd checked with my hotel contacts and found out the redhead was staying at the same hotel where Jayde had a room. Hoping to catch her, I sat in the lobby and watched. I needed to think again, anyway.

I was tired. I closed my eyes for a second just to rest. When I woke up, Hermione stood grinning in front of me, green eyes piercing right into mine.

"Hey, sleepyhead," she chuckled.

I straightened in the chair and shot her an embarrassed smile. "I was hoping to see you, Hermione. I want to run something past you." I stood, a bit unsteadily, shaking off the sleep.

"Why don't you take me to dinner?" she flirted. "We can discuss it over a meal."

She took my arm, and I let her lead me to the hotel's restaurant. The food was very good, if pricey. I had a twinge of conscience about the expense account I was going to present to Jayde. And a twinge of worry about my Visa card being declined if Hermione did not pay.

I made a lame effort to take the check. She didn't let me, and I was glad. I wasn't as uncomfortable with her as I thought I'd be. She wasn't as big a flirt as I thought she would be. She was also dogless. I asked her about it.

"Napoleon is taking a nap. He sleeps a lot these days."

"If he didn't hate me so much, I'd rent him from you to get rid of my landlord's rooster."

"Napoleon doesn't hate you, JJ. He just doesn't know you yet."

During most of the meal, we made small talk. She asked me about my family, which I don't have much of. (I didn't tell her about my sister's kids, though. I didn't trust her.) I told her things she could google and find out. She told me things that were probably manufactured in her imagination but were interesting nonetheless. Could have been partially true. I didn't let on that I knew her name was fake. She probably thought the movie star whose name she was using was unknown or forgotten.

Then, "Look, Hermione. I think we should come to an arrangement about this painting. We could all win."

"Aha, you've reconsidered my offer," she brightened.

"In a way. If you would pool your resources with us. With the piece of information you possibly have, we could most likely find the thing quickly and all . . ."

She shook her head in mock sadness. "Dear JJ, I don't want a finder's fee."

"But—" I began before she cut me off.

"Now, I have an offer for you to take back to your client. Not the agency she works for but her, the person. Tell her I would be willing to allocate a generous share of the proceeds of the painting's sale to her, and you, should she throw in her lot with me."

"She won't."

"She might. Will you present the offer for me?"

"Yes."

As we rose to leave, I accidentally knocked her bag off the chair next to me. Among the spillage was a miniature of the doll that had been placed at my door and Inez's.

"Where did you get that doll?" I asked.

"Quaint, isn't it? Some bit of folklore, I imagine. I found it leaning against my door as I was coming down. I can't imagine who left it there. Possibly a child dropped it."

"Maybe," I said, but I didn't really think so.

I walked her to the elevator and shook the hand she offered. As the elevator doors opened she turned back to me with a warning. "And, JJ, you are in the midst of a dangerous situation. Beware of the fat man."

I had questions, but the door had closed. So I called Jayde. No answer. I didn't leave a message. She wouldn't accept a deal with the old lady, of that I was certain. I called Jesse. He was home. He said there was no trace of Inez, and her mother hadn't been up to providing any useful information. Some mumbling about dolls, Jesse said. I told him I'd call him in the morning. Then I crossed the street and walked down to the beach.

The moon was full and white. I was there to think, but I decided not to. I would clear my mind and rest my soul instead. There were a few couples walking hand in hand along the sand. I found myself wishing I had a sweetheart. I wondered if I'd ever have one. That made my thoughts turn to Inez. Jayde I lusted for, but I could see myself wanting a real relationship with Inez. Too bad she didn't seem to feel the same about me. Like someone whose name I forget said, "Loving someone who doesn't love you back is like hugging a cactus. The tighter you hold on, the more it hurts."

CHAPTER 17

I watched Jayde's yellow convertible pull up to my yard's gate. She had called when she was already on her way, or I would have gone to her hotel. The front grille was dented from her accident, but not so badly that it was any kind of hazard. The front license plate was punched inward a little, although it was still legible. I opened my front door, looked left and right, then proceeded cautiously to meet her, with the gentlemanly intention of shielding her from my nemesis, Demetrius.

"Good morning," she beamed.

I looked around. No vicious poultry in sight. "Let's get to the house."

"What's wrong?"

"The rooster . . ." And as if waiting for the signal, Demetrius charged from behind the bushes near the fence, where I am sure he was lying in wait for me. I grabbed Jayde's arm and pulled her frantically toward the house.

"Hey!" She jerked free. "It's just a chicken." I froze in shock after I reached my door as she bent and extended her hand, palm up, to the bird. He actually pecked her hand gently, as if looking for food. "Sorry, bird. Don't have anything for you to eat." She stroked the bright feathers on his neck. Then she straightened. The great fighting cock pecked adoringly at her feet. I peeked out from the entryway where I was hiding, my mouth open in disbelief. "How did you . . .?" I stammered.

"JJ, he's just a little bird," she mocked scornfully. She sat and I spread the hand-drawn map on my desk. "Time to look at this and see if you have any ideas."

I leaned over the sketch. It was no work of art, but I could tell the key figure was probably a pyramid. There were lots of those in Central America and Mexico, if you counted Aztec, Olmec, and Mayan. Not enough detail on the map to tell what civilization it belonged to, even if I knew enough to distinguish among them. I said, "We should probably take this to a professor who knows about the peoples who built these things. They could at least give us an idea where it might be. I mean what country it could be in."

"If we have to, maybe. That's kind of a last resort. I don't want to give any academic a clue to what we're looking for. It could fall under a country's Antiquities Act or something, and they would claim it."

"Well, the artwork isn't very descriptive anyway. I don't think they'd get much more than we can from it," I agreed. "Those numbers there must be important. I wonder how."

"They surely must be," Jayde said. "If I put them together with my set of codes, and the set we stole from the fat man, they mean . . ." She slapped the paper in frustration. "Absolutely nothing!"

"Do you think Hermione's piece would make it work?" I asked. "Otherwise, we're at a standstill. Unless she has the third part of the code, like she says."

"She does. But only that. And I don't know how she got it."

"How did the fat man get his?" I asked.

"The cartel jefe had a trusted associate who turned out not to be so trustworthy. He sold off parts of the map and clues to people but made sure he was the only one who had them all."

"Maybe he has the artwork, then."

"No. He's dead. Got found out."

"Then . . .?" I began.

"Yes." She scooped up the map. "Let's go see Hermione."

I called the number from the redhead's card. To my surprise, she answered.

"Hermione, it's JJ here. I have Jayde with me. Are you OK with a sit-down? With me and Jayde?"

"With Jayde? What a surprise. A pleasant surprise. I would be delighted. Name the place."

I did. A simple neighborhood bar. Quiet and sure to be empty or close to it this time of day. We got there before she did and asked the proprietor to make fresh coffee.

The little mutt's yapping announced her arrival. She breezed in like a diva, gauzy green scarf flapping. "Darlings!" she sang. "How lovely that we're all together at last."

Jayde and I moved to stand, but Hermione stopped us with a motion as she sat. "No need for introductions, I think. We all know each other by reputation if nothing else."

Jayde reached toward the Chihuahua's rhinestone collar. "What a cute puppy. Does it—?" She whipped her hand back at Napoleon's snarl.

"Bite?" Hermione finished for her. "Yes."

I didn't say it out loud, but not for the first time I thought she looked familiar. Could be I saw her in my pre-Cancún days. Maybe it would come back to me.

"I guess we should get down to business," I said. "Does everyone want coffee?"

The women agreed, and I signaled the owner who had it ready to serve. I was grateful for the caffeine. It was obvious as the women sipped quietly that it would be up to me to lead the conversation. "One thing is sure, it seems to me. All parties involved seem to agree the . . . painting, portrait . . ." I looked around the empty café and lowered my voice "the thing we're after is somewhere in the Yucatán, as opposed to somewhere else in Mexico or in Central America. Is that right?"

Both nodded. I had hoped for words because I wasn't sure how to direct this get-together.

"I mean, it may be obvious, but is there a reason for this assumption?"

I could see the women were each waiting for the other to come clean about this.

Jayde gave in first. "All right. Mainly it's because El Chapo had a place in the jungle near here. He had other places, but not near a pyramid."

"Yes," Hermione chipped in. "Largely rumor, of course. But widespread enough to give it some credence. Of course, there is always the chance it could be a pyramid in Belize or even Guatemala."

"Neither of you think that, right?"

Their silence was enough answer. I had wanted one of them to lead the negotiation. Looked like that wasn't going to happen. "So if we had all the parts of the puzzle, we could likely find the object of our search pretty quickly, right?"

"That is, assuming the parts make a coherent whole," interjected Hermione. "We can't be sure of that without seeing the puzzle put together."

Jayde agreed. "Yes. And how do we accomplish that without revealing the location to each other?"

"That is the dilemma," agreed Hermione.

They both looked at me as if I could solve the problem. No quick answer came to me. I just said the first thing that came to my mind. "What if this thing is a forgery?"

The ladies looked at me as if I were as stupid as I felt. I wished I could suck my words back in, but it was too late. "OK, I know it might . . ." I sputtered. "Jayde, if the insurance company thought the thing was a phony, they'd kiss it off to a bad deal, right?"

"Hmmm, yes, but they agreed to the provenance that valued it in the first place. Twenty-five million estimated value."

That sank me. "No chance of bribing the guy, I suppose?"

"No," she smiled.

I exhaled loudly. No more ideas from me.

"He's dead," she went on.

I thought, but did not say, that lots of people seemed to be dead after being involved with this painting.

The redhead laughed. "Poor man."

"Do you know any valuers who could . . ." I started.

"Many," said Jayde. "For a price."

"Then we find a private buyer who's willing to wait a while until the provenance is reinstated or who doesn't care about that," grinned Hermione.

"Or we get a fake made. A good fake. One that looks centuries old and is made from materials, including paint, that is centuries old and can pass experts' tests to confirm that it is centuries old," offered Jayde. "Very hard to do. Perhaps not impossible."

Hermione and I both sat open-mouthed in admiration. Hermione spoke first. "My, my. What a devious mind you have, dear Jayde. I am in awe."

"I don't suppose you have your piece of the code with you, Hermione?"

"Ha, ha. No. I am trusting, not foolish. And you?"

Jayde smiled. "OK. Let's meet at my hotel tonight with the documents."

"You have a bodyguard, my dear. I do not. What is to keep you from taking my code and leaving me in the wind?"

"You have people here, Hermione. I think we have seen one of them. I am sure they will be hovering. We can meet in an open place. Let's say the hotel café an hour before the dinner crowd."

"Yes," she agreed and rose to leave. She shivered as she picked up her bag. "I get an odd feeling we are in for some stormy weather." And she left with a goodbye nod.

As we walked back to Jayde's car, I chuckled. "I feel bad about not trusting a little old lady."

Jayde smirked. "Those green eyes of hers are not old. She is cunning, I think. Hermione does not believe us, JJ. She is playing us."

"That's low of her," I said. "We were acting in good faith." Jayde didn't respond. I said, "Weren't we?"

She looked back at me and smiled.

CHAPTER 18

I told Jesse about our plan to meet with Hermione that night. I asked him to stay as inconspicuous as possible while keeping an eye on us. He'd been looking all morning for Inez. No luck. Her mother didn't remember him stopping by the day before, and she still had no information to give on Inez's whereabouts. She thought Inez had gone to the States, or "to the North," as she put it. She admitted that her daughter might have told her where, but if she had, it had slipped her memory. I think most things were slipping the old dear's memory. I asked Jesse to make a pass at the airport parking lot to see if he could spot Inez' car. He'd already called her friends, at least the ones we knew. Nobody knew anything. I wasn't sure why I was so worried. There was no reason she had to check in with me before she took a trip, although she normally would have, if only for me to keep an eye on her office.

Funny about Inez. I mean my feelings for her. I guess you could say I had a crush on her. But that makes me sound like a kid. My high school Spanish teacher, Mrs. Ragsdale, was from Mexico. She was my secret flame. I wonder if she knew. Sometimes your feelings are so strong you think the target of your romantic thoughts is bound to know. I wondered if Inez knew. Anyway, I was worried about her.

It was different with Jayde. That was pure lust. I had to laugh at myself. Unrequited love versus unrequited lust. I was such a wimp.

Jayde dropped me off at my house, and I snuck to my door without being attacked by the rooster. I played with the computer a bit, searching for pyramids in the area. Tulum was the closest. About eighty miles. Chichen Itza was thirty-five miles farther. Both had lots of tourist traffic, so the painting could have been discovered if it wasn't hidden very well. Surely there would have been news of that, unless the discoverer didn't know what he had. I crossed that idea off as unlikely. Anyway, I still had no firm cause to believe the pyramid in question was near Cancún, other than the area's proximity to the drug lord's jungle estate. I'd have to wait to see what the puzzle, once put together, showed us.

I had time to kill before the meeting. Best use of it might be to just cruise around and keep my eyes open. I didn't really think I was targeted for murder. That would be giving me too much credit. The more I considered it, the more I thought I was being warned by whoever shot at me. Maybe I was running a small risk by sticking with the case. But why would the killer run the risk of the getting caught, unless he believed I was really on to something? Even then it would be smart to wait until I found what the shooter wanted so he could take it from me.

Cancún was the same as always. Inez said she had a premonition that made her uneasy, but I didn't sense anything strange in the air. I mean, I'd seen a man killed and had been shot at myself, so there was that. OK, I'd been hired by two rival drug lords to find a serial killer who had come to town. And if either of them found out, no more JJ.

As I walked, I didn't see the flowered-shirt man who had killed the other stalker, and I was glad. I hadn't seen him since

Jayde and I passed him on the beach and he grinned at me. The recollection gave me goosebumps. I knew he was around somewhere. Most likely, he was the one who shot at me. I was horribly certain he could kill me if he really wanted to. I had to stop thinking about that or I'd have to quit the case. Coward I may be, but some small bit of manliness in my character wouldn't let me do that.

Jesse called with the news that Inez's car was in the long-term parking lot at the airport. I breathed easier. She'd flown somewhere. It was no surprise that her mother couldn't remember where she'd gone. Odd that Inez had not told me or Jesse or any of her friends we had contacted, though. For now, I would not worry so much about her.

I met up with Jayde an hour before the arranged meeting time of 5:30 p.m. Jesse was already there, seated at the bar with a good view of the restaurant tables. Hermione likely had us under surveillance, so I sat with Jayde at a fairly secluded table. She had the copy of the map with the hand-drawn pyramid, with numbers off to the side that we thought might be counted steps. Jayde had changed the numbers from those on the original map to confuse Hermione.

Jayde said, "She's a smart old girl, JJ. She'll have done something similar." She folded the paper and slid it back into her wallet. "The best we can get out of this meeting is a general idea of what she has. And maybe some insight into the overall directions to the painting. Remember it has to not only be well hidden but hidden in such a way that it's not damaged by weather or anything else.

"Is this meeting worth having, then?" I asked.

"Yes," she replied. "If only to make her think we're naive. Remember, her piece of the puzzle is the one we don't have. She won't be showing us the real clue, but we may get an idea of what the clue is. Is it numbers, another drawing, or what?"

But Hermione never showed up. We waited for two hours, calling her every fifteen minutes.

"She's not coming," I said, finally. "I think she may have had an accident, or . . ." I let the suggestion of harm hang.

"I think it's *or*," Jayde agreed.

"The fat man?"

"Most likely he's behind whatever happened to her," she said. "I don't know why he'd go after her now. Unless he knew she was making a deal with us."

"I think we should consider there may be others in the race," I suggested. "We're including only Hermione and the fat man right now. Don't you think there could be more?"

She considered for a moment before beginning to nod slowly. "There could be. El Chapo was no genius. He was successful because he terrorized people."

"That guy in the flowered shirt who killed the stalker may be part of a different group than Gutman's or Hermione's."

"That's right," she said. "You and Jesse better really start watching our backs."

As we got up to leave, I looked over to the bar to make sure Jesse was watching our backs.

Jayde went up to her room to call her employer. I decided to walk down the street to see if I could find the hotel where Hermione was staying. I suppose I should have done that before. I'd thought she was staying at Jayde's hotel, but I was wrong.

I could have prowled her room like I did Gutman's. It had been on my mind. If events hadn't exploded, I would have. The second hotel I walked into was the place where she'd checked in; however, the concierge, whom I knew slightly and always slipped a fair tip for info, told me she'd checked out earlier that afternoon. That would have been before our meeting time. I began to speculate on her reason for leaving. If she'd come up with a lead on the painting, I hoped she'd share. It was silly of me to think she'd feel obligated, though.

I started walking to my car, taking a shortcut through the hotel garden, and I'd just passed beyond the hotel's outdoor illumination when the flowered-shirt killer stepped out of the foliage.

In the instant before he slugged me unconscious with some sort of blackjack, I remarked mentally on his odd resemblance to someone I knew. And that he was wearing a black shirt, not a flowered one.

My brain was scrambled when I came to. My pockets were turned inside out, my wallet and keys gone. I stumbled to my feet and wobbled toward the hotel entry. I'd nearly reached it when a hand grasped my shoulder from behind.

"My God, man!" the fat man said with what seemed like genuine concern. "What has happened to you?"

I could barely stand, and my vision was blurred, but I could have sworn Gutman was holding a doll like the one I had been "gifted," except nearly twice as large. He was carrying it like one of those prizes you win at local carnivals. Then things went dark.

I woke up in a hospital bed with a saline drip in my arm and the fat man hovering. Even in the air-conditioned ward, he mopped perspiration from his face.

It was the nurse who spoke first. "How do you feel, Señor Tabasco?"

"Like somebody hit me on the head."

She gave a cute giggle. First thing I noticed was her figure, God help me.

"A good sign, Mr. Tabasco. Sense of humor is a good sign."

"Can you please give me my phone, nurse. I need to call my associate."

"It is in the nightstand beside you. I will tell the doctor you are awake."

She left and I turned to the fat man. "Mr. Gutman. What are you doing here?"

He gave a jolly chuckle. "It will come back to you, JJ. I brought you here."

"Oh." It was coming back, bit by bit. "Somebody whacked me."

"Yes. You have a couple of stitches."

"How . . .?"

"I was leaving my hotel and happened to see you in distress."

"Thanks. Did you call the police?"

"No. However, I believe the hospital has done so. They should be here soon."

"I have a friend there. I'll call him. I was robbed, I think."

"Yes. A mugging, I believe. Your pockets were turned out. Whatever was in them gone. The perpetrator left your watch, however. He must have overlooked it." Gutman grinned.

I looked down at my left wrist. Of course it was in the drawer with my phone. I blushed. My watch was a Walmart Timex. Not worth taking. "Yeah," I said. "They must have." My mind was gradually clearing. "Say, Mr. . . . eh, Kaspar, were you by any chance carrying a big doll when you found me?"

"Aha, very perceptive, even when injured. Private investigator's talent. Yes, I was. It is in my car. In fact, I was on my way to an acquaintance's home to inquire about it when our paths crossed."

"Where did you get it?"

"Oddly, it was leaning against my hotel room door. At first I thought it was a child's toy. And perhaps it is. Still, I would like an opinion from a person with knowledge of local lore. Would you perhaps know its origins?"

"Uh, no," I said. "Just seemed strange to see you with a doll instead of a lizard."

"Haha . . . I imagine so. Well, no matter. I can deal with that later." He moved to the door. "I imagine your associate will provide you with transportation when you are able to leave." He grimaced and rubbed his shoulder. "This weather plays havoc with my rheumatism. A storm coming, I think."

"Is everybody a weatherman?" I spat under my breath.

"I beg your pardon," he replied.

"Nothing. Yeah, he'll pick me up. Thanks for your help."

"My pleasure." The fat man paused in the doorway. "I will not press you in your present condition, of course, but I do hope you are considering my proposal." He gave a slight bow. "Good night, my friend." And he stood aside to let the nurse pass in before disappearing into the hallway. She was carrying a skeleton dangling on a string.

"What the—?"

She smiled mischievously. "A Day of the Dead decoration for your room. Only a few days away. I wanted to cheer you up."

I shook my head. "A skeleton to cheer me up. That is one Mexican custom I don't think I'll ever get used to."

CHAPTER 19

Tavi got to the hospital before Jesse, but I couldn't leave with either of them. The doctor wanted me to stay overnight to make sure there was no concussion.

I gave Tavi a description of the guy who slugged me and, as I did, I kept thinking I knew him or at least recognized him. Tavi told me it was unlikely the mugger would be caught, unless he tried to use one of my cards. He told me to cancel my Visa and Amex right away, which I did. The cash from my wallet was only twenty dollars or so in pesos. I didn't keep an exact count.

Tavi also recommended I change the locks in my house. As soon as I could, I'd follow that advice, as well. Nothing much I could do about the car without going to a lot of expense to change that lock. I'd just make sure my insurance was paid up.

The next morning, Jayde called and came by the office. I was touched. She seemed genuinely concerned about my injury, but she told me that her US office had no further relevant info for us. One thing, though. She said El Chapo's lawyers were pressing for the insurance settlement on the painting. They wanted to make sure they got paid. The drug lord couldn't claim any

for himself because in the US, the perpetrator of a crime isn't legally allowed to receive any financial benefits from it. So Jayde's employers were after her to speed up the search. They were sure Gutman wouldn't give up the location. If El Chapo escaped or bought his way out of prison, it might be the only thing left he could use to cash himself up.

She said we should make a stab at our step theory for finding the portrait by going to the Tulum pyramid, since it was closest. I agreed. She was paying. I just asked for a day or so while my head healed.

In spite of my headache, I spent the rest of the day in my office studying the parts of the map we had and trying to figure out what we might be lacking that Hermione's part would fill in. So far, it was just a crude drawing of a pyramid and some letters and a number that made no sense. I wondered if Hermione had the catalyst that made it click. I wondered if we'd ever see her again.

The nurse with her skeleton decoration had reminded me there would be a Festival del Día de Muertos in a few days. I wondered if the festival had anything to do with the Santa Muerte dolls that kept showing up at the doors of people searching for El Chapo's painting. And, if so, why. I believed Hermione and the fat man knew no more than I did, so I decided to go back to Mama Juana to see if she could tell me anything more, now that there was a kind of pattern.

I hadn't asked Jesse what Mama Juana had told him about the figure that was left at Inez's door. I would do that right away.

Jesse informed me that Mama Juana had googled "Santa Muerte doll" for more up-to-date information. Yes, I know. So I googled it myself. I found muñecas like the ones I and the others had been "gifted" with. But the internet info was too academic to be useful, and those narratives didn't have Mama

Juana's inside knowledge. My unanswered questions were: What are the dolls meant to do to or for us? And why were they given to the select few who had received them? Even Mama Juana didn't have answers.

I ran into the fat man the next day. Rather he ran into me. And Jayde. He wasn't carrying the doll, but he was leading his iguana.

Jayde and I were sitting at an outdoor table on the promenade, nursing morning coffee.

"You're sure?" she asked.

"I saw his face. It was the flowered shirt guy. The killer. I'm lucky he didn't kill me. He just wanted it to look like a mugging."

"Oh, no, here comes Gutman," she warned, "and his awful *pet*."

The fat man approached out table and doffed his hat formally. "Good day, dear JJ. May I join you?" He bowed to Jayde. "I am Kaspar Gutman, dear lady. If I am not greatly mistaken, you are Ms. Jayde Blackwood."

"I am," she answered.

"We have common interests, Ms. Blackwood. I am sure you know that."

He took a chair without waiting for permission. "Lovely day. If a bit warm." He motioned to the waiter and pointed to the coffee cups. "Otro café, mesero, por favor." He tied the iguana to the leg of his chair and set his hat on the table.

Jayde recoiled in disgust when the iguana brushed her leg. "My God!" she exclaimed. "What is that thing?"

"Herbert is my faithful and affectionate companion." He actually reached down to stroke the reptile. Jayde shivered at the sight.

"A lizard?" she asked incredulously.

"Iguana, my dear."

He turned to me. "How are you, my friend? Any long-term effects from the mishap?"

"I won't know until the long term. Did you find out anything about your doll?" I asked him.

"Yes and no. It is a kind of charm associated with the Santa Muerte cult. But I don't know who placed it or why."

"Some narcos follow that religion, if you can call it that," I said.

"Yes. However, I am reliably informed that this was not done by El Chapo's men or on his behalf," he countered. "If that is what you were wondering. I am not saying that it is impossible that a rogue element is involved, but my sources are excellent."

I threw a glance at Jayde, hoping the look would be enough to keep her from mentioning our own "voodoo dolls." It was.

"Just a prank, maybe," I said.

"Perhaps. At any rate, I am not concerning myself with it. More important matters are at hand."

A group of young people carrying brightly painted ceramic skulls stopped to admire the fat man's iguana. "Cuidado," he warned, "he will take a finger off." They took note and moved on, laughing. Jayde used her uninjured hand to self-consciously cover the one with the missing finger.

"Why are they carrying those skulls?" he asked. "I believe there is some sort of celebration coming up. Do they have to do with that?"

"Day of the Dead," I said. "First and second of November. First day is for departed children, second for adults. It's a national holiday now. Comes from a custom in place before the conquistadores."

"Aha," he acknowledged. "Interesting." His coffee came and he drank it in one gulp. "By the way, have you seen our flame-coiffed friend, Ms. Gingold, of late?"

I didn't know he knew about her. I stammered "I . . . uh . . ."

"Oh come, dear boy, there are no secrets in an enterprise like ours."

I blushed, I think. "Not for a while."

"Hmm," he considered. "Not like her to throw in the towel so early."

"Do you know her well?" Jayde frowned. "How?"

"Yes, yes, my dear. Not well, but it seems we are in the same line of work." He chuckled. "Colleagues, one might say."

He untied his iguana's leash. "In this case, I must agree with Hermione. I don't believe the item we seek is in this area. Indications are that it is likely in Belize. One of the older monuments. I am also abandoning this lovely place, I'm afraid." He picked up his hat and rubbed his shoulder. "My rheumatism presaged the weather channel, so it appears. A rather large disturbance is picking up strength in the Gulf and heading this way." Then he bowed and strolled off down the pathway.

"Do you believe him?" Jayde asked me.

"About the storm?"

"About his leaving."

"No."

CHAPTER 20

I must have left my phone on the desk in my office because I couldn't feel it on my bedside table where I usually parked it at night. I stumbled out of bed, bumping my shin on a chair in the dark. As I danced in pain, I glanced at my alarm clock. 5:30 a.m. Too damn early. I located the cell by the ring light on its screen. I reached for it but knocked it to the floor. When I finally got it under control, I was greeted by a familiar voice.

"JJ?"

"That you, Tavi? It's the damn middle of the night!"

"You said you wanted to be kept in the loop, my friend. You would not want to miss the latest artistry of our killer, I am sure."

"What?!"

"Come see for yourself."

"It's Sunday morning. My one day to sleep a little late," I complained.

"It appears our serial killer observes the Sabbath, too."

"What are you talking about?"

"The Cathedral. His latest work."

"You're kidding."

"Discovered by the priest who was scheduled to celebrate early Mass. He has called the bishop, who is on his way as we speak."

"I'll be there in fifteen minutes."

It didn't take me that long. But I had to park more than a block from the church. There were police cars crowded near the curb in front of the old cathedral, along with TV news, local and foreign press, and a bunch of curious gawkers ahead of me. I noticed the bishop's white limousine on the walkway to the open doors. His Excellency himself was with Tavi, and very unhappy by the looks of him. Tavi nodded humbly as the bishop took his leave and strode grimly back to his vehicle.

I looked up to the massive wooden doors and saw the reason for his unhappy mood. The killer's set decoration this time was even more confusing than his previous efforts. The corpse was dressed in an ordinary priest's cassock complete with Roman collar and biretta. He was seated in what looked like a mockup of a confessional, a Bible in one hand and, on his knee, a large Santa Muerte doll with his other hand up inside the back of the doll as if he were using it like a ventriloquist's dummy.

I searched deep into my vocabulary to describe my reaction and came up with "Wow!"

"Wow, indeed," echoed Tavi, newly arrived at my side. "It is the first time I have heard His Excellency use language that would make a drunken sailor blush."

"That's a Santa Muerte doll, isn't it?"

"Yes. A big one. That makes this an even greater sacrilege," Tavi said.

"Look at all those TV cameras. This is going to be all over the world's screens before we finish our morning coffee."

"Indeed," Tavi agreed. "If not already there."

Tavi moved one of his men who was protecting the display to give us a closer look.

I took a picture with my phone. "I have to give the devil his due," I said (which is a quote from one of Shakespeare's plays, I think). "Whoever's doing this is a real artist. Maybe a sick one, but still . . . he's good."

The oddest thing: Tavi blushed and looked down like a modest schoolboy. "Yes, I suppose he is." Then he caught himself. "For such an evil creature, imagine, a sacrilege like this, on the front steps of God's house."

"Do you think the cause of death with this fellow will be the same as for the others?"

"Of course, I can't be sure until he is autopsied, but I think so, yes."

"No progress?" I asked. "No DNA or fingerprints or anything?"

"Nothing. The killer knew how to keep things clean of identification. You need to tread very carefully, my friend. I know you are working for both the Río Seco and Luna Nueva cartels. If I know that, both of them will also know very soon. They will wonder if you are betraying one or both of them."

I didn't deny it. Tavi led me back out of the crowd, past the worshippers who had gathered for early Mass. I imagined the sight of the dead man would keep them saying their prayers faithfully for a long time.

I took leave of Tavi and headed for my truck. As I got in, I saw a black SUV with darkened windows. Little Sammy's—I was sure of it. Couldn't see who was inside because of the tinted windows, though.

Before I got home, my phone rang. The voice was familiar.

"I just came back from the Cathedral. I hate getting up this early," Little Sammy said. "I have not had my coffee. That makes me irritable."

"I know how you feel," I sympathized.

"No, Tabasco. You do not know how I feel. I have a business that is in danger of losing valuable employees. I would not care if these employees were not so important to my revenue. Opening an operation in a new market makes them even more essential."

"Sure," I said meekly. "I can see that."

In the background, I could hear his top man, Horatio. "Jefe, it is your wife, the pretty one, on your other phone. She says it doesn't matter if you are talking to the pope. She wants you on the line right now."

"Coming dear," he shouted, but submissively. Then he lowered his voice and said to me, "The dead man we have just seen at the Cathedral was not one of my men, God be praised. I would be even angrier than I am if he were. But, as you and the useless Cancún police have allowed the maniac doing these crimes to roam free, I can't be certain the next victim won't be one of my valued associates. I expect you to move quickly to find the killer. I am not a patient man."

He hung up before I could reassure him. Which was good because I had nothing reassuring to offer.

My next caller was even less patient. The corpse he was bemoaning once carried the vicious, but efficient, soul of a Río Seco sicario from Morelia. "This son of a bitch is killing my people all over the country!" he fumed. "What kind of maniac does that?! Does he do his slaughtering then send them to Cancún by FedEx?!"

I spoke without thinking. "Technically, Mr. Buendía, he doesn't slaughter them. He poisons them."

The explosion on the other end of the conversation nearly took out my eardrums. "I don't give a damn how he is doing it to my men, to people who belong to me!"

"Yes. Of course you're right. No matter what method he—"

"So, do your job! I expect immediate results. Do you understand me, Mr. Tabasco?!"

The second person in half an hour to hang up on me before I could answer. Must have been something annoying in my voice.

CHAPTER 21

In spite of fear for my life from Little Sammy and Buendía, I tried to put effort into Jayde's case. After all, she had hired me first. And she was a lot sexier.

We took Jayde's rented Mercedes to the Coba ruins about half an hour past Tulum. It was a much more comfortable ride than my truck, and the roads were pretty good. Nohoch Mul there was the tallest pyramid in the Yucatán. It would, I thought, appeal to the drug lord's ego. I had a theory that the number on our map indicated the level of the stone in the pyramid that the artwork was hidden beneath. One hundred and twenty steps led to the top of Nohoch Mul, and my piece of the code included a number with some squiggles following. The number looked like an eight. Didn't know if the squiggles meant "from top" or "from bottom," or something else entirely. Long shot, but with Hermione gone with her piece of the puzzle, it was all we had. And Tulum was the closest pyramid to El Chapo's jungle estate. Nothing ventured, nothing gained, they say. Besides, I had to make some effort to justify my retainer.

We had the top down all the way, and my nose was burned by the time we arrived. Jayde had offered me her sunblock, but I had to be "manly" and sacrifice myself to the gods of skin cancer. I wished I didn't feel the need to impress pretty women with how tough I was. It almost always backfires. My nose burned like hell.

I'd been to the Coba ruins before, but they still excited a sense of awe in me. I wondered what it would be like to be part of that society back then. Likely, I would be as ordinary as I am now.

There were three tourist buses there when we arrived. People with cell phones and regular cameras were recording every moment. I considered how I might get the painting out without drawing attention to it. That is, should I find it. About as likely as winning the lottery. I knew that. But I bought a lottery ticket every week.

Jayde had never been to these ruins, or any others like it, she said. So I indulged the tourist in her before we got down to work, and for a moment, I just let her alone while she breathed in the beauty. I started up the first few levels of the pyramid and waited for her to catch up.

The ruins of the ancient site gave a feeling of old ghosts looking at me from the stones. It was eerie but not frightening. I looked up at the pyramid of Nohoch Mul and struggled up the steps, trying to put myself in the place of a sacrificial victim about to die.

From the top, we looked out over the magnificent jungle landscape of Yucatán and wondered how many people had seen the same view as their last. It made my troubles seem petty. From her expression, I think Jayde was equally impressed. She gave me a brief look before we moved down.

"We should be careful," I said. "Mexico fines people who climb the pyramids."

The plan was to count up or down to the eighth step, then walk around the structure looking closely for any indication a stone was loose or disturbed. If we came across one, of course, we'd have to wait until the tourists had gone before we pried up the stone.

We walked down eight steps, then I started to my right and Jayde went left to circumnavigate the structure. I looked closely, but nothing appeared to have been disturbed for centuries. I focused intently. Too intently. That's why I bumped into the fat man.

"JJ, my friend," he said as he stumbled backward. "What a surprise!" Gutman was perspiring and wiping his face with a handkerchief the size of a dish towel. He lowered himself onto a step and fanned himself vigorously with the sweat-soaked cloth.

"I apologize," he puffed, short of breath. "I did not see you coming."

"Kaspar, I thought you were leaving." I was surprised, but not completely.

"Yes. Well, I thought I should have a go at least." He breathed deeply. "You also decided this area may have promise, I see."

I sat beside him. I wasn't fat, but I wasn't in the greatest shape. "Like you. I thought I might as well give it a try."

"Exactly. And what was your reasoning for examining this particular monument, my friend?"

I had to laugh a little at his audacity. "Come on, Kaspar. We're competitors."

He began to feign innocence, then gave it up with a grin. "We are, indeed. Though I have not given up hope that you will join forces with me."

Jayde rounded the corner and frowned when she saw me with the fat man. I waved. She didn't wave back. I stood, nodded to Kaspar, and walked toward Jayde.

"What was that about?" she asked.

"He's doing the same thing we are, but without the same clues, I think."

Gutman waved at Jayde and walked out of sight around the pyramid's corner. Jayde warned, "Let's avoid him."

There were lots of tourists crawling over the ruins. That was helpful because it probably disguised that Jayde and I were searching in a pattern. We took about an hour to inspect the two rows we had targeted. No success.

One of the buses that had been in the parking area when we pulled in was now moving quickly down the road. The fat man trotted, waving frantically in its wake. The driver was too far away to see him, I guess. At any rate, he didn't brake. Gutman stopped and wiped his face with his huge white handkerchief. I almost felt sorry for him. He rushed to one of the other two buses and spoke briefly to the driver. Must not have had any luck, because soon afterward, he backed away and marched purposefully to the only remaining bus. He spoke through the open door then stepped away from the bus, shaking his head in despair.

I couldn't avoid him on my way to Jayde's car. I knew before he asked what he wanted.

"Oh, my friend," he gasped, "I am so happy you are still here. My bus left without me. The other two have standing room only. In my physical condition," he grinned self-deprecatingly, "I would never make such a long journey standing in the aisle." He furiously cleared the moisture from his face, wringing out the handkerchief, and trying unsuccessfully to staunch the flow with the huge cotton cloth.

"I guess Jayde won't mind," I said as she came up from behind. She had heard and gave a kind of grudging assent.

"I am grateful to you, kind lady," he replied.

He sat in the back. I think Jayde left the top down so it would be harder to hold a conversation. I would rather have picked his brain, but I might have been overmatched in the slyness department. We dropped him off at his hotel just at sunset.

CHAPTER 22

Jayde dropped me off, too. I told her to stay in her hotel and not open her door to anyone. If she needed to go out, to call me, to use room service for dinner and ask the room service operator to give her the name of the waiter they were sending up and to describe him. She thought I was being overly cautious, but I bent down to show her the stitches in my head from the attack, and she agreed to do as I asked.

Jesse came by to take me to eat. I was tired but hungry. He was happy. He'd won 800 pesos in the lottery.

"Jesse, that's just forty dollars. You're acting like you won a million."

"Ah, yes, my friend. But I won. The amount is not important. I won. That means God is smiling down on me."

I could see why women liked him. He was almost childishly optimistic and happy about the most minor things. It was probably good to be Jesse.

"Does that mean you're buying dinner with your winnings?"

"Por supuesto! As long as we eat at a reasonably economical place."

"Tía's, then."

"OK." He ran right through a red light. Jesse was an adventurous driver. I was pretty sure I would meet my end riding with him one day. I crossed myself like the good Catholic I wasn't.

"Oh," he remembered. "Inez is back."

That was good news. I hadn't been able to get past the worry that she'd been hurt because of her friendship with me. "Did you talk to her?"

"No, but I saw her car in front of her office."

"I'll call her later. Or maybe we could stop by tomorrow if I can think of some excuse."

"You don't need an excuse, JJ. She likes you."

That was good for my ego. I just wished it was more than "like." But I decided I'd stop by the next day.

"All those people were right," Jesse broke into my reverie.

"What people?" I asked. "Right about what?"

"The weather. The storm. There is one coming. At least maybe coming. I saw it on the Weather Channel today."

"Why were you watching the Weather Channel?"

"I like it. Better than most of the stuff on TV."

I couldn't argue with that. And I knew what a hurricane could do to Cancún. We'd had them before. Not fun.

"Seems like lots of people feel bad weather is coming," I said.

"My mother was like that," Jesse said. "We didn't need the Weather Channel when I was a kid."

We were passing fairly close to Inez's office. "Why don't we swing by Inez's place and see if she's hungry?"

"Sure."

We were there in two minutes. I started to call to tell her we were outside rather than barge in on her, but there was a dark blue Audi parked next to her car.

"Whose car is that?" asked Jesse.

I looked up at her office window. The light was on, and I saw Inez pass back and forth waving her arms animatedly. "I think she's busy. Best not disturb her."

"Does she have a new boyfriend?" Jesse asked.

She'd had the same sweetheart for years, until he died in a car accident almost a decade ago. Since then, to the best of my knowledge, she hadn't been romantically involved with anyone.

"I'll call tomorrow," I said.

As I pulled out of the parking area, an off-road Jeep pulled in. The driver had a long scar on his face and gave me a once-over as he drove by. He and his passenger were short and dark. They were surely pure-blooded Indians, maybe Mayan or Nahua. In my rearview mirror, I watched him pull next to the Audi. I forgot about it quickly.

The restaurant was full. People were talking excitedly about two things: Day of the Dead celebrations and the impending storm. We had to wait a bit for a table, but the food there was worth it. We'd just found a place when two men, big guys, came in and gave us a menacing look as they sat three tables away from us. My back was to them, but Jesse could see them well.

"Híjole!" he whispered. "Those men look like hard cases."

I'd watched them walk past. They wore polo shirts like mine, one red, one blue, and khaki slacks. Their muscles looked firm and bulged tight in the sleeves. They were built more like boxers than weightlifters. In fact, the one in the red shirt looked like his nose had had frequent meetings with unfriendly fists. I didn't think they were close enough to hear in the raucous crowd, but I didn't want to take any chances, so I spoke softly. "They're sure not locals."

We hurried our meal a bit. I asked Jesse once or twice if they were looking our way. They were. And Jesse was getting nervous. Me too.

"Did you bring your gun?" I mumbled to Jesse.

"No. Do you think we will need a gun?" Jesse answered, a little too loudly.

"Shhh! OK. Let's just leave. If they follow . . . well, I don't really know. We'll have to play it by ear."

"What about your gun?" asked Jesse.

"At home." I rose. "Let's go."

We did. Unfortunately, the two men watching us did too. There was nothing to do but keep moving and get into Jesse's car quickly. But his doors were locked. He fumbled his keys and dropped them on the ground. A large rawboned hand cut in front of Jesse's and picked them up. Jesse straightened. I had to jolt myself with a quick shot of courage, but I came around the car to help.

The man in the red shirt held the keys out to Jesse, who took them nervously. The man's partner loomed behind him. The red-shirt man spoke to me.

"Are you J.J. Tabasco?"

"Yes."

He took a card from his pocket and extended it to me. "I am Special Agent Walter Purvis, DEA."

His card read: *Walter Lee Purvis, Special Agent, Drug Enforcement Agency* with a San Antonio address and three phone numbers. He didn't introduce his associate, nor did he offer a handshake. I stood without replying, waiting for him to say what he wanted.

"You have a Ms. Blackwood as a client, right?"

"I can't—" I began.

He held his hand palm up to interrupt. "OK. I'm not asking you to break any confidences. I just want to remind you that you are a United States citizen and subject to its laws. Including those involving obstruction of justice and lying to federal agents."

"I know." He was intimidating, but at least he wasn't the hood I expected him to be based on his appearance.

"We're going now. Talk to your client. Tell her we want to meet with her. Call me at the number on the card."

He started to walk toward a dark sedan. His partner called him back. "Hey, I haven't finished eating." The agent who had talked to me shook his head impatiently but followed his associate back into the café.

"That was weird," said Jesse.

"Most everything about this case is weird," I agreed.

CHAPTER 23

Instead of calling Inez in the morning, I got in touch with Tavi. He was in a meeting when I called, so I just dropped by. I had asked Jesse to search the internet to find the ten closest pyramids to Cancún. I didn't look forward to testing my far-fetched theory of the steps on that many, but I didn't know what else to do. I hoped a better clue would present itself.

Turned out, Tavi's meeting was about the Day of the Dead festival. I met Arturo Rivera and another member of the Chamber of Commerce whose name I couldn't recall as they came out the door. We exchanged greetings briefly, and I caught Tavi before he went back to his office.

"Hola, JJ," he sang out in his usual jolly manner. "How are you this morning?"

"Pretty good, Tavi. I just have a quick question if you've got a second."

"Cómo no. Dime."

I pulled out the card the DEA agent had given me and handed it to him. "Do you know if this guy is legit?"

Tavi studied the card and handed it back. His smile had dimmed. "Yes. Their office called from Texas and told me they would be here. *Told* me." He frowned. "Not asked me. Damn arrogant gringos. Sorry, JJ. I did not mean you."

"Never mind, Tavi. They are arrogant gringos. I just wanted to make sure they were real."

"I have not pried into your case, JJ. You always act reasonably and keep me informed of activities that I should know about. But you must be careful this time. I hear many things about very bad people interested in what you are doing. Some would say a man who is working for two rival narcotraficantes at the same time, while helping someone else steal the hidden treasure of another is almost surely suicidal."

"Thanks, Tavi," I said. "I'm grateful for your concern."

"Do you have anything you want to tell me now?"

I shook his hand. "Nothing now. I promise I will if anything looks bad."

Tavi was a good friend. He never gave me a hard time. And I never put him in a bad position with his bosses. I wouldn't do that this time. Unless I had to.

I thought about taking Jayde to breakfast, but she wasn't answering her phone. I stopped by her hotel. No answer on her room phone either. That worried me. I'd asked her not to go out without letting me know what she was doing. Of course, she didn't have to follow my orders. I couldn't protect her very well, though, if she didn't at least cooperate. Since I had nothing pressing, and she was my only client at the moment, except for two deadly cartel bosses, I found a comfortable chair and sat to wait.

I was dozing when she tapped me on the shoulder. I shook off my torpor and got to my feet. I was really out of sorts, but I tried to control myself. "I asked you not to go out without letting me know."

"JJ, I'm a big girl."

"First you want me to protect you, then you shrug it off."

"Don't be cranky. I met with the DEA men you told me about. I think they're pretty safe."

"We should have talked before you did that."

"Well, they called, and I have nothing to hide. They are just next door, anyway."

"What did you tell them?"

"I didn't give away our clues, if that's what you're asking."

I had calmed down a little. "Good. I mean, it's up to you."

She sat on the chair next to me. I took the cue and sat myself.

She gave me a knowing grin. "I found out something surprising. El Chapo himself does not know where the painting is hidden."

"How can he not know?"

"His lieutenant he entrusted it to was killed after he hid it, and whatever map or clues he may have had to its hiding place were not found on his body."

"You think the fat man killed him and took them?" I asked.

"Maybe, or somehow he got it from whoever did the killing."

"No wonder people are hounding us. They think we know more than we do. Could be that's true. Nobody knows a thing really, if it is."

She rose. "I'm hungry. Do you want brunch?"

"No, thanks. I've got things to do." I didn't. I just wanted to see Inez. "You go ahead. Answer your phone, though."

Things were happening that confused me. I admit I'm not a genius, but I'm not an idiot either. Events were swirling around me. I didn't have an endgame, and I needed one to anchor my actions. Times like these I felt as inexperienced as I guess I am.

My car was parked illegally in the fire zone outside the hotel entry. The doormen knew me and didn't mind as long as I moved it within a reasonable time.

I got stuck in traffic on my drive back to the office. Heavy traffic is not a normal thing for Cancún, but it was October 30, and the next day the Festival del Día de Muertos would begin.

The Day of the Dead celebration was put on every year by the city of Cancún from October 31 through November 2. It was a big deal. There were lots of performing artist groups that gave shows in different locations like Plaza de la Reforma del Palacio Municipal, Parque Las Palapas, and Parque Bohemia. It was worth seeing. There was a parade every day at 5:00 p.m.

It took forever to get to my turnoff, and I'd forgotten about Inez, so I backtracked to her street. Her car was in its usual spot, so I went up to her office without calling. I heard her arguing before I knocked. I had to knock twice before she acknowledged me. That was rare.

"Espérese!" she shot out. I couldn't remember Inez ever asking me to wait. Then her tone cooled a bit. "Vengo en un momento." She lowered her voice and spoke into the phone words I couldn't hear. By the time she opened the door she'd composed herself.

"Oh, hello, JJ. Come in." She moved aside to let me pass, then closed the door.

"Would you like some coffee or a bottle of water?"

"No, thanks," I said. "I just stopped by to see how you were."

"You could have just called." When she saw that I was made a bit crestfallen by her remark, she softened. "Sorry, JJ. I am very tired. I didn't mean to be short with you."

I could see this was a bad time to visit.

"Anything I can do?" I asked.

"No. I appreciate the offer," she answered. "I just need a little rest."

"Sure. I'll be going." But I had to ask. "I was out at the airport and saw your car parked in the long-term lot. A short vacation?"

"A business trip."

"You usually tell me when you're going out of town." She didn't reply, so we sat there for a few seconds in a strange silence. "You know I don't mind keeping an eye on your place."

"Sorry, thank you. I let my mother know. I guess she forgot to tell you. She is becoming . . . forgetful." Her eyes looked sad when she said that. I knew what she meant. I kissed her cheek and went to the door.

“Inez, let me know if I can do anything. I mean, I’m at your service. You know that.”

“Thank you, dear JJ.” She closed the door behind me.

CHAPTER 24

Something was very wrong with Inez. Possibly just worried about her mother's growing dementia, but I believed it was more than that. We were close enough that she surely would have let me carry some of the load. I had to put that out of my mind for now.

Not for the first time, I wished I did transcendental meditation, or something like that. I needed to clear my mind. I couldn't take a vacation, so I'd have to find another way to relax my brain. It had been a long time since I just enjoyed myself, so I called Jayde and told her to get ready, that I was coming by to pick her up.

As we walked into the Day of the Dead celebration grounds, a group of children with brightly painted plaster skulls passed by.

"I feel as if we are wasting time, JJ," Jayde warned as we moved among the colorful booths.

"We need to take a breath. What would we be doing otherwise? Sitting on our butts and coming up with nothing new?"

She laughed. "Probably. OK, let's have fun."

The whole area was filled with booths and performers. Paths between the stands were crowded with people of every age and social condition.

"Reminds me of the county fair in the little town where I grew up," I said.

"Yes, me too." Jayde smiled.

I looked at her as we walked. "Which little town are you from?"

"Brooklyn," she laughed. "We had street fairs."

I saw Jesse in the crowd and shouted him over.

"Hola, amigos! Are you having a good time?"

"Just got here," I said. "I thought you'd be at the cemetery."

"I was. I put a new coat of paint on my abuelitos' graves." He saw the question on Jayde's face. "There are painted cement blocks on top of the dead. We paint them every year in my family. To show affection and respect."

"I understand that. We decorate our loved ones' graves, too. The difference is we're usually sad about the passings. Here, the relatives look happy."

"Of course we grieve, too." Jesse grinned his handsome grin. "But why not take this opportunity every year to celebrate their lives and keep them in ours? In Mexico, we look at death as a part of life."

"Well," she replied. "I suppose it is, really."

"See you two later," he said and was quickly swallowed by the wave of revelers.

"The Mayans call this holiday Hanal Pixan," I said. "Food for the Soul."

"Why Food for the Soul?"

"Maybe because of the food offerings they make in honor of their ancestors. I should ask Jesse."

"Well, I'm already glad you made me come with you." She smiled.

So was I, but I didn't say so. And from the looks I got, men thought I was lucky to have such a beauty with me. More likely they were wondering how an ordinary guy like me rated a woman like that. Who cared? I liked the rare feeling of being envied for my date.

"What is this place?" Jayde asked me.

"It's Parque Las Palapas. It is always a fun place, but during this celebration even more so."

She turned toward a couple walking by, stuffing what looked like tortillas into their mouths.

"What's that?"

"That's a local fast food known as garnachas."

"What's in it?"

"I don't know. I'm afraid to find out exactly what. It tastes too good not to be bad for me in some way."

Jayde was fascinated by the altars with pictures of the departed relatives, sugar skulls, and many wooden and ceramic skulls and skeletons.

She said, "It's amazing, all these morbid things look kind of jolly in the fiesta's atmosphere."

Jayde and I strolled around for an hour or so, if stroll is the right word for moving around in such a large crowd. It really did have the effect of clearing my mind. Only it didn't fill the emptiness of my mind with any useful ideas. On that, I was no better off than when I started the evening.

"This is cool. I guess you know lots about the culture down here," Jayde said. "I mean, you've lived here a while."

"I know a few things, I guess."

"What do you like best, then, about Mexico?"

"Mexicans."

That just came out. I realized it was true. I really did.

But there was a kind of substratum of violence here that couldn't be denied, and it worried me.

"Should we paint our faces like skeletons too?" Jayde threw out with a laugh.

"We could. But it's hard to get all that makeup off," I answered.

"Just kidding. Fun, but no chance I would do it."

I watched the swirling mass of people and sucked up their energy, and in that moment, I wished I hadn't taken the case. I wished I was doing something else entirely for a living. But wishes weren't what kept me fed. I was a mediocre private investigator involved in a problem well above my ability to resolve.

Just then, I decided to bite the bullet and do the best I could. No. More than that. I determined to solve the case, find the painting, and earn my fee. As someone once told me: "Always give one hundred percent . . . unless you're donating blood."

We passed a booth with an old bruja selling charms. Jayde stopped to look. "Tell her we need one to bring us luck."

I did and the woman held up a small carved skull.

"Cien pesos," she said. "Muy buena suerte."

I paid her and gave the skull to Jayde. "Thanks," she said.

"I'll list it on my expenses."

As I started away, the old woman pulled on my sleeve. She held a very small doll just like the one I'd found at my door. I shook my head, but she persisted. "OK, cuánto?"

"Un regalo," she said.

A gift.

"Para protegerle."

She pointed at the cloudless sky. "La tormenta viene."

I took the doll reluctantly.

Jayde noticed. "What's the problem?"

I smiled over my anxiety. "Nothing really. Just that there's a lot of bizarre stuff happening lately. And that old witch was just another bit of creepiness."

Jayde tapped my arm and nodded toward a booth where the two DEA agents who had confronted me at the restaurant were cramming themselves full of food and cold beer. They saw us and smiled a phony greeting. I returned the favor.

Jesse rolled up with a very pretty young girl. I was glad for the interruption and for Jesse's nearly permanent smile. "Hey, buddy," I greeted. "Is this lovely another of your cousins?"

"Haha. No this is Esmeralda. My true love. For today."

Jayde slapped his arm playfully. "You're in trouble."

"No. She speaks no English at all," he said, laughing.

The girl grinned. "I went to college in Dallas."

I thought Jesse was going to faint.

Pretty Esmeralda was loving his embarrassment. She was a female version of Jesse, good-looking and happy.

The sky was sparkling with stars, and the crowd was sparkling with delight. Except for me. I had a dark feeling I couldn't shake.

Jesse began holding forth on Mexican customs. He had the women enthralled with his explanation of the Day of the Dead and its variations in the many regions of Mexico. He was very knowledgeable about the myriad indigenous groups. That's why, when I saw a group of young men flowing almost in synchronization through the crowd, I asked his opinion. They looked dangerous to me, not that I could pinpoint the reason. Save for the fact they were the only people I could see who weren't smiling. I watched them snake, seemingly purposefully, in our direction.

"Jesse, you see those guys coming our way?"

He followed my eyes to the group. They were all dressed in black, which in itself was odd. It was also strange that they seemed to be heading toward us. "Yes," he answered. "They might be a performance group or something."

Their progress wasn't fast, but it was steady. The hawk-nosed man I thought must be their leader stopped a few feet from me and stared into my eyes. I froze. There was a threatening aura about him I couldn't really grasp. It only lasted a moment before the group moved on.

Jayde asked Jesse. "Are those men local Indians? I mean Mayans or like that?"

"No," Jesse answered, his expression no longer jolly. "Nahuas, descendants of the Mexica, otherwise known as Aztecs."

"How do you know that?" she asked.

"They had Aztec amulets around their necks. At least the ones I could see."

"Amulets?"

"Yes. Those small gold medals. Folklore says they were forged by the demon Tezcatcatl. I haven't seen many." He had a worried look on his face that was rare for him. "We have a lot of indigenous people grouping together these days. Political, mostly."

Jayde motioned to another group. Hard-looking men with dark shirts and evil grins. "What about those guys?"

"No. They are mestizos. They are not here for the celebration, I think."

"What then?"

"Narcos," Jesse responded, grim-faced.

He glanced at me and nodded imperceptibly at my warning look. I didn't want to talk about the cartels in front of Jayde. I didn't recognize any of the sicarios in the group we were talking about, either. I hoped they weren't from a third group thinking about moving into our town.

I saw the DEA agents stalking the narcs, not trying to keep out of sight. I wondered if they thought they looked like tourists. They didn't. They looked like cops.

After a while, we forgot about the Indians and the narcos. I was finally infected with the gaiety of the occasion and relaxed. Later, I recalled looking up at the bright-starred moonless sky and marveling at how peaceful I felt because of it.

CHAPTER 25

My phone rang early. Jesse had news.

"Those two DEA agents?" he began. "Muertos."

That shocked me. "Dead?"

"Killed," he elaborated. "Assassinated. Tavi called."

"How?"

"The usual cartel method. Bullet to the back of the head. They were tortured first. Ears cut off. Dumped on the beach. The narcos are sending a message, I think. Maybe to us. Tavi says it was not Buendía or Little Sammy. Not sure how he knows."

"Man," I whispered. "This is bad. Killing DEA agents, even in Mexico, is damn risky for them."

"They must think the risk is worth it," he continued. "But why?"

"I don't have any idea. Do you think it has anything to do with our case?

"No sé, jefe. But it could be."

"OK, I'll call Jayde and meet you at the police station. First, I'll call Buendía and Little Sammy. They might know if any other cartels are sniffing around."

"Bueno," he agreed. "One other thing. The Weather Channel said they named the storm in the gulf."

"What?"

"Celia."

* * *

The rooster was standing in my yard when I opened my front door to head out. He didn't threaten me, though, as he usually did. That confused me. Until I looked down and saw that a package had been left on my doorstep. It was a small box, so I didn't think it was a bomb. I picked it up delicately anyway and opened the lid. Ears. Human ears. Four bloody ears.

I went back inside and grabbed my .38.

Jayde and Jesse were already at the police station when I arrived. I dropped the box of sliced-off ears on Tavi's desk. Jayde and Jesse jerked away from the desk in disgust. Tavi spat, "Híjole, JJ! Qué barbaridad es este!?"

"On my doorstep this morning." I thought I might be sick, so I looked away. "What you want to bet they're from the DEA guys?"

"Carajo! This is not usual for Cancún. What the hell have you brought to our town?"

"That's not fair," Jayde threw out. "Bad people brought this here, not us!"

"Lo siento, señorita. You are right."

Tavi picked up his phone and called his assistant, who appeared in an instant. "Cuida de estos," Tavi said as he pushed the box at the young corporal.

He recoiled as if the bloody container held a cobra. "Ay, jefe! Tanto sangre. Qué quiere que hago con . . .?"

Tavi slapped his desk in frustration. "Entrégalos al médico forense, idiota!"

The corporal grabbed the box and scurried out.

None of us spoke for a moment. Jayde broke the silence. "Who do you think did this, Tavi?"

"Es obvio," he answered low. "Narcos."

Jesse agreed. "Pretty sure we saw them at el parque last night, Chief."

"How do you know?" Tavi followed.

Jesse shrugged. "I know. They were not Cancún people."

The chief grudgingly nodded in agreement. "Sí. Desgraciados."

I shook my head. "Killing US federal agents . . . this is very bad. Crosses a line. Not like popping off soldiers from a rival cartel. Nobody cares about that. But this . . ."

"Yes." Tavi frowned. "I will have every gringo federale in Texas here by tomorrow."

Jesse said, "They won't let up until they find the asesinos, Jefe. It surprises me that the cartel bosses would approve such a killing."

Jesse wasn't the only one confused. It was an incredibly stupid act.

"Yes," Tavi said. "I find it very hard to comprehend." He looked hard at Jayde. "Is it possible that your search is something the narcos are worried about?"

"I can't see why," she answered. "I mean, it concerns El Chapo. So, maybe. But why kill the DEA people?"

I said, "Maybe they thought the DEA was helping us."

Jesse looked at me with concern. "Then we are in danger, too."

Tavi knitted his brows. "I don't want to know more. JJ, carry your pistol. Yes, I know you have one. You don't need to deny it. You won't be charged with an offense if you are caught with it. But I cannot protect you from the people who shot at you."

"It's in my truck," I admitted.

"Good," he agreed, then spoke directly to Jayde. "If I were you, señorita, I would fly home right away. Your job is not worth your life."

She chuckled. "You don't know my boss."

I led her to the door but held back until she was out of earshot and then whispered to Tavi, "It wasn't Buendía or Little Sammy. I checked."

⁂

Jayde, Jesse, and I met back at my office. It was closer than her hotel, and we needed a confab.

"Tavi was right, Jayde," I began. "Why risk your life for this? Your employer wouldn't ask you to do that. This case has gotten too hot. We could all get killed."

"Do you want to drop me as a client, JJ?"

I looked at Jesse for his opinion. He just shrugged. "No, I guess not," I answered reluctantly. "But promise me you'll be more careful. And we need combat pay. Tell your company this is no longer a 'Do-It-Yourself' job."

"I will. I agree you deserve more."

"OK, since we're still on the case," Jesse interjected, "I should tell you that on the way to see Tavi, I think I saw Hermione at a hotel. I can't be sure. But I think it was her."

"Maybe there's still a chance of getting her piece of the puzzle," I suggested. "Do you want to try?" I asked, turning back to Jayde.

"I guess it's worth it. Not that I think she'll settle for a finder's fee," she answered. "In the meantime, do you want to try your step theory on another pyramid? Long shot but might be worth a gamble."

"Maybe. Let's think about that. And Jesse really needs to stay close to you, given the things that are happening. I'll check out Hermione. What hotel, Jesse?"

"Conquistador."

"I'll drop by."

As he held my front door open for Jayde to leave, he turned back to me.

"Your rooster is not around."

"Yes," I replied. "Strange."

"It's because el huracán is coming soon. Animals know." Then he grinned. "Also I saw it on the Weather Channel."

As I drove to "hotel row," I considered how I'd approach the redhead. I couldn't see her making a deal that didn't give her control. Craftiness isn't my strong point, but I knew I'd have to trick her somehow into letting me see her clue. I was straining my brain with the matter when I saw the flowered-shirt killer flit past on the sidewalk. I pulled over and jumped out of my truck. It was a reflex action. I had no idea what I was going to do. I sure as hell wasn't going to attack him. Even if I had been brave enough to run the man down, he probably would have killed me like he did his fellow stalker, when all the craziness began.

I saw him slip into a beach cabana tent and close the flap, so I stopped at the top of the steps that led from the sidewalk to the sand and watched. There were crowds of people on the beach, so I calculated the danger of his attacking me was small, until I recalled he killed the other stalker in the midst of heavy foot traffic on the promenade. I couldn't force myself forward.

I thought I was hallucinating when Hermione emerged from the cabana fully garbed in her wild attire and carrying her dog. I didn't move for several seconds. She'd entered the building before I could unfreeze myself. My curiosity slowly overcame my fear, and I crept carefully toward the tent. At the entry flap, I looked around in all directions to make certain there were potential witnesses to whatever might happen. I threw back the flap and jumped aside.

The cabana was empty except for a lounge chair and a small table.

There was no place to hide. The killer was gone. If he'd slipped out, I didn't see how. I wondered if it was just my imagination. And what about the red-haired Hermione? Did I imagine that, too? I needed a drink.

Chuey Medina's "El Gato" bar was nearly always full, anytime day or night. In spite of that, it rarely saw fights or even verbal assaults. It was populated mainly by patrons who wanted a drink or two in a peaceful but not celebratory atmosphere. Right then I sure fit that description. I called Jesse to meet me.

"Were you drunk?" he naturally asked after I told him what had happened.

"Damn it, Jesse, no. And I'm not drunk now either. Not yet. But I want to be."

Jesse didn't drink much, so he nursed his beer. "Well, you have had a lot of stress lately, so . . ."

"Crap, Jesse," I sputtered. "I was sober and calm. Well, not calm, but damn! I know what I saw."

"OK," he pacified. "I believe you." He took a half-hearted sip of his Corona. "I've seen the old red-haired lady myself. The assassin is a different matter. If he was there, he probably went out the back of the cabana just as you got to the front."

"Yes," I replied. "I guess that could have happened. But what was he doing in there with Hermione?" I considered that for a moment. "Unless he works for her."

"Ah, sí. That is possible."

"Do you think we should drop this case? It's gone way past what we're used to dealing with. I mean with Buendía and Little Sammy . . . we can't drop them and stay alive."

He gave me a reassuring smile. "I think we can handle it, JJ. We just have to be careful." He fished a crumpled bill out of his pocket and dropped it on the bar. "And you have to admit the money's good."

"Sure, if we stay alive to spend it."

CHAPTER 26

I left my bedroom window open that night. Sometimes I do that, if the weather isn't oppressive. I like the night sounds. The insects and the occasional bird. It's not just relaxing; it's kind of therapeutic.

My landlord entrusted me with feeding Demetrius, his homicidal chicken, while he went to Mexico City for a few days. I was tempted to withhold the animal's corn and starve him to death, but I was afraid the bird would find a way to take his revenge. He's a very violent and vengeful rooster. I complied grudgingly by throwing his food toward his coop after dark.

That night the moon was full and beaming sweet through my window. Living on the outskirts of Cancún, as I am, is good mostly, if not for that damned rooster. It is quiet at night, except for nature's music. Sleep usually comes easy.

But most nights, if I'm not overly tired, I have a short conversation with myself. I try not to take myself too seriously, though. I'm only an ordinary man. And I pray to be a better one. That is, I talk to God, wondering why he puts up with me. I did all that this night, and it made me feel peaceful. But just as I was about to slip into a good, deep sleep, I heard firecrackers. Sounded not too far off in the jungle nearby. Left over from Day of the Dead celebrations, I guessed. Then I closed my eyes and slept.

Not firecrackers, as it turned out.

Jesse called me just as the sun was struggling over the thick tropical growth. I shook the drowsiness off and asked him to repeat himself.

"Dead. All of them, I think. Tavi said we could come look if we hurry."

I hurried. If it was the narcos we saw on the Day of the Dead, I needed to know. When I arrived at the gory scene, which was less than a mile away, the Chief's and two other squad cars were there, lights flashing. Jesse was there, too, talking to Tavi. I parked and hurried over.

Six bodies lay in a neat row. The jungle growth protected them from the view of anyone who wasn't passing nearby. "Did you do the arrangement here?" I asked Tavi.

"No. This is how I found them. Well, a housekeeper walking to her employer's house found them. She had no cell phone, so she ran to the house to report it. She was terrified, of course. No information to add to what you see here. Are these the men you and Jesse saw on el Día de Muertos?"

"Yes," I answered. I noticed a small Santa Muerte doll in the Chief's hand. "Was that here?"

He held it out to me, but I was reluctant to take it. "Yes, it was standing at the feet of that body in the middle, the only one with his throat cut. The others got a small-caliber bullet to the back of the head."

"When do you think this happened?" Jesse asked Tavi.

"Just after eleven last night," I interjected before Tavi had a chance to respond.

They both looked at me quizzically. "Pretty sure I heard the shots. I thought it was firecrackers."

A uniformed cop walked up to us with a pillowcase squirming in his hand.

"Mire, jefe," he said, pulling the bag open. A yappy bark I was sure I recognized announced a skinny Chihuahua with a rhinestone collar.

CHAPTER 27

Who killed the narcos? They were Sonorans, so they'd likely been taken out by one of the small Yucatán groups, we thought, worried about the northerners encroaching on their turf. As far as I could ascertain, it wasn't Little Sammy or Buendía. I was surprised whoever did the murders hadn't also gone after those two.

The DEA coming here was unusual. Their killing was even more rare. It was going to bring incredible heat down on the drug lords who kept haciendas in the Yucatán. And this mass execution right on the heels of the DEA murder was incredible . . . and frightening. Were we going to become a free-fire zone like Nuevo Laredo and Juárez? One thing for sure: our search was getting more dangerous by the day.

Jesse had tracked Hermione to the Conquistador Hotel. So when Tavi released her dog to me (of course he bit me), I stuffed the vicious midget wolf back in the pillowcase and drove to the hotel, wondering what the hell he'd been doing at the murder scene. I had to grudgingly admire the tiny mongrel, since he was

the only living being who seemed to strike fear into Demetrius, the rooster psychopath.

Hermione came right down when I called her room.

"Oh, my darling!" she gushed. Not to me. To her "baby," Napoleon. She pulled him out of the pillowcase and hugged him. He jumped from her embrace to the floor and proceeded to urinate against a chair leg.

"I have been so worried," she said, looking lovingly at her dog. "Where did you find him?"

I studied her face for signs of duplicity. She seemed genuinely relieved. I didn't think she knew about the killings.

"There was a shooting, of some drug cartel soldiers."

She was either a great actress or she truly didn't know what had happened. "My God! What would my Napoleon be doing with people like that?"

Now she was showing true form. Not the murder she cared about, but her silly mutt's being around unsavory types. "I can't answer that," I said. "The cops found him in this pillowcase at the crime scene. I thought he might have been kidnapped."

"Ahhh. If that was so, they had not yet contacted me for ransom, which I would certainly have paid."

"Maybe they wanted to find out all you know about the painting."

"Then I am surprised they did not reach out to me. Napoleon is worth more to me than a painting, no matter its value."

Just then a large figure approached us. The fat man doffed his hat. "A very good morning, friends." Before we could reply, his iguana strained at his leash and snapped at the Chihuahua. Hermione snatched up her pet and hissed at Gutman, "Get your cursed reptile away from my Napoleon!"

He stepped back in fear of the redhead's wrath. "Come, Herbert. It appears we are not wanted here." He gave a brief nod and continued on his way.

"So you know nothing at all about the . . . incidents?" I asked. "The one last night or the DEA people?"

She gasped. "How would I?! I have nothing to do with violence . . . certainly not assassinations!"

"Just thought I'd ask. No offense."

"You suspect these crimes are related to our search, don't you?"

"I'm not certain. They could have to do with the narcotics business. But they're very unusual for Cancún." I rose to leave. It seemed I had a lot to do, but I couldn't figure what exactly. "If I set up a meeting with Jayde and Gutman, would you come?"

She seemed surprised before her expression changed to appreciation. "I would strongly consider it. Let me know."

"I will."

The sooner the better, I thought. I hurried to see if I could catch up to the fat man. That wasn't hard to do. He moved his bulk slowly. I rounded the hotel drive and approached him on the sidewalk.

"Kaspar," I called. He stopped and turned to me. His iguana turned, too, straining on his leash toward me. I held up. Iguanas have a savage war face. "Your lizard isn't getting ready to bite me, is he?"

Gutman chuckled (evilly, I thought). "Oh, no. He's just watching out for me."

I relaxed a little. "Good. Kaspar, if I asked you to a meeting with Jayde and Hermione, would you come? There is a lot of very bad stuff happening, and we need to work out something, or we may all end up dead."

"I heard about the slain cartel people," he said with a newly serious expression. "Yes, I will come to the meeting, although I make no promise of cooperation."

"I just want all interested parties to talk. See what happens," I said.

"Let me know the time and place," he smiled and turned to go.

"Say, Kaspar," I called after him. "Does your little dinosaur eat chickens?"

CHAPTER 28

Inspector Gustavo Maximiliano Huerta was shorter than Little Sammy, and his taste in clothing even worse. When I walked into Tavi's office at the police station, I thought the jolly fellow in the loud green and yellow Hawaiian shirt, sandals, and board shorts was a Midwestern American tourist.

"Come in, JJ," Tavi invited. "This is Inspector Gustavo Maximiliano Huerta, from the Federal Police in Mexico City."

"Please to meet you, Inspector," I said and shook the smiling cop's hand, then sat.

"Just Gus, please, JJ. Chief Fuentes here has told me about you."

"Well, I hope good things," I said.

Tavi seemed eager to make a good impression on his visitor. He was freshly shaved, which was unusual for him, and his uniform was pressed with sharp creases on shirt and pants.

"Yes, I have explained how you have helped identify similarities among the killings and strange displays of our recent murders. Of course, you do not know, but the head of the Federales in our capital has kindly lent the services and talents of Inspector Huerta to help us find the serial killer and bring him to justice."

"I see," I said. "We will all be happy when that happens."

"And Gus here is their foremost expert on serial killers. He can see clues where the majority of investigators cannot."

Gus shook his head in false modesty. “It is true I have had some success in this area. Perhaps due to luck as much as anything.”

“Oh, no, no, no, Gus,” said Tavi. “I am fully aware of your well-deserved reputation.”

I could almost see Gus glow. I thought I might as well throw some more fuel on the fire of his ego. “I’m sure you’ll make short order of our local monster, Gus. If there’s any way I can help, I’m at your service.”

“Allowing me to practice my English is a welcome help, but I would like to spend some time in conversation about your impressions of the victims . . . more specifically, about the poses they were arranged in after death.”

“Of course. I’ll make myself available anytime you like.”

“Excellent. There is a football . . .” Gus chuckled. “Soccer match that I absolutely must watch this afternoon. If our killer is not a completely depraved soul, he will be watching, too. He will put his evil impulses on hold for a couple of hours.”

The inspector must have taken note of my staring at his outlandish wardrobe. He nodded and laughed. “I see you are wondering about my outfit. No, it is not the new uniform of the federal police.” He lifted the untucked front of his shirt to reveal a holstered .32 caliber revolver. “For one thing it conceals my weapon.” He removed the pistol and offered it to me.

I took it briefly and handed it back. “Not very big,”

“No. Then again, it will do if I am close. I do not intend to get into gunfights. My real weapon is my brain. That is how I will defeat the perpetrator.”

“Gus is famous for outfoxing the foxes,” said Tavi.

“You see, my clothing is a costume. I am dressed like a simple tourist. The murderer, and, oh, yes, I am certain he is still amongst us, would never suspect someone like this tourist to be looking for him.”

A quote from Raymond Chandler popped into my mind: *He looked about as inconspicuous as a tarantula on a slice of angel food*. "Unless he thought you looked *too* touristy," I said before I could stop myself. Tavi was shocked.

Gus held up his index finger. "Aha! You are very perceptive, young man." He closed his eyes briefly in appreciation. "But because it is such a very outlandish outfit, he would think that no policeman with any brain at all would wear it to escape detection."

I waited for a beat to see if he was kidding. He wasn't. Then a quote from Albert Einstein shoved itself into my consciousness: *Two things are infinite, the universe and human stupidity; and I'm not sure about the universe.* "I see," I said.

"Yes, young man. I must admit I am considered a master of disguise. You may walk past me on the street without the slightest glimmer of recognition. So, if a stranger whispers a greeting to you, it may well be me." The inspector picked up his Dallas Cowboys hat and wrap-around sunglasses from Tavi's desk and stood. "Oh, one thing. I understand that all of the victims of this killer were active members of cartels."

"That is true," said Tavi. "If you—"

"I have no interest in cartels. I will focus my complete attention on the serial killer. If I have questions about the cartels, it will only be as to why they might have been targeted by the murderer. Enforcement of other laws is completely in the hands of your local police."

CHAPTER 29

Jayde said OK to the meeting, even though it would almost surely not be approved by her company. Like me, she felt the violence was exploding all around this hunt, and we were likely to die if we didn't get the painting right away and get it out of the reach of whoever was doing the bloodletting. I had only a general idea about an agreement, and I had little hope it would be accepted by all parties. But I had to try.

It wasn't even noon when I parked in front of my gate. I'd forgotten to feed the rooster that morning in my rush to the scene of the narcos' killing. I couldn't believe I felt guilty about it. It was only a damned chicken, after all. Actually, I was more fearful than guilt-ridden. I knew Demetrius could hold a grudge, and he hated me anyway. Before I opened the gate, I did a visual recon of the yard, with special concentration on the path to my front door. The feed was just inside, but I had to stop and unlock the door to get to it. When I was certain the bird was nowhere around, I bolted through the gate and down the path.

There was something of the occult about that bird. I was barely halfway to my door when his horrid shriek ripped my eardrums. Terror fueled my feet, but he got in two good pecks with his dagger beak while I shoved my key into the lock. I kicked him off, slid inside, and slammed the door.

I enjoyed my escape for a second or two before I remembered my obligation. I reached down and picked up the bag of chicken feed, opened the door a couple of inches, and threw out a handful of the pellets. No sooner had I completed the throw than the psychotic bird slammed into my door. I turned the deadbolt and backed slowly into my living room, wondering why I wasn't run off by hired assassins, one of whom had beaten me senseless, but was paralyzed with fear of a damned chicken.

I looked through the peephole in the door and watched Demetrius gulp down the feed pellets. I thought, not for the first time, that Demetrius was proof the Devil existed.

There were messages on my answering machine. Unlike most people my age, I kept a landline as well as a cell. Mostly, I got telemarketers on my landline machine. Tonight was different.

"We only warned you before," said the heavily accented voice on the machine. "If we had wanted to kill you, it would have happened. Stop helping the gringa now, or next time we will kill you. Believe this."

I believed it.

But I wasn't going to quit. I may be something of a wimp, but I'm also stubborn. If I'd quit the case, my reputation would have been so torn up I'd have ended up looking for another line of work, and I wasn't qualified for much. So I organized the meeting of all interested parties for the next night. I didn't really trust any of them, including Jayde, to stick to any treaty we worked out. On the other hand, it was the best option I could think of.

There were three "interested parties" that I could identify, and at least one that I could not. That was a wild card I knew would be hard to deal with. And that group was the deadly one. Maybe not the only deadly one, I thought. It was possible I was over- (or under-) estimating the others. They might be a lot meaner than I gave them credit for.

People think I'm kind of a tough guy because of what I do for a living. But that caricature comes from TV and movies. A PI really just does research, something any graduate student does very well. Of course, I didn't disabuse my clients of the notion that I was a hard case. It was good for business. Not really me, though.

Right then I wished I really was tough. I was pretty sure there would be a need for some stern stuff before it was all over. Whether or not I was up to the demand was an open question.

I hadn't really thought much about the value of the painting we were hunting. Not just the dollar amount, although I knew that was in the multi-millions. But I realized I hadn't thought about the painting's cultural value, either. I wondered how much the Smithsonian and its cousins would pay. See, I can't help my mercenary tendencies. Just the way I am.

CHAPTER 30

Sometimes when you get what you wish for, you wish you hadn't wished for it.

That was how I felt the moment I got the group together. Hermione, Kaspar, Jayde, and I agreed faithfully to pool our resources and find the painting as quickly as possible. And I knew in my heart that not a single one of us was sincere. As soon as we found the painting, if we did, the quickest, stealthiest, and "fastest on the draw" would make off with it. But maybe not. Maybe we'd find it, sell it, and split the proceeds amicably. And maybe it would snow in the Yucatán this Christmas.

We did agree to meet at my office the following morning with each individual's piece of the map. From that, we would come up with an action plan. If you think the idea was dumb, so did I, the more I thought about it. Better than sniffing around bogus leads, though. Better than continuing to get shot at.

Jesse arrived before the others. I was glad because I wanted to discuss with him, face-to-face, the ethical problem we had representing Jayde as a client while working with the others to find the artwork.

"She agreed to it," he said. "I think that makes it OK for us, don't you?"

"I guess so," I answered. "I'm not really comfortable with it, though."

"Since when are you so high-minded," he grinned. "Our client agreed to the deal, and she's paying us every week. Stop thinking so much."

He was right. Now I had to figure out how to keep the painting from being stolen by the fat man or Hermione. As soon as we could prove the painting had been found, Jayde's company was off the hook if she could find a loophole that let the company end their commitment to insure the piece. Or maybe they could simply refuse to renew the policy. Keep it guarded until the policy's annual expiration date, and she and her company would be free and clear.

They all arrived at the same time. Kaspar and Hermione brought their damned pets, but I held my tongue about it. "Be best if you tie your animals far enough apart so they can't eat each other," I suggested, and they obliged by moving their chairs apart past the length of the combined leashes. I felt better and hoped I wouldn't have to clean dog and lizard waste off my floor. I reflected for an instant that I'd never seen a pile of iguana dung. There are times when I just cannot control my mind.

"OK," Jayde said. "Let's get started."

I cleared off half my desk and we all stood around it. Beginning with my client, each of them laid their torn pieces of the clue sheets side by side, and one thing quickly became obvious: the pieces of the puzzle *didn't* fit together.

I almost laughed at the expressions on the faces around my desk, like holders of pieces of an assumed winning lottery ticket with all the numbers, *except one*! Fate sure knows how to put us puny humans in our place. Then the expressions turned angry, and I knew something had to be done. After all, it was my lame idea that led them to this point, giving up what secrets they had in return for . . . well, not much at all.

The fat man roared, "Ha! We are no better off than before! All our goodwill adds up to nothing, it seems."

"Don't be so hasty, Kaspar," Hermione cautioned. "This may simply require some study."

"Wait a minute," Jayde broke in. "JJ thought these numbers might be the number of steps that lead to the hiding place."

"So? These are just more numbers," the fat man scoffed. "Do you think we should try this theory on every pyramid in Yucatán and Central America?"

"No, my cynical friend," countered Hermione. She pointed to a number, 85k, on her list of clues. "This number may be a distance. Possibly a distance from El Chapo's hacienda. Not a number of stones or steps."

I pulled a map of the Yucatán peninsula out of my desk drawer and motioned to Jesse to come closer. "Can you find where El Chapo's place is on this map?"

He moved in and frowned in concentration. Then he pointed to a spot in the jungle. "Here, I think. I can get the exact location of the property on the internet, I believe. If not, at the deed registration office."

I picked up a pen and marked the spot with an *X*. Then I took a piece of string from my drawer and gauged eighty-five kilometers along its length from the legend at the bottom of the map. Holding that length, I tied the string around the pen, held the beginning point on the *X* I'd marked on the map, and drew a circle from that point with a constant eighty-five-kilometer radius. "Somewhere along the circumference on this map is the pyramid we want," I said. "I think."

The group was quiet for a minute. Then Gutman spoke. "You may have discovered an important element of the clues, dear JJ and dear Hermione."

"One problem, though," Jayde said. "I don't see any pyramids, or any ruins at all, along that line."

"That doesn't mean there aren't any there," Jesse offered. "My friend at the university just last week discovered a large Mayan complex under the vegetation. They used some kind of laser technology."

I said, "And El Chapo might have found something like that on his property, or near it. And it's likely he wouldn't have reported it."

"How do we find it?" Jayde asked. "Do we just try to follow the edge of that circle all around?"

"I don't know," I answered. "We might have to."

Jayde said, "That looks like it's all jungle."

"She's right," the fat man broke in. "Be realistic. That route is all heavy vegetation. To make a trek along that circumference would take us years. And I certainly could not make it."

Hermione grinned. "You would have to trust us, Kaspar, darling."

Kaspar rolled his eyes.

"We could fly," Jesse said. All eyes turned to him and waited expectantly for him to continue.

"Osvaldo?" I queried.

"He was killed last month, remember?" Jesse replied.

"What are you talking about?" Jayde asked.

"Osvaldo is, was, a friend of ours with a small plane," I answered. "He worked both sides of the fence. Someone put him down. El Chapo's soldiers or the federales. Who knows? Too bad. He could have flown us along the circumference. He flew for Guzmán on some drug runs, and he was familiar with Shorty's land. I don't know what we'd see, but it would have been worth a try. And Osvaldo was the only pilot I know we could trust."

"Rosa?" Jesse asked me.

"Who is Rosa?" Gutman asked.

"Osvaldo's wife . . . widow. She was his copilot sometimes."

"Call her?" asked Jesse.

"No," I said. "Better a personal visit."

Jayde smiled. "An old sweetheart, Jesse?"

"Cousin."

"Will she fly with the storm coming?" I asked.

"She is a brave woman," Jesse replied. "And she really likes money."

CHAPTER 31

Jesse had no trouble organizing Rosa and her plane for our search. I wanted to set out right away, but I found a text on my cell from Inspector Huerta setting a meeting first thing in the morning at his hotel.

I arrived on time and asked for him at the front desk under the name he was using, Joe Smith. (Real tricky, huh?) There was no answer on his room phone, so I called Tavi to get his cell number. No response there either. I left a message, got his room number, and went up to see if he'd slept in. After I knocked loud and long and still couldn't raise him, I went back to the lobby to see if I could get someone to open the room. The concierge was new, and since he didn't know me, he was reluctant to disturb a guest. I called Tavi and asked him to come help.

Something didn't seem right.

I met Tavi at Huerta's door. I wanted to make sure neither the inspector nor anyone else left the hotel room or entered it before Tavi and I got a look. I figured, since the federal cop had been so specific about the time and place, he'd have texted me about any changes.

"You got the keycard?" I asked.

He motioned me aside and held the card over the lock plate until we heard a click and the green indicator light came on. He

stuffed something into his left ear, then changed gun hands and did the same to his right. Tavi pressed down on the door handle. Gently and slowly, he pushed it open. He crouched cautiously as he inched into the room.

The curtains were pulled back, so the figure sitting on the bed nearest the open door to the balcony was clearly visible. Tavi held up his hand to keep me back and held fast while he took in the situation. The bright green and yellow shirt with palm trees and pink flamingos was the one the inspector was wearing when I first met him. The blue cap was the same, too, although he was facing out toward the balcony and away from us, so I couldn't be sure about that.

"Inspector Huerta," Tavi called out. "Are you . . .?"

We moved closer. It wasn't the inspector. It was a life-sized Santa Muerte doll dressed in the inspector's clothes, staring out at the beach below through the "expert" serial killer hunter's wraparound sunglasses.

"That's not a person," I said and relaxed. Tavi paid no attention. I tapped his shoulder, and he flinched back toward me, his gun aimed at my gut.

"Tavi, take out those damn earplugs!"

He smiled meekly. "Haha. Oh, yes. I forgot."

Tavi and I found a dirty laundry cart and hid the "body" under sheets. While he pulled his car around, I rolled the cart to the delivery doors, and we stuffed the body into his trunk.

"You going to call the federales about this?" I asked.

"What would I tell them? That their expert on serial killers changed into Holy Death?" He shrugged.

"But he was only here a day before . . . before whatever happened to him happened. It's their fault."

"Not exactly—I asked for him specifically. He hasn't solved a case in years."

"But why . . .?"

"I did not want someone who would quickly solve a case that I should have wrapped up. I thought I might lose my job. So . . ."

"What if his bosses get worried when he doesn't check in?" I asked.

"They will call me, and I will think of something by then." He opened his door and sat behind the wheel. "If we work hard, we may arrest the maniac before Mexico City even misses their Inspector Huerta."

He began to pull away, then stopped and rolled down his window. "Maybe you could see if Buendía and Little Sammy have heard anything."

"OK," I said. "I'll come by your place tonight."

"Not tonight," he said, rolling up his window. "I have book club."

I just stood with my mouth open as the Police Chief of Cancún drove off to pursue improvement of his mind. My world was becoming weirder by the day.

CHAPTER 32

Rosa's plane was a Beech Bonanza G36. It was twenty years old but well maintained. It had a range of just over 920 nautical miles, so the distance we planned to fly wouldn't be a problem. She was happy for the business. Osvaldo hadn't left her much besides the aircraft, and the upkeep and storage fee ate into what little she had.

I knew Rosa fairly well. She was a good woman, good to her kids, good to her friends, and a good pilot. She often flew when her husband had been too drunk. In fact, like most pilots, she loved to fly, to soar out over the earth, leaving fears and worries on the ground.

The fat man sat up front in the copilot's seat. Small planes have a balance problem with heavy cargo, and Kaspar was indeed heavy cargo. Jayde, Hermione, Jesse, and I sat in back. It was a little cramped, but not too bad. Hermione had wanted to bring her dog, but Rosa wouldn't allow that. She said she didn't want the animal smelling up her plane. Hermione was offended but complied. I'd brought two extra binoculars and passed them to Kaspar and Hermione. Jesse and I had our own.

"You and I can share," I told Jayde.

"It might be better just to use the naked eye. I'm happy with that," she replied.

The sky was clear, and the plane rose up smoothly. Cancún is beautiful from the air, and I'd grown to love the town and the folks who lived there. Most of the bad people I ran across were from other places. I got lost in the view until Rosa spoke.

"You want to head for El Chapo's place, right?" she asked me.

"Yeah. We can get our bearings from there."

"You don't want to tell me your actual destination? Maybe I know a shorter route."

"Sorry, Rosa. If you don't mind, just get to Chapo's hacienda first."

Rosa turned and smiled at me. She was a pretty woman. I'm sure she could have gotten any info she wanted from me with a smile like that. Sometimes I think I should castrate myself. I have no defense against the smile of an attractive woman. Luckily, Rosa didn't press me.

The flight to the hacienda took half an hour. No one talked much. We were all entranced by the jungle below, lost in whatever thoughts the thick tropical forest below inspired in each of us.

At last, Rosa spoke up. "There it is," she said. "The ranch. I don't want to go too low when I pass over it. They know my plane. Might think I am flying DEA or federales."

"We don't need to do that. What we're after isn't here," I told her. "Just take a bearing from this point and fly out eighty-five kilometers."

"In what direction?" she asked me.

"Doesn't matter. Any direction will do. Just go eighty-five K and maintain that distance from the ranch headquarters in a full circle. Can you do that?"

"Por supuesto." She took a pad and pen from her map holder and figured for a minute. "That will be about 530 kilometers and will take us just over an hour and a half to fly."

"Ok," I said. "Let's do it."

The jungle canopy hid well what lay in its shadow. I had to keep myself from being so hypnotized by the uniformity of the landscape that I'd doze off. I was grateful for the occasional village with tile and tin roofs for the visual diversity. Each time we passed over a village, Jesse marked it on the map he'd spread on his lap. When he wasn't sure of the identity of a pueblecito, he asked Rosa about it. So we knew we were pretty well holding to the eighty-five-kilometer circumference we'd targeted.

"That's a full circle," Rosa said when we completed a revolution. "What now?"

"Has anybody sighted anything that looks interesting? Something we should go back and look closer at?" No one responded. I thought for a minute. "Should we try again?"

"We're up here. I think we should make another pass," Jayde offered.

"I agree," Kaspar followed.

Hermione nodded. "Until I have to go to the ladies' room, fine with me."

"OK, Rosa. Another pass, please," I said. "But in the opposite direction."

"Good idea," said the fat man. "A different perspective might well bring something to our attention that we overlooked."

So Rosa did a wide turn and came back on the heading that would take us on the return flight path. I did my best to focus. The binoculars didn't really help. Too jerky. Jayde was right. The naked eye was better.

We passed over the same villages, and the same scattered Mayan ruins we'd seen on the first roundabout. I thought I saw a couple of stone piles I hadn't noticed before but nothing like a pyramid or any other type of structure. I found it harder and harder to focus. My eyes were getting tired and dry. After about an hour, I asked, "Anybody got anything?" They all just shook their heads.

"Unfortunately," Kaspar said, "we may have to revisit our interpretation of the clues."

"It could be the pyramid is just covered by too much foliage," Hermione offered.

"We might have to search on foot," I said.

Jayde shook her head. "Over five hundred kilometers? In the jungle? On foot?"

She was right. We may have struck out. I had no good ideas at the moment.

Rosa turned back to me. "You're looking for a ruin? A pyramid?"

"That's right," I answered.

"Why did you start searching from El Chapo's place?" she asked.

I had to trust her. "We had a map that showed us a ruin eighty-five kilometers from his main ranch buildings."

"I know where there is a pyramid. But it is much closer to Chapo's place," she said.

"How close?"

"Maybe eight to ten kilometers."

Hermione looked at me. "Eight *point* five kilometers. We misread the clue. Or whoever wrote it forgot the decimal."

I high-fived Jayde. It was a bit of hope anyway. "Can you take us over it, Rosa?" I asked.

She turned the aircraft sharply. "Fifteen minutes or close to that," she said. Nobody talked. Everybody smiled.

* * *

It wasn't long before Rosa motioned downward with her finger. "See? Just past the clearing."

There it was. A pyramid. If she hadn't pointed it out, it would have been easy to miss. Vines covered most of the surface, and tropical trees grew right to its edges. Rosa made a low pass as slowly as she dared. Then she flew around and came in again from another direction.

I leaned forward to get a better view. "Is that a trail to the west of the ruin?"

"It looks like it, but I have never been down there."

"Could we try to follow it, Rosa?" Jesse asked.

She turned and trailed the path through the trees for a few miles until it joined up with a crude dirt road.

"Mark that on the map, please, Jesse," I asked.

"Got it," he said. "Now where does the road lead?"

"I will find out," said Rosa and banked off to the east.

In no more than ten or fifteen kilometers, the dirt track hooked into a two-lane blacktop.

Jesse pointed to a spot on the map. "That road is right here!"

"Think we can find our way, then?" I asked.

"Should be no problem."

"Thanks, Rosa," I said. "We can head back."

At that moment, I was happy with the turn of events. Later, I'd wish we'd never found that damned pyramid.

CHAPTER 33

I calculated it would be a two-hour drive to the dirt road turnoff and maybe another hour from there to the trail leading to the pyramid. We had to rent a four-wheel drive big enough to carry all five of us, and we settled on a new Toyota Land Cruiser. We figured we might have to spend the night, so we dug up sleeping bags, cots, and mosquito netting that could be set up over the cots. Also flashlights, food, and water.

I didn't ask anyone to bring guns, but I knew that everyone, except Jayde, had a pistol hidden somewhere. With luck, we wouldn't need them for anything more than scaring off a jaguar. We agreed to meet at Jayde's hotel at 6:00 the next morning and hoped we could get to the pyramid early enough to finish our search the same day.

Jesse and I went shopping for food. Nothing fancy. Bottles of mineral water, canned chili, tortillas, cheese, and ham, along with some candy and sundry other edibles. Probably too much, but there was no supermarket in the jungle. No need for food for the iguana and Hermione's dog. I was adamant they wouldn't go. Jesse found babysitters for the beasts.

When we set out, the sun was just giving a stingy glow of pale orange to the new day's sky. The fat man had the same outfit on he always seemed to wear, white shoes, white shirt, white

trousers, and coat. For a heavy man who was constantly perspiring in the tropical heat, it seemed a suicidal wardrobe choice. It crossed my mind to mention it, but I thought he might find my well-intentioned advice rude, so I kept my opinion to myself. The rest of us, even Hermione, wore shorts and polo shirts. Much better in the humid heat, as long as we were liberal with insect repellent on the exposed skin.

I took the first shift at the wheel. Everyone seemed kind of nervous in anticipation of the trek we were about to take, but the cool air from the air conditioner soon lulled all but me to sleep. I didn't mind. I was enjoying the drive. No traffic at that time of day, not that there was ever much in Quintana Roo. A pair of headlights stayed in my rearview mirror for several miles. They turned off before I got worried, but something about the vehicle preyed on my mind for a few minutes. As I turned off the city road, I noticed a bright red Honda motorcycle behind me but not really on my tail. It hung well back, which I thought was odd. I was going just under the speed limit. In my experience, bikers usually flew by at death speed. When I turned onto the two-lane blacktop, the bike sped past me and disappeared ahead. I shrugged off my paranoia.

By that time we were well out of the city and the highway was fairly deserted, with the exception of a few farm trucks carrying fresh produce. It was only when the sun was fully above the horizon and we were going through the villages that dotted the route that activity increased.

"How about stopping for coffee?" Jayde asked as she stretched off her doze.

"Good idea," Gutman agreed.

"Sure. I'll find a place." I was in need of a caffeine hit, too. A few minutes later, I saw a tourist bus parked outside an open-air café and a few dozen tourists of various ages beginning to board the vehicle. That was a good sign. Tour drivers make sure to stop at clean, friendly places. I pulled in as the bus was leaving.

There was an old off-road Jeep parked behind it, and two men I slightly recognized sitting at a nearby table. One had a jagged scar down the left side of his face.

"Jesse, do those guys look familiar?" I asked.

"What guys?"

"At the table . . . by that Jeep."

"Maybe. Hard to say."

"Didn't we see them at Inez's office? Not inside, but in the lot."

"Could be. Not sure. Is it important?"

"No," I admitted. "Probably not."

The mesero came for our order. We all wanted coffee, and Gutman also chose some sweetbreads. We hurried a little because we still hoped to return to Cancún before nightfall. Just as we got up to leave, the red motorcycle I'd noticed earlier drove in and stopped by the scarred man's table. The rider pulled off his helmet and glanced at me before sitting with the two from the Jeep. His skin was dark, almost certainly full Indian, but he didn't look familiar. I couldn't help feeling something wasn't right with those three, but I was distracted by a sightseeing helicopter flying low over the village, so I shoved the thought way back into the recesses of my mind.

From the café, it was a quick trip to the intersection with the dirt road where we would turn south. The coffee had enlivened my passengers, so there was some small talk. Turns out the fat man was once an operatic tenor. He had the build for it. Hermione said she'd been an aspiring actress in Hollywood but was never able to get the role that would have catapulted her into stardom. I didn't know what kind of role that could have been. I couldn't attest to her acting ability, but she would have to have been a lot more attractive back then to have landed top billing.

As I turned onto the dirt road, another, or maybe the same, tourist helicopter flew low. The *chop chop* of the blades was loud enough to be heard over our air conditioner.

"What's that?" asked Jayde.

"Tourist chopper," I answered. "I hope our 'hidden' pyramid hasn't become a tourist attraction."

The dirt road was bumpier than it looked from the air. We were close to being on the travel time estimate I had given, so I didn't feel a need to make us more uncomfortable by going faster. Half an hour after the turnoff, we came to the end of the road. There was a small turnaround clearing where it looked like the undergrowth had been manually cut out of the jungle. From there began a thin path that was, if our reckoning was solid, the trail to the pyramid.

We got out of the SUV and Jesse and I took up the backpacks with water and a few tools to work on the ruin's stone. The heat and humidity hit hard after the cool comfort of our air-conditioned vehicle.

"This weather is unbearable," Gutman complained only seconds after stepping out of the Toyota. "I hope my heart can take it." He began mopping his face.

"For God's sake, Kaspar," chided Hermione, "Don't be such a baby. Take off that ridiculous coat and tie and roll up your sleeves."

He grudgingly followed her advice. "I am not accustomed to such primitive conditions."

"You can wait with the car," I offered. "If it gets too hot, you can turn on the air conditioner."

"Haha, no, my friend," he shot back. "That would give you all a chance to conspire against me should you find the painting. I need to protect my interests."

"Look, we all subscribed to the deal," Jayde said. "I'm the one on the short end here. I'm still not sure how I'm going to work things out with my company."

"We better get going," Jesse warned. "If we want to try to get it done in one day. Otherwise, we get to sleep with the bugs and snakes."

Hermione shuddered. "I can bear bugs. Snakes are another matter."

I ignored her and waved to my partner. "Take the lead, Jesse."

He started down the path cutting into the jungle. I heard chopper blades close overhead. Looking up, I saw the same helicopter we had seen earlier. I slapped a mosquito the size of a vulture and called out to Jesse.

"Jess, did you see any other route to this pyramid when we flew over?"

He stopped and looked up. "No. I'm pretty sure there was no other trail, at least. I suppose a person could break through the jungle, but that would be hard."

"That tourist helo worries me," I said. "I hope we don't get to the ruin and find a bunch of day-trippers having a picnic."

The jungle wasn't quiet. Birds a little way off and up in the trees sang their territorial challenges. Funny, I found their calls soothing. But, after a few minutes, I heard a dissonant sound in the background. I tapped Jesse on the shoulder.

"You hear that?"

"What?"

"I don't know, exactly. Stop and listen. A motor or machine."

"I thought I caught some sort of clatter behind us," Jayde said.

Kaspar shrugged. Hermione shook her head.

I said, "Could be from the highway, I guess. But that's pretty far off."

Kaspar waved me forward. "Let's keep moving. This heat is murderous. And the storm is coming."

I nodded to Jesse and we kept on. All of us were quiet, and for a while I enjoyed the jungle sounds again. The birds were a talented orchestra: toucans' hollow *click*, and small, colorful birds with a whole range of whistles and chirps. Must have been a dozen types of parrot squawks that, mixed with the other music, were uplifting rather than annoying. A bird let out a squawk between a heavy chuckle and a full laugh. What I was pretty sure was a howler monkey set the rhythm with a guttural boom. I guessed most people would call the noise cacophony, but it set my mind at ease.

We trekked on silently for about twenty minutes. I heard the fat man huffing behind me, and I hoped he'd make it. He really should have waited with the Toyota.

"Would you please pass a bottle of water back, good man?" he wheezed.

I took one out of my backpack and tossed it to him. He downed the whole thing in seconds and asked for another. We began to stumble a little in the humid heat, so I was glad to see the several feet of clearing that opened up on the pyramid.

Jesse turned back to me, smiling. "Ya estamos!" he grinned. "Al fin."

We spread out around the base of the monument.

The fat man dropped his bottle of water and reached down to pick it up. Jesse shoved him hard.

"What?!" Kaspar grunted angrily.

Jesse held him back and pointed to the bottle he'd been reaching for. Slithering away was a gray and black snake over six feet long.

"Nauyaca," Jesse warned. "The deadliest snake in the Yucatán."

Kaspar pulled out his revolver, but I grabbed his arm. "It's gone," I said. "A gunshot would just draw attention if anyone is in the area."

Hermione jumped up to the first step of the pyramid. "My Napoleon would have made short work of that slimy creature."

"Be glad he wasn't here," Jesse answered. "If that snake got his fangs into the dog, he would not even have time to yelp."

"Be careful where you step and where you put your hands," I cautioned.

"Let's get this done," said Jayde. "This tropical setting is lovely, but—"

"I agree," said Hermione. "You have the clues, JJ. Where do we start?"

"We need to count up eight steps first, then search around the whole structure on that level," I told them.

The gray weathered stones were covered heavily with vines and other foliage, which is why it was so hard to see from the air.

"It rises above the canopy a fair bit," Gutman offered.

Jesse stepped up to the first level. "The Mayans made sure their pyramids' summits were above the tops of the tree line. They used the pyramids for navigation. It's always been easy to get lost in the jungle."

"Looks like someone knocked the point off the top," said Jayde.

Jesse slapped a bright green insect away and kept crawling upward. "No. The tops are usually flat. The Indians used the summit for altars and special celebrations."

"Human sacrifice?" cringed Hermione.

"Lots of that," laughed Jesse.

I looked up at the clear blue sky and wondered if what I was seeing was the scene the sacrificial victim saw just before the jade knife sliced into his chest.

"Let's get going," ordered Jayde.

I snapped to. She was the one writing checks.

Jesse was the first to make it up eight steps. "Eight right here."

"OK," I said, hurrying up to him. "You go around that way. I'll go the other. We'll meet up."

"I think we should all look," said the fat man, grunting up to the starting step where I waited.

"I think you don't trust me, Kaspar," I accused him with a laugh.

"Not at all, my young friend. That is to say, I do trust you. However, it is possible that more eyes scouring the stones could reveal a missed sign."

"He's right," Jayde agreed. And she started up. Hermione, too, but more slowly. We must have made an odd sight. Kaspar stopped suddenly.

"What is it, Kaspar?" asked Hermione. "Have you found something?"

"Do those snakes climb stones?" he worried.

Jesse laughed. "You are too big for them to swallow. Don't worry." So the fat man pressed on, but cautiously.

It didn't take long to make the circuit of the eighth step. No stones looked like they weren't permanently attached, so we traversed it again, single file, all eyes focused on the stones. I found a loose one, but there was nothing beneath it. We made a third trip and a fourth.

"This is pointless," Gutman complained, wiping sweat from his face with a soaked handkerchief. "There is nothing here."

I reminded him, "What if it's not eight steps from the bottom? What if it's eight steps from the top?"

Jesse practically ran up to the summit and began stepping down, counting as he went. When he reached the eighth step from the top he held up. Jayde hurried up to meet Jesse and began to circle the pyramid.

"Hey, JJ! Look!" she shouted down. "There's something under this!" She'd found a dislodged and loosely replaced stone next to the southern corner.

Jesse and I reached her quickly. Jesse pried up the stone with a huge screwdriver and levered the stone up enough to get his fingers under it. He strained while everyone else crowded in. "Give me some room," he said. Finally, the stone gave way. "Aargh!" Jesse grunted and pushed the block aside.

Underneath, in a clear plastic bag, was a rolled canvas and some sort of paper with handwritten notes. I bent down and lifted it out.

"At last!" Hermione gasped.

"Is that it?" asked Jayde in awe.

"Wonderful!" exclaimed the fat man.

I wiped the accumulated grime off the plastic with delicate reverence. This was a real treasure, something far beyond the scope of my mundane experience, and I felt honored to have found it, or have, at least, been instrumental in its discovery. I stuffed the paper inside my shirt pocket to go over later, then passed the rolled-up canvas to Jayde.

She unrolled the scroll, hands shaking with barely controlled expectation. The actual portrait was protected both front and back by plastic that was joined at the edges, front shield to back shield, to guard against moisture. But we could see the face of the lovely Aztec woman through the protective covering. Jayde studied it closely. Then her expression darkened.

While we were all basking in our good fortune, we didn't notice we had visitors approaching. Just as Jayde passed the painting back to me, I saw them. Three Indian men, the same I'd seen at the café where we stopped for coffee, stood spread a few yards apart just inside the small clearing at the base of the pyramid. Two of them held AK-47s. The third, who had been on the red motorcycle, had an automatic pistol stuck in his belt. He smiled and waved. I didn't return his greeting.

The man with the scar running down his face motioned upward with his rifle. We lifted our hands obediently. I hoped no one would pull a gun. We would all die if they did. No one spoke. We were frozen in place. The Indian holding the pistol aimed at the canvas I was grasping in my raised hand. I nodded. He gestured for me to throw it to him. I did, but I overshot, and it landed near the jungle growth. The Indian bent down to pick it up and then screeched in pain. "Dios mío! Culebra!"

The nauyaca was fastened to the man's hand by deeply imbedded fangs. The Indian tore it off and pulled his pistol, firing wildly at the slithering snake, but the reptile was too fast.

The man's comrades rushed to him. One grabbed the painting. The other lifted his wounded friend across his shoulders and struggled back down the trail. The scarred man glared at us and backed onto the path, disappearing into the jungle.

For a moment, our group just stood on the pyramid steps, transfixed. It had happened so fast. One by one, we lowered our hands.

"Should we go after them?" Jesse asked me.

"No," ordered Jayde.

"But they have the painting," Jesse insisted.

"They'd kill us," I said. "They have automatic weapons."

"But . . ."

"Not worth it," laughed Jayde.

"I am amazed you find humor in our predicament," the fat man growled. "We found the pot of gold at the end of the rainbow only to have it snatched from our hands."

"Not a pot of gold," Jayde kept chuckling, out of nervousness, I thought.

"Maybe we can get it back," I said.

Jayde grinned. "Don't want it back."

Hermione gave her an exasperated look. "I wish you would stop your insane laughter, dear woman."

"Sorry. I should explain."

"Explain what?" I asked.

"It's a fake. Like we talked about doing ourselves, JJ, remember?" Jayde laughed even harder. "Those men will be very disappointed if they try to sell it."

We all stared at her in silence for a long moment, each of us processing this news. Then, since there was nothing more we could do at the pyramid, we all climbed down, some more slowly than others. We trudged back to the Land Cruiser in silence. Our hopes were dashed. The robbers didn't get the original, but we didn't either. We were a defeated army ambushed and shamed.

I should have set one of us out as a sentinel on the path. Leaving no one on watch was stupid. Nobody accused me of incompetence, but I would have accepted the criticism if they had.

We passed the red motorcycle on the way to our vehicle. Our attackers must have been in too much of a hurry to get the rider to help to have worried about the bike. I doubted they'd get their buddy to medical attention in time. The snake was too deadly.

* * *

We were silent most of the trip back to Cancún. Finally, I spoke. "Jayde, are you sure that painting was a fake?"

"Yes. Cortés would have used materials available to the Aztecs at that time for the portrait. The painting we found was done in recent oils. The colors gave it away through the plastic."

"Why would anyone bother to hide a fake?" Gutman asked.

"From my experience, there are a few reasons. The first being insuring a fake as if it were an original and claiming it was stolen or destroyed," she answered.

Hermione nodded. "I can see that."

Jayde continued, "It could be sold at the value of the original, while the owner kept the original for a later sale, or just to hold."

"Yes," the fat man agreed. "Then again, perhaps hiding it was meant to stop the search. If it had not been identified as a fake by an expert like Jayde, whoever found it would be convinced that it was the original."

"Pretty dumb to think an expert wouldn't see what Jayde did," I said. "But not a lot of criminals are Rhodes scholars."

"Which of those three do you think it was in this case?" asked Hermione.

"I'm leaning toward the phony that is insured as the original and a false claim lodged," answered Jayde. "But maybe that's just because I see that a lot in my line of work."

We pulled into the drive of Jayde's hotel. She opened the door and got out. "I don't want to think about it tonight," she said. "We could meet tomorrow early if everybody wants to."

"Yes," said Hermione. "For now I need to get to my sweet Napoleon. He'll comfort me."

"Good Lord," scoffed the fat man.

Hermione gave him a scornful look. "You wouldn't understand, Kaspar. Who could cuddle a lizard?"

I didn't return the Land Cruiser to the rental office. I thought we might need it again, although I was way too tired to think about another foray into the jungle just then.

When I got to my front door there was another of those damned dolls waiting for me. This time I wasn't scared of it. I kicked it out into my yard and smack into the beak of that equally damned Demetrius. I almost laughed when the rooster squawked and ran off. At this point, I was too tired to be intimidated by voodoo dolls or crazed chickens. I needed a hot shower and some food. It dawned on me that we'd had nothing but water since coffee at the roadside café. I opened a can of soup and ate it lukewarm.

When I took off my shirt to shower, the paper I'd shoved inside it at the pyramid fell onto the floor. I hesitated before I picked it up. It made me uneasy. A childish sketch of a pyramid was topped with some numbers I didn't understand. I decided to leave it until the morning.

I called around early in the morning. The whole gang, including Jesse, had been gifted with a Santa Muerte doll. I couldn't figure out the significance, other than it being an attempt to intimidate us. If that was the motivation, it wasn't working. But it made me decide to confront Inez about the scar-faced Indian I'd seen pulling out of her parking lot. Maybe she didn't know him, but it was at the very least a suspicious coincidence. I called Jesse and asked him to arrange a meeting of our group.

When I turned the corner to Inez's place, she was pulling out in her car. She didn't see me, and I didn't want to chase her down. I couldn't be absolutely sure, but I thought it was scarface in her passenger seat. Now I was really confused. Answers would have to wait, though. I headed to Jayde's hotel for the meeting.

I was late. The rest, including Jesse, were seated at a large table in the hotel restaurant.

"Sorry," I said, pulling up a chair. "I went by Inez's place on the way."

"What did she have to say?" asked Jayde.

"I missed her. But I saw her driving off with one of the men who attacked us."

"What!?" Kaspar barked. "What would she be doing with those people?!"

"I don't know. Let's leave it for now. Jesse and I will talk to her later."

I pushed up to the table and tossed my doll into the middle. "This is the one I found last night. Did anyone else bring theirs?"

No one had. "Were they all just like the ones you got before?"

"Mine was nearly a duplicate," answered Jayde.

"As was mine," said Kaspar.

The others nodded agreement.

I said, "I might go see Mama Juana again. I can't figure out if someone is just trying to run us off, or if there's more to it."

The fat man's iguana nipped at my leg. "Dammit, Kaspar. Do you have to bring that thing to breakfast?" I asked.

"That *thing*?" He actually reached down to caress the reptile. "Do you think Herbert has no feelings?"

That question was too stupid to deserve a response. I just shook my head and motioned to the waiter for coffee.

Hermione suppressed a look of disgust, even though her own pet was actually sitting on her lap. "What is our next step, JJ? The prize is still out there somewhere, and we are not, it appears, the only ones searching for it. Those bandits will soon find out they have stolen a phony."

Something about her seemed off. I couldn't pinpoint it. Her hair seemed tilted, but I didn't dwell on it. The waiter began pouring my coffee, then snapped back at the sight of the Santa Muerte figure on the table. The hot liquid splashed all over my pants.

"Hey, man! What's wrong with you?" I jerked back in my chair.

"Lo siento, señor," he begged, frightened, but not of me. "La muñeca." He pointed at the doll and backed off without even wiping the mess from my leg.

"Well, it sure scared him," I said, cleaning my pants with a napkin before reaching into my pocket and pulling out the piece of paper I'd found with the copy of the portrait.

"This was with the painting they stole. I'd stuffed it down my shirt pocket, but I forgot about it." I gave it to Jayde first. "Pass it around." They all looked at the paper, but one by one, disappointment spread over their faces.

"This is only scribbles," complained Gutman, tossing the paper back to me.

"I think it's more than that," I said, pointing to the pencil marks. "First of all, that's another pyramid. Might be a childish drawing, but you'll have to agree it's of a pyramid."

"JJ dear," Hermione sighed. "It's probably just another false clue. I don't think there is a real portrait, if you want to know the truth."

"What do you think the numbers mean, JJ?" asked Jayde.

"I need to think about them, but I was hoping all of you could help come up with ideas," I answered. "I have a feeling about this. Why would this have been hidden with the copy if it didn't mean something?"

The fat man exhaled his exasperation. "I tend to agree with Hermione. I think this will lead nowhere."

"I can't believe you're so negative," I complained. "It's the only lead we have." I folded the paper and put it back in my pocket. "I know everyone feels let down and tired of this search. But we can't just give up."

Kaspar said, "I think we would do better tracking down the Indians who robbed us. I am willing to bet they know some things we do not."

"All right," I conceded. "Jesse and I will talk to Inez and see what's what. Remember, Jayde cut you guys into the deal. She didn't have to, and you can leave anytime."

"I want to go with you," said Jayde, rising from her chair. "Don't forget, I'm still paying you." She smiled sweetly at Gutman. "But you can pay for breakfast, Kaspar."

CHAPTER 34

I called Buendía the following morning to follow up on Inspector Huerta's disappearance. He swore his people had nothing to do it, but it sounded like something the "savage" Sammy would do. He said bits and pieces of the inspector would be scattered all over Quintana Roo by now and that Sammy probably thought the federal cops would quickly find the Luna Nueva group was behind the killings, trying to scare off Río Seco.

Then I called Little Sammy, who said Buendía was probably behind it because he'd found Buendía's people were doing the murders.

I said, "But Sammy, Buendía's men have been targeted, too."

"That bastard Buendía would sacrifice his mother for business," he countered. "He has no morals."

I was pretty sure neither one of the drug jefes knew what had happened to the inspector. But I knew it wouldn't be long now before they'd start warring. When that happened, Cancún would be put on "Do Not Visit" lists around the world. I would have to try to keep the cartels from bloodshed while Tavi and I tried hard to find the serial killer. And I needed time to work on Jayde's case. I felt we were getting close there.

Trouble was, I couldn't think of a plan for any of these problems that didn't have big holes in it. Still, I think somebody once said, "Don't let the perfect be the enemy of the good."

* * *

I called Tavi.

"We're going to need them, both of them, if we're going to catch the killer," I said. "They'll have to trust us and each other if they're going to work with us to find this guy. I'm pretty sure it's neither of them doing it. We need to set some sort of trap and lure the killer into it. But first we need a truce. If they start killing each other, we won't have much hope of trapping him."

"I suppose we can try," Tavi said. "I am not optimistic about getting them together. We would have to find a place to meet. We can't do this over the phone."

"I have a neutral ground in mind."

"Don't say my office, JJ. It is true I may look away at many cartel activities, but I cannot be seen having a conference with them. That sort of hypocrisy is a way of life here in Mexico, and it must be adhered to."

"No. I have a better site in mind. One at an organization that serves the interests of all parties and has an interest in seeing the serial killer stopped as much or more than any of the factions."

CHAPTER 35

I couldn't get the two cartel chiefs to come without their entourage of sicarios, and I was answered with belly laughs when I asked them to come unarmed. Never-the-hell-less, as my old Pop used to say, I did get them to agree to meet. I'd like to think it was my marvelous rhetorical skills that moved these two violent men to consider a peaceful accommodation, but the truth, I think, was their egos were stroked by being invited to the Chamber of Commerce boardroom—even though the meeting was to be held after dark, and no members of the actual Chamber would be present.

To be honest, it was as much in the Chamber's interest as anyone's to have peace between the two cartels (at least temporarily). That applied to finding the serial killer, as well. Tourism was already beginning to suffer and wouldn't likely improve until the lunatic was stopped.

Tavi stationed four patrol cars to guard the jefes' SUVs in case some local teenagers decided they wanted to take on the cartel drivers guarding the vehicles and drive off with the prizes. The cops were there mainly to keep would-be carjackers from being sent to the great chop shop in the sky. Bad publicity if kids, even delinquents, got splattered against the curb.

Jesse offered a suggestion that almost certainly avoided bloodshed. It was brilliant, and I was ashamed I hadn't thought of it: place cards making clear who would sit where without feeling snubbed. Narcos are sensitive people. About some things.

The legations from Río Seco and Luna Nueva arrived in front of the chamber building at 10:00 p.m. exactly. Both had insisted they should exit their vehicles and enter the boardroom at the same time. As my old Texas friend Kinky Friedman said, "If you're paranoid long enough, sooner or later you're going to be right."

The boardroom table was a long rectangle of expensive wood, I think mahogany, and the surrounding chairs were covered in soft light suede. The side of the room opposite the entry had a panoramic view of the hotels and fine restaurants of the tourist area, as well as the Caribbean beyond. A large whiteboard was pulled down from the ceiling in case we needed it. The Mexican flag hung on the back wall, larger and in the center of the flags of many nations that spread out on either side.

"Welcome, gentlemen," I greeted as Jesse led Buendía and Sammy and their men through the entry to the boardroom. There was stony silence from the capos and their guards (each boss had brought three in and left one with their SUVs). They all ignored me and kept their gaze fixed on their counterparts, as if they expected to be drawn down on any second. Jesse pointed Buendía and Little Sammy to the chairs at the ends of the table that held their name cards. Their men stood behind them. Tavi and Jesse closed the door and guarded it, Tavi inside and Jesse on the other side.

"I'll get right to it," I said. "I've been hired by both of you to find out who's killing your employees. You suspected each other, I know. But I promise you that is not the case. Someone outside your organizations is doing it. I am working with the Chief of Police to find that person."

Little Sammy banged his fist on the table. "I should kill you right now for working for this Buendía bastard behind my back!"

Buendía jumped up with his pistol drawn. "You damned savage! Watch your mouth, or I will put a bullet in it."

Little Sammy pulled both his pistols. Buendía's head bodyguard, Ernesto, and Sammy's Horatio both aimed their weapons and were an angel's breath from firing. I swore to God if I lived through this I would go to Mass every Sunday. Or every other Sunday.

When bullets weren't immediately fired, I changed that to every Christmas and Easter. Every Easter, anyway.

The bodyguards were the last to reholster their guns. But not without some lingering spite.

"You are lucky I did not splatter you all over the wall, you sissy jota," Ernesto spat at Horatio.

Horatio chuckled his contempt. "I doubt you could see past that disgusting growth that you call a beard."

"This from a tulip whose hair is a rat's nest full of vermin," Ernesto shot back.

I was almost certain they would start blood flowing, bosses' orders or no. Then a condescending smile grew on Horatio's face. He looked down at his hands as he calmy took a seat. "I would tear your wretched head from your disgusting body, but I just had my nails done and you are not worth the risk of my breaking one."

I thought I'd better jump in while the opportunity presented itself. "Please, all of you! I know you have a legitimate reason to be upset with me, but I had no choice. If I had refused you, you would have killed me. Right?"

They didn't answer. But at least the rest of the men sat down, so I hurried to say what I wanted before something else set them off. "All I'm asking is for you both to give your word that you will not start a war with each other until we find the serial killer. And that you'll help me with that."

Buendía spoke first. "What help?"

"Lend me your men . . . only one from each of you . . . to patrol and question anyone you think is acting suspiciously." I raised my hands, pleadingly. "Please no violence, though. You can intimidate all you want if you don't do physical damage."

Sammy growled, "If we find out this cabrón Buendía is behind it, I will take back my word and kill him!"

"You . . . you damned hijo de puta! The same applies to you," hissed Buendía. He got up from his chair. "Now, I wish to leave the presence of this unbathed mongrel. I leave Ernesto with you, JJ. Instruct him, and he will call when he is ready to come home."

Little Sammy followed his lead. "I will leave Horatio."

They left in icy silence, but at least nobody was killed. I nodded to the two sicarios they left behind. I thought they could sure as hell scare information out of people. I just hoped they didn't cause any heart attacks.

CHAPTER 36

Tavi called me on my way to my truck.

"Good news," he said.

"About the killer?" I asked.

"In a way," he laughed. "Ernesto and Horatio seem to be getting along very well."

"What do you mean?"

"Some of my cops are telling me they appear to be laughing and joking and buying each other drinks."

"That's great, but I hope they find our serial killer, or our two cartel jefes won't be laughing and joking with me."

I called Inez to tell her we were coming, but the machine answered at her office, and her cell went right to voicemail. I decided to head over to Mama Juana's. She didn't go out much, so a bet that she'd be home was a pretty sure thing.

"This doll came from someone who does not want to harm you," said Mama Juana, holding the doll close so her failing eyes could inspect it. "It is Santa Muerte auténtico, pero no es para hacer más que asustar. It is only to frighten." She handed it back to me.

Jesse and I glanced at each other briefly before I looked back at Mama Juana. “So we shouldn’t be worried?”

The old woman laughed. “I cannot say that. Those who made the dolls may become more dangerous if they see you are ignoring their warnings. But this doll is not a muñeca de muerte. A killing doll.”

“Do you know anyone in Cancún who could have made these dolls?” I asked.

“Oh, señor. Many. Pues, creo que fueron hechos por indios puros. I think by pure Indians.”

“From here? I mean local Indians?” Jayde pressed.

“I think from more to the west” Mama Juana responded. “I think Nahua.”

“Not narcotraficantes?” asked Jesse.

“Tal vez, pero no lo creo. I don’t think is true,” she answered.

I left a few hundred pesos on the old woman’s table. She nodded her appreciation as we left.

“Nahuas?” wondered Jesse as we walked back to the car. “That’s strange, because they don’t live around here.”

“Yeah,” I said. “But the portrait is of an ancestor of theirs, right? An Aztec princess or whatever she was.”

“Anyway, how were the people who left the dolls, whoever they are, clued in to our search?” Jayde asked. “How would they know anything about it?”

I opened the Land Cruiser’s doors and waited until we were all in before I responded. “I don’t know, but I bet Inez does.”

And that’s where we headed.

She still wasn’t there. I knocked on her door in case she was just avoiding the phone, but her car wasn’t in the lot, so it was unlikely she was hiding. Something was wrong, though. I could feel it. It wasn’t even noon, so I took us to my office. If we all studied the paper with the pyramid and numbers on it, maybe we could come up with something useful.

The fighting cock was there, but he'd seemed a bit wary since our encounter of the day before. I knew his timidity wouldn't last, so I took full advantage while I could. I even intentionally angled toward him on the way to my door. He took a couple of false charges at me, and when I didn't give way, he backed off. I was inordinately proud of myself. I think I may have strutted. Whatever my posture, it drew laughs from Jesse and Jayde.

In the office, the first thing I did was spread the mysterious sheet of paper on my desk. Jayde and Jesse pressed in for a better look.

"There must be something here," Jayde said. "I can't believe it's just to mislead."

Jesse traced the drawing with his index finger. "The person who drew this picture was no artist. He couldn't be the same person who painted the portrait copy."

"I agree," I said. "Maybe it was an afterthought, or a mistake. Maybe it wasn't meant to be stored with the painting. On the other hand, maybe it was. Maybe it was intentionally placed there by El Chapo's man to lead to the real portrait but in such a way that only someone he trusted would know what it was pointing to."

Jayde pointed to a rust-red smudge at the corner of the paper. "Blood?"

I took a magnifying glass from the desk drawer and held it over the spot. "I can't tell. Maybe."

"I suppose that doesn't matter as far as finding what we are looking for," she said. "But these markings may offer something."

I held the glass over the marks. "Looks like someone wrote them in pencil, and the lead was smeared by rubbing or some kind of moisture. See the stain over them." I circled the discolored portion of the sheet with my finger.

Jesse tilted my desk lamp closer to the writing. "These are numbers." He looked at me for affirmation.

I nodded and looked closer. "You're right, I think. But what about the scrawly bits next to them?" I asked.

"I know this sounds crazy, but it looks like some kind of mathematical formula to me," Jayde said.

"Let's write the numbers out and see if they start to make sense," Jesse suggested.

I set a lined legal pad next to the paper and began to write, calling out what I was writing as I did. "Two, one, then a period or maybe a decimal point, zero, seven, eight, one, then some kind of small circle, then what looks like an *N*, then an eight, a six, another period, two sevens, a four, a nine, another little circle, and what I think is a *V* . . . wait. Part of that looked kind of faded. I think it's a *W*."

"OK," said Jayde. "I think you got all those right. Except, I don't know about that *W* at the end. I still think it may be a *V*."

"Could be," I admitted. "Either way I don't know what it means."

Jayde furrowed her brow. "I'm short on ideas here. Maybe it will come to us if we don't think too hard about it."

"Yeah," chimed in Jesse. "Gestalt."

Jayde and I both looked at him quizzically.

He shrugged. "You know, when something kind of blossoms into an answer without a person knowing why," he said.

I shook my head and looked at Jayde. "Ever since he joined Inez's book club, he comes up with highbrow stuff that just goes over my head."

"I read a book on logic. Syllogisms and things," he smiled.

"OK," I surrendered. "I hope you're right. I hope one of us gestalls or whatever."

"Gestalt," he corrected gently.

We took a break. Jesse made coffee while I tried Inez again on her cell. No answer and I didn't leave a message. I sat in front of my computer and googled random things. No real purpose. I sometimes did that. It relaxed me as I filled my brain with useless trivia. I googled "maps" and was hit with a pile of information. I settled on a world atlas. The first page was a map of the world with lines of latitude and longitude. *Gestalt!* Or maybe just luck. I was hit so hard it took me a moment to say, "I know what the numbers mean!" I realized I'd shouted like a kid who'd just seen Santa coming down a chimney.

Jesse and Jayde rushed to me and bent down to see the screen.

"What?" Jayde asked impatiently.

"A map?" Jesse looked up at me.

"Just look for a minute. Tell me what you see," I teased, savoring my triumph.

"I see a map of the world," said Jayde. "What are you getting at?"

"What's on the map?" I led on.

"Countries," offered Jesse. "Oceans."

"Lines," I gave in, tracing the longitudinal lines with my finger.

"Longitude?" Jesse suggested.

"So . . .?" began Jayde.

"So, look at what I wrote down."

They looked over the paper again, and the answer seemed to dawn on them both at once. Jayde voiced it first. "Map coordinates. Probably latitude and longitude of the ruins where the painting is hidden."

"That's my guess," I said.

We converged on my computer, and I found a site that delivered map locations for corresponding coordinates. I typed in the numbers and pushed *enter.* Our faces fell as one.

"That can't be right," Jesse complained.

"That's the middle of Cancún," Jayde said. "Run the numbers through again."

I did. The results were the same.

"Are there any pyramid ruins in Cancún?" Jayde asked.

"No," said Jesse. "Only those four heaps of rubble on the tourist map, the ones we drove by. No good place to hide what we are looking for."

"I'm missing something," I conceded. "But what?"

"Do you think any of the numbers are wrong?" pressed Jayde.

"Look closely," I said. "I don't see the mistake."

"You're pretty sure about it being latitude and longitude?" Jesse pushed.

"I'm not sure of anything. It just seems the most logical thing to me."

We studied the paper and compared it back and forth with the numbers I'd written down. Studied until we all had headaches from eyestrain.

"I have a thought," said Jesse at last. "Whoever wrote this either made a mistake with one of the numbers or didn't know how to identify the longitude and latitude of the pyramid."

"You can get Google to come up with the longitude and latitude of just about any point on the globe," Jayde said.

"Most narcos aren't that smart." I stretched and sighed. "Only one thing I can think of now." The two of them looked at me expectantly, but my suggestion was less than awe-inspiring. "We get a list of every pyramid in Mexico and compare their coordinates with these numbers. We might find the mistake."

They didn't look elated. I didn't blame them.

"You know how many there are, JJ?" Jesse asked.

"We can start with the closest to El Chapo's hacienda and work outward," I said. "If we don't find something likely, we move on to Belize and Guatemala."

Jesse and Jayde grabbed their cell phones, sat down, and started tapping. I used my laptop. Finally, we came up with half a dozen sites that were closest to the coordinates I'd copied from the paper. It looked like we'd just have to go through the hard slog of going to each one and checking the stones on the steps like we did when we found the false portrait.

"What if the number of steps isn't the same as on our original clue?" Jayde asked.

"That could be, but, if that turns out to be the case, we'll just have to check every step," I answered.

"We will not be able to do that on each one. Not in one lifetime," said Jesse.

"We might have to split up, and then we could cover three times as much," I said.

"Oh, man," Jesse collapsed in his chair.

I shrugged. "I'm open to ideas. I don't think we can count on help from Kaspar or Hermione, though. I'll ask, but I don't think either of them is in shape for the physical activity the hunt will take."

"Then the deal with them would be off," said Jayde.

"We should at least make the offer." I took Jayde's silence as assent. "I'll call them. Anyway, I'll make up a list of pyramids for us tonight. So we can get started."

The two of them looked tired. I knew this was a task none of us really wanted.

"Look, let's take a break," I said. "We can go by Inez's again. I want to see what she can tell us about the Indians."

"I'll call to see if she's back," offered Jesse.

"No. Don't worry. If she's not there we can wait. I have a feeling she's avoiding me, so I don't want to give her any warning."

"Should we board up the windows here?" he asked.

"What?" asked Jayde.

"The storm," I answered. "No, Jesse. I'm far enough inland not to worry, I think."

We hadn't eaten since breakfast, and it was mid-afternoon, so we stopped for tamales on the way to Inez's. I called Hermione and Kaspar to tell them what we'd decided and how we were going to approach the matter. I asked them if they were still in. Hermione was noncommittal. She said to call her if we found the painting, and she'd work something out. Kaspar said the heat would kill him if he tried to search alone, but he was willing to go along with one of us to assist. I told them both I'd get back to them.

Jayde said, "If that's really the best they can do, the deal is off."

I said, "I agree. We can decide what to do if we find it."

After we inhaled the tamales, we drove to Inez's office. Her car wasn't there, nor was the Indian's Jeep.

"What now?" Jayde asked.

"Let's go up to her office. She could be up there even if her car isn't here."

"Call her?"

"No. I don't think she'd pick up."

She didn't answer my knock at her door either. I thought she wouldn't even if she was there. She wasn't though, unless she was being very quiet. I pressed my ear to the door. Nothing.

"What now?" asked Jayde.

I took out a credit card and stuck it into the doorjamb.

"What are you doing?" worried Jayde.

"Getting in, I hope." It didn't take much. The lock gave, and I opened the door. The blinds were open, so, even though the office lights were off, the afternoon sun provided plenty of illumination. Unfortunately, that also exposed us to view from outside. Inez hadn't yet closed her hurricane shutters. We were on the second floor (top floor, really, it was only a two-story building) so it was unlikely, however, that anyone would see us unless we were near a window, and there were only two. Jayde and Jesse were holding in the doorway, and I waved them in. "Come on. Someone might come down the hall." They moved in cautiously. I closed the door and locked it.

Jesse flipped on the light switch. I reached behind him and turned it off. "We don't need the lights. Someone could see them."

"What are we doing, JJ?" Jayde asked, looking even more worried.

"We are breaking the law, amigo," Jesse cautioned.

"We won't be long," I said. I moved to Inez's desk and scanned the scattered papers on the large oak surface. I didn't have a firm idea of what I was looking for, but I figured I'd know if I saw it.

Jesse voiced my thoughts. "What are we looking for?"

"I'm not sure. Something that might tell us what Inez's relation with the Indians is."

Jayde frowned. "Let's be quick. I don't like this."

I nodded my assent. Nothing on the desktop looked interesting. Only a couple of yellow sticky notes with a new real estate client's cell phone and address in Monterrey and a reminder about her mother's birthday. I pulled on the desk drawers, but they were all locked except the thin middle one that held writing and note pads, pens of two or three colors, and paper clips. In a tin were the kind of breath mints I liked, so I took one.

The filing cabinets were also locked, all four of them. To me, it seemed like a lot of security for a real estate agent.

Then Jesse pulled on the corner of a sheet of paper sticking out of a file cabinet I'd checked, but not well, I guess. "Mira, JJ." Jesse held up the paper.

I took it and looked closely. It was blank except for the cheaply printed letterhead that read *Asociación de Pueblos Indígenas de México* followed by a Mexico City address and phone number. "Association of Indigenous Peoples of Mexico," I translated. "Must be a group she has something to do with. Probably a charity of some sort. She does a lot of that kind of thing."

"You think those robbers were with this group?" asked Jayde.

"Robbers don't have letterheads and offices," I scoffed gently.

"Guess not," she admitted.

I slid the paper back through the edge of the locked drawer and took a final look around.

"We'd better go," I said. "I don't know what I was hoping to find, but it's not here."

A stifled gasp twirled me around. Jayde stood with her mouth wide at the opened door of a small coat closet. At her feet were four Santa Muerte dolls in various stages of assembly.

CHAPTER 37

All three of us had theories about why Inez had the dolls in that closet. None of us were sure of anything.

"I just can't see Inez mixed up in anything criminal," I said.

Jesse stood looking at the dolls. "I know. Still, I've seen good people seduced by narco money."

Jayde said, "Well, I don't know her, but having these dolls in her closet is very suspicious, you have to admit."

My cell rang. It was Hermione. "I've decided I want in," she said without preamble. "Let me know what you want me to do."

"Go down to the beach bar at your hotel. We'll meet you there in half an hour."

"Why not my room? It's hot outside."

"Maybe I'm getting paranoid, but your room might be bugged. We just found . . . never mind. I'll tell you when I get there."

I hung up and said to Jayde and Jesse, "Hermione. She wants back in. She can ride with me or Jesse when we search the pyramids."

"I'll take her," offered Jesse. "If she doesn't bring that useless dog."

"Jayde, you'll be stuck with Kaspar then. I'll go solo."

"We'll need two more four-wheel drives," Jesse said.

"Yeah," I said. "Let Kaspar and Hermione get those. We, I mean Jayde, is paying for enough."

"Don't worry," she said. "The company will eat it."

I parked on the street before the hotel so I wouldn't have to tip a valet. I try hard not to overbill my clients.

We walked around the hotel entrance and down the path to the beach bar. Gutman and Hermione were sitting side by side on bar stools and laughing heartily. Both their obnoxious pets were on leashes at their feet. The Chihuahua was sniffing the iguana, who didn't seem to mind at all. Not for the first time, I wondered why I gathered such odd people around me.

"Ah, JJ," greeted the fat man when I drew close. "Good to see you."

"Hello, Kaspar. Let's get a table."

Hermione and Gutman slid off their stools and followed me to a small round table away from the bar. A waiter followed our group closely and stopped to take our orders.

"A round of margaritas," commanded Kaspar. Then more gently, "Is that satisfactory with all?"

No one disagreed, so the mesero nodded and left.

"So, fill us in," said Hermione.

I told them about what we'd come up with at my office, how we needed to get started on the new search, and what we had found at Inez's office.

"What does all this mean?" asked Hermione.

I laughed. "With all my great detective skills, I must say I don't understand a damn thing about this case. And every day, I know less. It wouldn't surprise me if there's no authentic portrait and the whole thing is a setup to help pass off the fake portrait either as an insurance loss or for a fast sale to a not-too-clued-in buyer."

"I could see that," said Kaspar. "However, I still am of the opinion that a genuine painting exists."

"I feel the same," agreed Hermione. "At any rate, we've come this far. What do we need to do, JJ, to complete the mission, one way or another?"

"Well, Jayde, Jesse, and I have worked out a search plan. It's a pain in the butt. Still, I can't come up with anything better. If anybody else does, I'm open."

The fat man dropped some sort of treat to his lizard. "Tell us, JJ."

I realized what it was. "Kaspar, did you just drop your iguana a cricket?"

He smiled paternally at his pet. "He loves a snack in the afternoon. But that was a bit of fruit. Herbie is an herbivore."

Somehow I didn't believe him. "Could you please hold off feeding him till I leave. I don't want to be sick," I said in disgust.

The fat man said nothing but complied with an insincere smile. Hermione hugged her chihuahua to her breast protectively.

"We have a list of potential pyramids, arranged in order of proximity to Guzmán's ranch. We've broken those down into three target groups," I continued, passing copies of the list to Kaspar and Hermione. "Kaspar, you'll go with Jayde, if you agree." He nodded. "Hermione, you'll be with Jesse, OK?"

She smiled coquettishly at my handsome associate. "Sounds good."

"Kaspar, you and Hermione each need to rent a four-wheel drive for the trip. That's only fair. Jayde has been covering costs to now. Any problems with that?" They shook their heads. Kaspar wiped the ever-present perspiration from his face with his handkerchief.

"Just ask the concierges at your hotels," Jesse advised. "They can have the vehicles waiting for you in the morning."

"Fine," said Hermione. "You will have to drive though, Jesse dear."

"Sure."

I was tired, so I asked Jesse to drive, too. We dropped off Jayde, then headed back toward my place. The late afternoon was still humid and hot, but we left the windows down in the Land Cruiser, and the breeze was relaxing. We were driving in light traffic on Boulevard Kukulkan's hotel zone when something caught my eye. It only registered in my subconscious, but I knew it was important. "Jesse, do me a favor and make a U-turn."

"Did you leave something at the hotel?"

"No, I think we just passed something we need to see."

"What?"

"I'm not sure," I laughed in embarrassment. "I hope I know when I see it."

We retraced the last few blocks, and there it was. It had been right in front of me from the start. Now the pieces of the puzzle fit.

It stood tall in the sunset's glow, white, fresh, and taller than any of the pyramids we had set down on our sheet or visited. "That's it," I announced, my voice almost reverent. "It was right here, all along. Everything makes sense now."

Jesse pulled over to the curb, and I pointed to the left. "The hotel?" he asked incredulously.

"It's a pyramid, isn't it? Looks like one, anyway."

"Of course!" he exclaimed. "That's why it's called Pyramid Grand Oasis!"

"How much do you bet the coordinates for its location are exactly the ones we have on the paper we found with the phony portrait?" I asked.

"Let's get to the office and run the address against Google Maps."

I didn't talk on the way. I was absolutely certain this was what we'd been looking for. I gave silent kudos to whoever had crafted this trick. They were smarter than most narcos, anyway. I thought about calling Jayde, but I wanted to make sure. When I did match—if I did—the coordinates, I'd call Hermione and Kaspar and tell them to cancel the four-wheel drives for now.

It was just getting dark when we got to my house. Demetrius scratched the dirt aggressively when I opened the gate, but I was in no mood to be trifled with. I stood and stared until he turned meekly and slunk back into his coop.

The coordinates matched those of the Pyramid Grand Oasis address, as I was sure they would. I called Jayde first, then the other two. Everyone was excited, but I said we should wait and meet the next morning at Jayde's hotel. I didn't want to botch things by rushing in without a plan. We'd worked too hard.

Jesse asked, "What should we do? We can't just search a hotel."

"You have cousins in every hotel in this town. Don't you have one at the Pyramid?"

"It's true. My family has done the world the favor of spreading our seed generously. At that particular hotel, I only have a second cousin."

"Can he, she help us? Will he, she help us?"

"He owes me money. And his wife is what they call 'high maintenance.'"

"OK, partner. Give him a call."

CHAPTER 38

It's never a harbinger of good news when my cell phone chirps before the sun is up, so I didn't expect to hear, "Congratulations! You have won the National Lottery!" But in the past month I'd become used to early calls. So after a curt "Hello," I listened politely.

"Good morning, sweetheart," sang a vaguely familiar voice. "Did I wake you?"

"Who is this?" I mumbled.

"Horatio, dear, with sad tidings."

"What do you mean?"

"Ernesto and I have stumbled upon another one of these theatrically posed murders. Actually, *stumbled* isn't the right word. We were doing our night patrolling and came upon the person . . . really, it seems, 'persons' in the act of setting up a grotesque diorama."

"Did you call your bosses?"

"No. We have decided we hate our jefes. They have been extremely abusive of their workforce lately, particularly us. We like you, though. You are cute. Admittedly, we tried the Chief, Octavio, and your pretty partner, Jesse, but they are not picking up. *Lazy.*"

"Where?"

"You know the golf course on the side of Nichupté Lagoon, where the road goes past to Hotel Row?"

"I know it. I'll be there in fifteen minutes. I'll call your bosses. And Horatio, please keep people away until I get there."

"That's no problem. For some reason, law-abiding citizens tend to give us a wide berth."

I called Jesse and asked him to call the jefes.

"I'll call them right now. What about Tavi?"

"Yeah, call him, too," I said. "Is your phone OK? Sounds like some kind of noise in the background."

"Not sure. I've been having a little trouble with it. It works, though."

"Right. I'll see you there."

Tavi arrived a few minutes after me. I expected him to already be there, since he lived closer, but he may have found it hard to get out of bed. He'd been pushing a hard schedule. I was already questioning the two head sicarios when he walked up. He examined the "display" before he turned back. "Buendía and Little Sammy?"

"On their way, I think. Jesse called them."

He nodded to Ernesto. "Jesse said you two saw the murderers. He said there was more than one."

"Three of them."

"Could you identify them?"

"They were far away. All dressed in black."

Horatio interrupted. "They were getting into a boat when we saw them. By the time we got here, they were out on the water, and we had no hope of catching up."

Buendía and his guards slid to a halt with Little Sammy and his close behind. Buendía berated his lieutenant first. "Ernesto, why did you not call me?"

Ernesto started to snap back but thought better of it and responded mildly. "JJ said he would call you, Jefe."

"I pay your wages, damn you! Not this private detective's."

"Sí, Jefe."

I walked back to the corpse. The mortuary ambulance drove in and parked right in front of the dead man. "Move that away until I tell you," Tavi ordered the driver.

Little Sammy's big SUV crunched to a halt right behind us. Sammy jumped out and screamed at Horatio.

"Who do you report to, you freak? Me or this . . ." He pointed to me but apparently couldn't come up with a sufficiently demeaning insult.

Horatio raised his hand, palm out, placatingly. "Dear Jefe, you know how it distresses me when you speak harshly to me." The tone was meek, but the look in the sicario's eyes was sharp, hot steel. Sammy walked away to save face and headed to the corpse. He stopped when he was almost upon him and reached out to touch the face.

"Don't touch!" Tavi warned.

Little Sammy whirled around angrily, hands on his pistols. Tavi smiled his apology. "Please," Tavi added.

"I recognize this man," Little Sammy said. "He is one of mine, from Michoacán. Julio Benavides. Not much good. No real loss, except for the insult of killing a sicario that belongs to me."

"What is that knife in his hand?" I asked.

"A K-bar fighting knife, like the US Marines use," Tavi answered. "The rifle in his other hand is an M4 carbine."

"Those are hard to get," said Sammy. "If he stole that from me, I will kill him! Or I would if he was not already . . ."

"The men we saw were dressed like that. All in black," Ernesto said.

Buendía frowned. "When my men find out there are three serial killers, they will panic. They already believe some sort of demon is doing this."

"Yes," Little Sammy agreed. "We must keep it from them." He pointed into the faces of Ernesto and Horatio. "They will not know if you two do not tell them."

"It will go very bad for you, if you do," reinforced Buendía.

"Maybe no one has to know there has been another killing," said Sammy hopefully.

"Can you keep your people quiet?" Buendía asked Tavi.

"Maybe . . . but." He looked at a procession of headlights coming down the road. "Here comes the press. No way to silence it now."

"If you don't mind a suggestion, gentlemen," I began to the two cartel honchos, "you might want to take off before the press gets here. Probably not good to see you with the chief of police. Not good for him, either."

They both hesitated briefly before hurrying back to their vehicles.

Jesse arrived just as I was leaving. "Had to stop for breakfast?" I asked.

"Trouble with my battery. Remember, we have a meeting this morning."

"I'll be there. I'm going to go home and shave first. Still plenty of time."

"See you there," he said and took off without asking me about the new dead man. Odd for Jesse.

CHAPTER 39

We sat around the two tables the waiter had put together for us. It was early, 7:00 a.m., but there were already scores of people in the hotel restaurant. An international convention of financial advisors packed the tables. Buses were lined up at the hotel entrance to take them on one sightseeing tour or another. They looked excited and ready to travel, but there was worry, it appeared, about traveling in spite of an imminent hurricane. Not to mention a famous serial killer on the loose. I had to lean in so the others at our table could hear me. Conventioneers were passing all around us and greeting each other with gusto, and while they would not have any idea what we were discussing, I was very wary after all that had happened. Two Policía Turística armed cops waited near the lobby. There had been a rare drug hit in the local hospital a few weeks before, and the tourist commission was making sure tourists and convention participants were safe—or felt safe, anyway.

"My guess is it's on the eighth floor, not the eighth step," I said.

"How the devil can we search the entire floor of a major hotel?" the fat man sputtered. "Impossible!" I held up my hands, palms forward, to shut him up. Gutman frowned and wiped his face, despite the fact that the day's heat had not really begun.

I was grateful he and Hermione had left their animals in their rooms, so I humored his cynicism.

I could tell the others agreed with him. I smiled knowingly and paused for dramatic effect. "We may not have to search an entire floor. Only one suite."

"What do you mean?" Jayde asked.

"Jesse has a cousin who works there. For a small bribe, he told us there is one suite on the top floor, which is the eighth floor, and it's been booked for a year. Since the first week of that rental, no one has occupied it, as far as he can tell. At least, according to the housekeeping staff, no one has slept in the bed or used the shower."

Hermione looked especially pleased. "What suite is that, dear boy?"

"Eight O Five. When things settle down for the day, we can search it."

"Do we have a key?" she asked.

"It will be under the vase in the hallway. The one closest to the door," I answered. "By the way, I expect you and Kaspar to chip in on the bribe money. Jayde shouldn't have to wear all of it."

Gutman grinned. "Willingly, JJ. Willingly."

Jayde snapped her attention to her right and half lifted herself from her seat. I frowned at her. "What's wrong, Jayde?"

She shook her head. "Nothing. For a second I thought I saw that scar-faced man. I was wrong. This serial killer business is playing on my nerves. Those damned dolls somebody slapped us with is bad enough." She sat back down. "When do we go?" she asked.

"In two or three hours. After housekeeping is done with that floor. They still clean the room every day. Jesse's cousin will call us."

"In that case, I have time to go up to my room," Hermione said, rising. "I feel the need to check on my Napoleon. He frets when I am away from him for long periods."

"OK, but don't call anybody," I warned.

"Of course." She left the table and headed for the elevators.

"All right," I said. "How do we get up to the room?"

"Not as a group," warned Kaspar. "That would definitely look suspicious."

"There is a beach entrance," Jesse said. "It leads into a floor used for functions. The elevators are right there, and nobody is usually around."

"Great. Good idea," I said. "We still should go in singly or in pairs."

"Why not let JJ go alone?" said Jayde.

Kaspar shook his head in feigned amusement. "Not that I don't trust young JJ, but our search will be shortened with all of us helping."

I nodded. "He's right. The less time spent in the room the better. It's not likely, but possible, that someone will come along. There are other suites on the floor. We'll have to be quiet."

"Hopefully the people in those rooms will be out for the day," said Jayde.

"Yes, hopefully, but not certainly," I said.

"Are we just going to sit here and wait?" asked Jayde.

"We don't have to. Maybe we could meet at the Pyramid Oasis in, say, two hours."

"I think best if we meet here," said Gutman. "In case circumstances change."

"OK," I said. "We'd better wait for Hermione to get back before we break up. No, I'll just call her." I took out my phone and dialed her number. It rang several times, then went to voicemail. "She's not answering. I'll wait here for her if the rest of you want to go."

"I should see about returning my vehicle," said Gutman. "They delivered it this morning in spite of the message I left." He stood up then flinched at the crack of gunfire that transfixed the entire restaurant. "What the?!" he spat out. The rest of us were speechless for the moment it took for the attack to register.

"That's a gun!" Jesse shouted. "Get down!"

I rolled to the floor and rose up just enough to see what was happening. Jesse and I crossed ourselves at the same time, then

Jesse drew the pistol he was carrying and began to stand. "Stay down, Jesse!" I shouted.

I saw the shooter coming toward us. It was the killer I'd seen stab the man in the flowered shirt. He advanced on us with no doubt as to his intention. He was deadly calm. His right hand held a semi-auto pistol. I saw his cold blue eyes, and I froze.

The restaurant echoed with screams from the diners.

The gunman closed in, raised his gun, and aimed at me. It would be hard for him to miss at that range.

If I hadn't been shoved aside by a man hurtling in flight from the next table, I would have taken a round to my gut. The man who pushed me took the bullet instead. He moaned and fell.

Jayde was frozen in place. I grabbed her arm and dragged her down with me. The fat man bowled over chairs and knocked over tables in his wild bid to escape. The pistol barked after him, but the rounds felled those around him instead.

People tried to help the wounded but seemed to be held back by their fear of being shot themselves.

Jesse took a firing stance in spite of my warning. He got off two rounds before lead smashed into the post beside him. He dropped to the floor and fired again but the round passed wide of the attacker.

The gunman was so close I could almost reach out and touch him. He was firing at all of us at the table, but the melee was diverting his aim. The cops who had been waiting for the conventioneers finally returned fire. The fusillade stopped the assassin's advance.

I'd left my pistol in my desk, so I was useless. I reached up, grabbed a glass from the table, and threw it from my cover. To my amazement, it actually hit the shooter's gun. It shattered and a piece hit him just above the hairline. I thought for a second I saw blood run down his face. He hesitated and threw rapid shots at the cops to keep them at bay, before he fled down the steps to the beach.

The restaurant was paralyzed in silence, waiting for more shots, which did not come. Then the dam of shock which had held the fear in check burst. The conventioneers stampeded to the hotel entrance and out the doors.

The cops ran down the stairs after the gunman. I looked around, and seeing no one in our group was hurt, herded them to the lobby. Kaspar was already there, hiding behind the check-in desk. He only ventured out when he saw us.

"That was for us," Jayde whispered.

"Yes," I agreed. "I know he was after us, but I don't know who sent him."

Jesse nodded. "I would bet on the cartel. El Chapo's men. Which means we better hurry up if we want to find the painting."

"You're right," I said. "Let's head for the Oasis."

"Do you think the police will question us? Do you think they realized we were the target?" asked Gutman. "If they do, we could be held for hours, or more. We need to get to the Pyramid Hotel, find the painting, and leave the country on the first available flight."

"You're right," I said.

"Let's go to my room," suggested Jayde. "It's just across the street. We need to agree what to do with the painting if we find it."

"Don't worry," said Gutman. "I have lined up a number of buyers."

"OK," I said. "I'd better call Hermione and tell her where we'll be."

Hermione still wasn't answering, so I left another message, more urgent this time.

She didn't call me back, but half an hour later she knocked at Jayde's door.

"About time," Gutman scolded. "Why haven't you returned our calls? We need to make haste."

"I heard the gunfire," she said, walking into the room. "People were scurrying all over my hotel like frightened ants."

"Had you been there, you would have been frightened, as well," he said. "And what are you doing with that enormous bag?' He asked, pointing to the straw shopping bag she was carrying.

She sneered at Gutman. "It may well rain. And I do not intend to remain in wet clothing. I have a delicate constitution."

"Were you near the shooting?" she asked Jayde.

"We were the targets. We were very lucky not to have been killed."

"My God!" Hermione exclaimed. "What if my Napoleon had been with me?! Only good fortune that I left when I did."

Jayde touched Hermione's shoulder gently and softly advised, "Your mascara is smudged. There are makeup lights in the bathroom."

"What? Oh, thank you dear. I was in a . . ." without finishing she hurried toward the bathroom.

Gutman sniffed, "You and your silly pet!"

Hermione would have hit him, I think, if she hadn't been afraid he might hit her back. She scowled at him and spat, "Who are you to talk!? What sort of person keeps a pet lizard on a leash?!"

Gutman advanced a step toward her, so I stepped in. "OK. That's enough. We have to get organized."

"I agree," said the fat man. "We have little time before it becomes too difficult to enter the room."

Hermione popped into and back out of the bathroom and then looked at me. "And what if the room you believe is the hiding place is not the right one after all? What then?"

"I don't know," I admitted. "Let's cross that bridge when we come to it."

"So how do we proceed from here, JJ?" Jayde asked.

"OK. Assuming we find the real portrait, one of us will have to hold it. That means the others will have to trust that person. Who should that be?"

"Since I gave the final and most crucial part of the clues, I think I should be entrusted with the painting," offered Gutman. "In addition, I have already lined up likely purchasers."

"Ha!" Hermione snapped. "That is exactly why you should *not* be the holder. You could easily run off and sell it, leaving the rest of us high and dry."

"I think Jayde should hold it," I said. "She has the most to risk. She'll get fired and probably jailed if what we're doing gets out. You and Kaspar would only have to make a phone call to her office to really mess her up."

"Hmmm," Hermione said. "I see your point."

"No," said Jayde. "It should be JJ. He's the only one, he and Jesse, that are . . . no offense . . ." she turned to me. "Well, they are the only ones not sophisticated enough to do a deal for the portrait on their own."

I did take offense, but she was right. Jesse and I wouldn't have the least idea how to offload a nearly priceless piece of art.

"Oh, very well," conceded Gutman, wiping the gathering sweat from his face.

Hermione chuckled. "Goodness, Kaspar. You perspire even in the air-conditioning."

"Yes, it's true." He shook his head. "I am not built for tropical heat."

Jesse interjected, "JJ, there could be people going in and out of the hotel elevators, and maybe some on the top floor."

"Yes, we would have a difficult time explaining ourselves to the police," worried Hermione.

Jesse shook his head. "It's not the police I worry about. Chapo could have a guard in the suite."

"One other thing to consider," I threw in, "is we'll need some basic tools. The portrait may be stored behind a wall. We'd have to cut it open. That would be noisy."

"I will get my cousin to leave a drywall saw at the end of the hallway," offered Jesse.

"And a hammer and maybe large and small screwdrivers," I added.

Jesse nodded. "What do we do about the noise?"

"I don't know."

"And I hate to press you, JJ," Jesse continued. "But a hurricane is coming. If it does not hit Cancún directly, it will be close."

"You and your Weather Channel," I grinned. "But you're right. We'd better get a move on."

Kaspar went to the ice bucket near the room's fridge. "No ice," he complained. "I am miserable. I keep my room's thermostat on sixty-five."

I watched him wipe his face and run cool water to soak his handkerchief. "Thanks, Kaspar. You've given me an idea." I turned to Jesse. "Could your cousin knock out the air-conditioning at the hotel for a couple hours?"

"I could ask him. Why?"

"The hotel would turn into a sauna in a very short time, and the guests would get out to find cooler places. That would pretty well reduce the chances of any noise we make being heard. Unless the hurricane hits. They won't venture out in that. But in that case the storm's noise should cover us."

"That's a great idea," Jayde said.

Jesse went out on the balcony to make the call. I could see him arguing through the glass. He turned and stuck his head back into the room. "He wants a thousand dollars. And we have to be quick. He is in charge of hurricane-proofing the hotel."

I looked at the others. Kaspar shrugged. Hermione nodded. Jayde said, "OK."

"Tell him to do it right now, if he can," I told Jesse.

When he came back in, he said apologetically, "My cousin is greedy, so he's in. But he could lose his job if he is found out. He needs some time to pull it off."

"That's OK," I said. "When?"

"Fifteen minutes from now. Half an hour to be safe."

"How long can he keep it off?" asked Jayde.

"He is fairly certain he can keep it down for at least two hours."

I said, "People will start feeling pretty miserable in an hour or so. Then we'll have an hour to search."

"That is not much time," worried Hermione.

"We will have to be quick. Split up and search assigned areas. All right?"

"You're all welcome to wait here until we leave," said Jayde. "I can call room service if you want anything."

"I want to find the ice machine and fill this bucket," said Gutman.

"Just past the elevators," said Jayde.

I turned on Jayde's TV to watch the news. A local news van and several police cars with lights flashing were parked in front of the hotel. I stood on the balcony with the door open so I could pay attention to the news broadcast and the activity on the street at the same time. Jayde came out with me and started to say something when she stopped short. "Hey! That's Kaspar down there, isn't it?"

I focused where she was pointing. No doubt it was the fat man. He was getting out of his rented vehicle across the street.

"Jesse!" I yelled. "Gutman is going for the Pyramid. He could be trying to screw us. Call your cousin quick. Make sure Gutman can't get into the room without us."

"I'll go get him. I'll call on the way," said Jesse.

"Good. And call me when you find him."

A quarter of an hour later I saw Jesse escorting Gutman back across the street to Jayde's hotel. Five minutes after that they came through the door. I was about to berate him, but Hermione got in first. "What the hell were you playing at, you rotten scoundrel!" she spat. "Trying to cut us out, weren't you?!"

Gutman raised his hands in appeasement. "Nothing of the sort, my friends. I simply wanted to perform a brief reconnaissance of the area to avoid problems later. Also, I wanted to be ready for a quick escape should that be required. I could hardly leave Herbert abandoned in my hotel room."

"You and your lizard," said Jayde in disgust.

"Then why did you sneak off to do it, Kaspar?" I accused.

"It was simply a spur of the moment impulse. That's all," he pleaded.

Hermione glared at him. "People die for that sort of betrayal, Gutman. I will keep my eye on you."

The fat man shrugged sheepishly. "I can tell you that the air-conditioning is off. I could already feel the heat increasing."

"All right," I said. "Let's give it another thirty minutes, then go one at a time to the back entrance and up to the eighth floor. Jesse, call your cousin and make sure he puts the keycard under the vase."

"Who goes first?" asked Gutman.

"Certainly not you," Hermione snapped.

"OK, OK," I interceded. "Jesse will go first. If there's a problem, he can call his cousin. Then Jayde. Hermione next, then Kaspar. I'll come last."

No one disagreed, so we sat in silence, alternating between watching the news on TV and looking out at the street activity from the balcony. Police cars with flashing lights were still lined up in front of the hotel where we were attacked. And crews at all the hotels were scurrying around, boarding up windows to protect against the coming tempest. The fat man said he wanted to go for ice again, but the others shouted him down. I went myself and came back with a full bucket. Kaspar soaked his handkerchief and filled it with ice before pressing it to his forehead.

After half an hour I stood up. "OK. Let's go. Jesse first."

Onc at a time, we slipped to the beachside door of the Grand Oasis Pyramid and took the elevator to the eighth floor. Jesse got the room keycard and opened the door for the rest of us from inside. It took nearly half an hour for all of us to gather.

Jesse warned, "I can't be sure, JJ, but I think I spotted Inez and the Indians driving past."

"Did they see you?" I asked.

"I don't believe so."

"OK," I said. "We don't have time to worry about her right now."

I divided the search into the four rooms of the suite: bedroom, living room, kitchen, and bath. There were five of us, so Jesse guarded the door. The suite was huge, with a view of the beach as well as the neighboring hotels. Probably a great view at night. The side view also looked down on some of the parking area to the front of the hotel. I saw the Land Cruiser Jesse had pointed out to me as the fat man's in one of the spaces.

"Jayde, could you watch with Jesse for anyone that looks like a potential problem?" I asked.

"I'll take the back view," she said. "If Jesse is monitoring the hallway, he's closer to the side window."

We were pretty miserable in the suite because of the lack of air-conditioning. I turned on the overhead fans in the living room and bedroom and opened the door to the balcony. It helped a little, but not much. The fat man was soaking in sweat after fifteen minutes, and the rest of us fared little better.

"I can't take much more of this, JJ," Gutman groaned.

"It's bad, I agree," I said. "Why not go back to Jayde's room. I'll call you if we find the painting."

"Ha," he scoffed. "If you find it, I doubt I would see any of you again."

Hermione wheezed. "This will take days if we don't focus. We may have to tear off all the drywall and rip up the tiles."

Gutman found the thermostat for the suite and turned it to *fan*. "At least we can have some breeze. Better than nothing."

He stood on the bed and lifted his face as high as he could toward the air-conditioning vent. When he could feel no air blowing out, he slammed the vent with his fist. "Damn thing doesn't work!" He stepped down and went to the living room, where he moved the coffee table to give him access to a vent high up on the wall. "Ah, at least this one is open."

While he comforted himself in the flow of air from the vent, Hermione chided him. "Kaspar, get down and help us find the damned portrait! You are such a baby."

Jayde touched Hermione's forehead. "Are you bleeding?"

Hermione recoiled but quickly regained her composure. "My little Napoleon scratched me. Excuse me for a moment." She rushed into the bathroom and closed the door.

I stood immobile for a moment. Something was slapping my brain in the face, telling me I was on the verge of a major realization. Then it hit me. "Kaspar has found the portrait," I said softly.

Jayde said, "What are you talking about?"

"I think Kaspar's need for relief from the heat has paid off." I stood on the bed where the fat man had unsuccessfully tried to open the vent. "There's no air coming from this vent," I announced. "I would bet it's blocked by what we're looking for. I need a screwdriver."

Jesse found one among the tools his cousin had left for us and tossed it up to me. I removed the screws holding the vent and dropped it down to Jesse. Inside the cavity a plastic-wrapped package was blocking the airflow. I twisted the parcel around until I could pull it free and hopped down to let everyone else see what I had.

"May I?" asked Jayde, reaching for the rolled canvas I had just removed from the plastic. She unrolled the scroll carefully onto the bed and bent down to examine it closely. After a quick minute, she looked up. Her smile told us it was authentic. For a second, we were all quiet. I could tell by the faces around me that we were afraid we might be dreaming.

"Well, then," Gutman said at last. "It appears we have found it."

"Yes, thank you," said Hermione. "And I'll have it now, thank you."

But when we turned to the voice it wasn't Hermione speaking. It was a man in a flowered shirt and cargo pants, grinning widely and pointing a .45 Auto in our direction. On the couch beside him lay a bright red wig and what appeared to be facial plastics, including the tip of what had been Hermione's nose.

"You!" I spat. "Damn! Your eyes!"

"Yes, yes." She—he—grinned. "Are they not a lovely shade of blue? Those green contacts were killing me. Ha ha . . . killing the killer." No one else laughed. "What?" He frowned theatrically. "No sense of humor."

"You're the assassin!" I whispered.

"Yes, I guess you could call me that. Fortunately for you all, my assignment doesn't include harming you." For a minute his expression turned firm. "Unless such action is necessary."

Jayde shook her head in sad disbelief. "How could . . .?"

". . . I be a hired killer?" he finished for her. "Well, the pay is good. I get to meet many interesting people, although the friendships rarely endure." He motioned us back with his pistol as he moved to retrieve the painting. "I think some people are looking for us. But, in my case, the little old lady they would be alerted to no longer exists. The rest of you must care for yourselves."

"Who—?" I began.

"Who hired me? Let me remind you that El Chapo has enemies. And these enemies see this as a way to hurt their rival while making a good deal of money."

He held us at bay while he pulled a cell phone from his purse and dialed. The call was answered quickly. "I have it," he spoke into the phone. "Have the plane ready. And don't forget my dog." He paused to listen. "Yes, damn you, my dog! Do I make myself clear?" He threw up his hands in exaggerated despair. "Good help is so hard to find these days."

The killer smiled with a false friendliness that was more frightening than a scowl. "I have grown fond of you all. It would pain me greatly to kill any of you. However, that is what I do, so, if any of you come after me, I will certainly terminate with extreme prejudice, as they say. Please do not make me do that. And the noise would be distracting. I hate loud noises."

He backed toward the door slowly and would have made it had the hurricane warning siren not startled him. He stumbled for only an instant, but the fat man, moving faster than I would have imagined possible for someone of his bulk, used the disorientation to kick the gun from the killer's hand, propelling him backward. The killer's head hit the floor hard. With a second burst of amazing agility, the fat man scooped up the gun and grabbed the painting. "Tie her . . . or him up with something," he ordered, shouting over the blaring of the siren.

Jesse retrieved the drywall saw from our small collection of tools and cut the curtain cords to use for binding the assassin. I helped him tie Hermione's hands behind his back, then his feet. He was coming back to his senses and glared at us all in turn, but he focused on Gutman. "You great tub of guts! This is not over!"

"Oh, my dear, I have been threatened by better men . . . women . . . whatever . . . than you. And yet I manage to sleep peacefully at night. You are fortunate I do not find you intimidating or I would have to kill you now. However, should we meet again, I may reconsider my largesse."

I had to laugh as I reached out to Gutman for the artwork. He just tilted his head and smiled indulgently. "Oh, no, my dear JJ. I will be holding on to this lovely work. While I am not a connoisseur of fine art, I am greatly appreciative of the money it commands."

I should have seen it coming. I had told Jayde we couldn't trust Hermione or Gutman. I'll never know if Jayde would have honored the deal, but I like to think she would have.

Gutman backed to the door and opened it to make sure the hallway was clear. Then he ducked back in quickly. "I thought the suite next door was unoccupied," he accused, frowning at Jesse.

"It is," Jesse answered. "Unless it was just booked. Why?"

"Never mind. I hope for their sake they don't come out while . . ." He stopped and gave us a final warning. "Like Hermione, I am fond of you. If you try to follow me, I will only shoot to wound you. Fair warning though, I am not a good shot. If I aim at your leg, who knows what I will hit. I recommend you stay in place until you look out that window and see me driving off." Then he slid out and closed the door quietly behind him.

The rest of us stood looking after him until we couldn't hold ourselves back and rushed to the door in a wave. I was closest so I got there first. I gripped the doorknob, working up the courage to ease the door open. No one spoke, maybe waiting for a gunshot to break though the warning wail of the sirens. When there was none, I eased the door open and started into the hallway.

I was stopped by a revolver pressed hard into my stomach.

"Inez!" I spat out in shock. "What the . . .?!"

She pushed the gun farther into my belly, forcing me back into the room, until she was in far enough to close the door.

"What are you doing?" I raised my hands without being asked, although I was sure Inez wouldn't shoot me. "Why are you here?"

"The same as you, JJ. For the portrait of la Malinche."

"That painting is la Malinche?" asked Jesse incredulously.

"Sí, hermano. La desgraciada."

"I'm completely lost here," Jayde spoke up. "Could someone please fill me in?"

"Of course," agreed Inez. "That portrait—or what it portrays—is a source of shame to our nation. The woman called la Malinche was Cortés' interpreter and mistress. She was the traitor who helped the Spanish conquistadores overcome our Aztec ancestors."

"Inez, that's crazy," interrupted Jesse. "No one cares about that anymore."

"Jesse, you and I are mestizo, mixed race, like almost everyone in our country now, so many generations later. La Malinche gave birth to the first of our kind, to La Raza, with her bastard son Martín, whelp of Hernan Cortés."

"Why are you here, though, Inez?" I asked.

"Because I am with the Organization of Indigenous Peoples of Mexico. The woman in that portrait disgraced us. She was the whore who collaborated with the European invader—yes, she was sold into slavery and gifted to Cortés as a mistress, but she then chose to collaborate with him. We do not want the painting to be admired by the public. We will not destroy it, but it will remain secured from the eyes of the world."

Jayde walked up to Inez and took the gun from her hand. "You're not going to shoot anyone, Inez. That's not who you are."

Inez didn't resist. She nodded and pointed to the window overlooking the parking area. "Look down. There is no need for me to shoot anyone."

We all moved to the window. The scar-faced Indian and his partner had Gutman and were pushing him into the back seat of his Land Rover. I wondered if his pet iguana would protect him. I didn't think so. Lizards are not particularly loyal. The scarred Indian climbed into the driver's seat and sped out of the parking area and onto the avenue.

The downpour was just starting. I couldn't tell if the hurricane was going to slam directly into us, but at the very least, we were going to get sideswiped.

Inez looked at me. "JJ, I hope you will not chase them."

"That's up to Jayde. She's my client. But we are about to get the hell knocked out of us by this storm. We'd better all get away from the windows and cram ourselves into the bathroom."

Jayde set the pistol on the table and looked out the sliding doors to the waves slapping more and more forcefully onto the beach. "It's not worth chasing them," she said. "Probably the only people who have a real claim to that painting are the Indians anyway. At least, that's the way it feels. I'll tell my company it's stolen—and I'll make it a good enough story that they'll allow me to stop looking for it. I don't feel sorry for them. They were stupid enough to insure a painting for a drug dealer."

"I hope you don't lose your job," said Inez.

"I probably need a change, anyway."

"You can work with me and Jesse," I offered.

She chuckled. "Thanks for the offer. I'll think about it."

"What about me?" I'd forgotten Hermione, who lay trussed up on the floor. "You are being so generous, why not let me go?"

"Hermione, or whoever, you killed some people," I said. "It's true you're not the serial killer we've been searching for, but you still did plenty of bloody work."

"They were narcos. I did the world a service."

I shook my head. "Murder is murder. I have to call the cops."

"I'll be out by tomorrow. My employer has influence in Mexico."

"Great, good for you. But I have to turn you in. Ethics."

"What about my dog?"

"Is that really your pet?" I asked. "Or just part of your disguise?"

"No. Napoleon is my friend. Long-term friends are hard to find in my line of work."

"Won't your associates, the people you called, take care of him?" Jayde asked.

"Ha, those people have no heart. They will probably throw him out the window when they learn I have failed in my mission. At least let me call them. I will threaten them with a fate worse than death unless they treat Napoleon well."

"All right," I conceded. "Jesse will dial the number for you in a minute. Let's get into a room with no windows quick."

Inez picked up her gun. "I'll take this back if you don't mind." She grinned. "Cancún is becoming a dangerous place."

"Sure. If you have trouble with the narcotraficantes, Jesse and I will be there for you."

"She will have no trouble with them," Hermione said. "I see no need to mention Inez to my employers."

"Thank you," said Inez.

"You are welcome, my dear. Perhaps we can exchange makeup tips down the road. Haha."

"I will go now," Inez said. And to Jayde she extended her hand. "I am grateful."

"Inez, not in the storm," I pleaded.

"I will be fine," she said.

Then she left.

I reflected again later that I have a talent for becoming involved with strange people.

CHAPTER 40

We holed up for three hours in the bathroom of the suite. The worst of the hurricane hit up the coast.

The case was over. Jayde wrote me a check and kissed me on the cheek. She didn't know what she was going to do with her life next, but I told her the invitation to join our small detective agency was open. I didn't tell her we went for long periods with no clients. I thought she could help us with that.

I felt OK about the results of the job, even though my client lost out. The people who most deserved the painting were in possession of it. They were also in possession of the fat man, but I thought he'd probably surface unharmed. His damned lizard, too.

The resort town had been wounded by the storm, but it could have been much worse. Crews were already clearing debris from the roads, and the hotels were cleaning up scattered plants and broken glass. According to the media, no one had been killed or even seriously injured. When I drove down the long road to my casita, I had to swerve around branches that had been torn and scattered by the high winds. I made a mental note to arrange for them to be swept up. I knew it would be a while, though. Cleanup workers were going to be in heavy demand after the storm's fury.

I was bone tired. Not just physically, but soul-tired. The kind you get when you've been playing in a league you're not ready for. But maybe I would be next time.

When I got out of my car, I scanned the pathway to my door for an angry fighting cock. I had faced dangerous humans the past few days, and yet that rooster still worried me. On a whim, I'd bought some small-grain corn at a feed store I passed on my way home. I thought it might come in handy with Demetrius. I could scatter it and pray he was hungry. Hopefully it'd keep the bird from attacking me.

There he was. He stuck his head out of his coop and stood boldly, like a bull ready to charge. He scratched the dirt and headed for me. In a panic, I threw the grain at him, and to my surprise, the rooster actually stopped to peck at the corn. When he'd eaten what was before him, he cocked his head to the side, as if he wanted more. For reasons I can't begin to explain, I lowered my hand with the grain in it as if I were trying to attract a puppy. Demetrius took a couple of hesitant steps toward me, then a couple more, until he was in pecking distance of the handful I held toward him. He poked at the meal, taking care not to wound me. I couldn't believe it. I reached out with my other hand to pet the bird. He squawked and backed off.

Oh, well. It was a beginning, I said to myself.

I dropped the grain so he could feed and started back to my door. I froze when I saw what was waiting on my doorstep. A Santa Muerte doll.

Cautiously, I approached it. It was very like the ones I'd found before, with a significant exception. This doll had a smile painted on its face and a sign attached to its body with a single word, *Gracias.*

CHAPTER 41

Somehow I'd forgotten I still had a client. Actually, two clients. Two mean, nasty clients who would likely have done me harm if I didn't perform according to their expectations. And one of them was banging on my casita door.

My phone showed 3:30 a.m., an hour when civilized people were sleeping soundly, recovering from their hard day's work in service of their country, their family, mankind . . . or just a hangover from a late night out.

"Get up, you lazy, incompetent fool!" There was no mistaking Buendía's angry baritone. "If you do not open up this instant, I will break your door into pieces!"

"I'm coming," I shouted back, but by the time I unlocked the door it was showing early stages of splintering. What crossed my mind was that I would be left at the mercy of Demetrius, the rabid rooster.

Buendía grabbed me by my shirt front (in my exhaustion, I had not even undressed the previous night before collapsing on my bed) and shook me. "You had better have some results on the killer, or you will be the star of a murderous scene yourself!"

"What is going on, Mr. Buendía?" I croaked. "With the storm . . ."

He slapped me across the face and turned me loose. His top lieutenant, Ernesto, gave me a sympathetic look and his boss a look that said Buendía should start sleeping with a gun under his pillow, if he didn't already. "I don't care about the damned storm! The killer put one of those scenes, whatever you call it, right at the front gate of my house. Now my men think the serial killer is a ghost because they saw nothing until they changed the guard. They are panicking and threatening mutiny. I may have to shoot one or two to restore order. And I am short-handed as it is."

"Do you want me to call the police?"

"I want you to come with me right now and lie to my men about how close you are to catching this maniac."

"Of course. I'm a very good liar." I caught a warning glare in his eye. "Oh, no, Señor Buendía, not to my clients."

My cell phone played its little melody. Tavi. I answered. "Yeah?" I couldn't believe what he was telling me. "Hold on a sec, Tavi." I turned to Buendía. "Tavi says Little Sammy has one of the theatrical sets in front of his place, too. The dead man on it is one of his own sicarios from Sonora."

"Mine, too! The corpse is one of my men from another town."

I told Tavi. He said he had personally been patrolling both cartel houses and had seen nothing. I passed that on to Buendía.

"Then, damn you both, maybe it *is* a demon!" He grabbed my arm and hustled me out to his car.

"Tavi, Mr. Buendía is taking me to his estate to talk to his men. Maybe you should do that with Little Sammy's crew if they're running scared. Call Jesse, too, please. We'll get together later today."

When we arrived at Buendía's Río Seco compound, every light in the house and all the security lights in the drive and yard were screaming brightness for miles around. We approached the mise-en-scène where the new body was enshrined. There were at least a dozen armed guards around it, but they were standing a good way back as if it might grab them with its spell if they got too close.

"Mr. Buendía," I tapped his shoulder in the front seat.

He spun around and glared at me. "Yes?" he shot back.

"If you don't mind a suggestion, maybe you should cut off some of these lights. They will attract attention we don't want, especially the media."

He didn't grace me with a personal response. "Ernesto, turn off all outside lights," he ordered.

The SUV came to a halt right in front of the posed cadaver. I stopped to take it in. I held up my phone to Buendía seeking his OK to take a photo. He nodded and I did.

The fellow on the stage had a sneaky grin painted on his face and was dressed in a three-piece suit of dark blue. A necklace of crypto coins was strung around his neck, and the word *Ponzi* was embroidered on the handkerchief hanging from one hand. "Mr. Buendía, this is one of your men?"

"Yes. I told you."

"Do you think he was killed like the others? Fentanyl?"

"Of course! And what kind of depraved assassin would cowardly poison a man who is simply trying to earn food and shelter for his family?"

"Oh," I said. "I'm sorry. So he was a family man?"

"Yes, very much a family man. In fact, he had three families. He took care of them all and was training several of his children to work for me after they finish third grade. I insist all my employees learn to read and write."

"Do you have any idea what his being dressed like this means?"

"No. That is what I'm paying you to find out. Now, inside!"

It was like walking into an armed camp. Actually, I'd never been in an armed camp, but I'd seen movies with armed camps in them. Lots of weapons and angry bad guys holding them like they are looking for someone to blow away.

Buendía took me a third of the way up the staircase linking the entry hall to the second floor so his people could see and hear me. For close to ten minutes, I prevaricated, lied, and made things up. By the time I'd finished, Buendía's men were convinced I would have the serial killer (or evil demon) behind bars or destroyed. They gave me a hearty round of applause.

Buendía said a few words in Spanish so quickly I could not understand them and led me back to his SUV. He turned me over to Ernesto. "Take him home. Then hurry back here."

"Excuse me, Señor Buendía," I said before he was too far away. "What was that last thing that you told your men? I didn't catch it."

He turned for a second, smiled briefly and said, "I told them they could be sure you would find the killer before the end of this week, because I told you that if you did not, I would put you in one of these scenes."

It was still dark when I caught up with Tavi at Little Sammy's fortress. Jesse was standing with Tavi, Little Sammy, and Horatio in front of a scene much like the others. This one had the corpse clothed in a Roman toga with a dagger in his hand raised above a mannequin with a gold leaf laurel crown on his head and wearing a purple-striped toga. The mannequin's hands were raised as if to ward off the corpse's attack.

"One of your sicarios, Mr. Sammy?" I asked as I walked up to them.

He gave me a curt nod. "This has gone on too long." He waved at the score of heavily armed men around the estate's house and garden. "My men think it is a demon now. No one saw or heard the killer set this up. Only when our sentry changed did they find it."

I noticed Tavi had no other police with him, and his patrol car lights weren't on. "Buendía's scene like the previous one?" he asked me.

"Yes. I guess this body, too."

He nodded.

"You want to keep this one out of the press?" I asked.

"Yes," he said. "We don't need any more publicity. I'll get it taken to the morgue under wraps. Take it out of the costume."

"Buendía's?"

"His, too."

"I'll take a photo," I said. "I printed the others out. Maybe they'll tell us something useful."

"What will be useful is for you to find this maniac before all my people panic," spat Little Sammy. "You are not giving me my money's worth of your so-called *expertise*. I will consider other measures to ensure your performance, all three of you."

I saw Tavi bristle at the threat, so I jumped in. "Horatio, did you and Ernesto notice anything odd during your patrol tonight?"

"No," Horatio said. "Only your chief of police here, and your pretty boy Jesse round the same time. We stopped looking about two in the morning. We were tired."

Sammy raised his hands as if asking for delivery from my foolishness. "I even give you my top man to help! I am too generous." He turned and began to stalk away. "Now you three get rid of that monstrosity in my yard and go do your jobs."

Horatio gave me a sympathetic look and a brotherly tap on my shoulder before he followed his boss.

"If I were doing my job," Tavi said under his breath, "you would be sitting in one of my cells, you narcotraficante cabrón!"

When I was sure Sammy was out of range of my voice, I asked Tavi, "What do you make of these two on the same night?"

He started to say something but held back, then shook his head. "I don't know."

"There have been nine of these killings now," I said. "That's a lot. And we've got a missing, maybe dead federal investigator. Every federal cop in Mexico is going to be down here soon."

Jesse looked down at the ground and then turned his head to Tavi, who, I thought, appeared to be signaling him to be quiet. "What is it, Jesse?"

"Nothing. It will keep. I will see you back at the office."

When Jesse got to the office he was carrying a much-welcomed bag of enchiladas. While stuffing our mouths, we discussed what our next move should be.

"We did all we could for Jayde, JJ." he said. "We found what she was looking for. The fact that it was stolen again was not our fault."

"I don't know if her company will see it that way," I said. "I feel bad for her. I should have thought about keeping the painting secure once we got our hands on it."

"We can't really go after it now without hurting Inez."

He set a book he was carrying on my desk and pulled a paper towel from a roll to wipe the drippings from his chin.

"That's some book, Jesse."

"It's from my book club."

"You have a meeting today?"

"No. I just want to finish it."

I stood up and went to my angrily beeping cell. A text from Tavi. I called him back.

Tavi was watching for us at the front desk of the police station. I found it hard to believe when he told me over the phone that Federal Inspector Gustavo Maximiliano Huerta, presumed dead serial killer expert, had shown up dazed and hungry but otherwise unharmed at Tavi's station less than an hour earlier. He was sitting in Tavi's only comfortable office chair when we came in. He started to get up, but Tavi stopped him.

"No, Gus. Rest. Rest."

"Inspector," I greeted. "It's good to see you although . . . I mean . . . I thought . . ."

"As did I, my friend. I am as surprised as you, although probably more pleasantly so, that this day finds me still drawing breath." The inspector was wearing the tropical shirt and Dallas Cowboys cap that he wore when we first met. The sunglasses were on his lap.

"I see you retrieved your clothes, unless you pack spares," I said.

"My friend, Chief Octavio, restored them to me. No need to have them in evidence."

"What happened, Inspector? Did you see who took you?" asked Jesse.

"I have given Chief Fuentes here an initial report. I will add details when I am a little recovered from my ordeal."

"He is indeed lucky to be alive," Tavi interrupted. "I am convinced he was in the hands of our serial killer."

"Yes, I, too, believe so. I cannot understand why he did not dispose of me. He, or they, it may well be there is a colleague, even two, helping our killer."

Tavi laid his hand on the inspector's shoulder. "Gus was held in a makeshift cage of wood and wire out in the jungle."

"Did you recognize any of the surroundings or landmarks on the way there?" I asked.

"I was slugged from behind, and a cloth bag was thrown over my head. The jungle was just dense foliage. Food and water were thrown to me when I was sleeping. I never saw anyone. They must have drugged me before I was packed up and brought here. I woke up on the sidewalk out front." He got up slowly and stretched his sore muscles. “But now I will go to my hotel and rest. Tavi graciously phoned to make sure they had my room ready.”

We walked with the inspector to the patrol car Tavi had waiting. Gus looked up at us as he slid into the passenger seat. “Tavi says there are no new developments regarding the killer.”

I shook my head apologetically.

“Don’t worry, my friends,” he smiled. “I have returned. We will track the maniac, or maniacs, down and destroy him . . . or them.”

CHAPTER 42

I woke to the sirens of multiple fire trucks and the red-orange glow of what looked like dawn to the north and south of me. I thought at first I was dreaming, but, as I shook off my drowsiness, I could see sharp plumes of bright yellow flames shooting high from both directions.

Before I could recover my senses, I was startled by an insistent banging on my door. I ran to my bathroom and retrieved my pistol from the toilet tank. I moved cautiously into my office and stood to the side of the door in case whoever was there decided to fire through it.

"Open up!" yelled a familiar voice. "We don't have much time."

I slid over to my front window and peeked as much as I dared without exposing myself. A white SUV was parked at my gate.

"Open, damn you, JJ, or I will kick the door in." What had my door done, I wondered, for it to be so frequently threatened with annihilation. Even in anger, the musical tone of the voice identified the speaker, well, the yeller. I opened the door gradually until Horatio pushed it in and me to the side. Ernesto followed on his heels.

"I don't suppose you have coffee made," he asked.

I just shook my head numbly. "No, I was asleep . . . What?"

"We are leaving this lovely city, JJ. Our sicarios have mutinied against Buendía and Little Sammy."

"What!? How . . .?"

"Even ruthless people like ourselves have a limit on the ruthlessness they can bear. So we have cast off our chains and disposed of our masters."

"And the rest of the sicarios?"

"Ernesto and I have divided up the cash the cartels had on hand among our associates. Of course, we kept a reasonable share for ourselves."

"What about the killer?"

"We don't care about him. It seems he was going after only our cartels. Now that those cartels no longer exist, it is likely he will fade away. But, if not, that is not our concern. Our sole kowtow to Christian charity is informing you of the situation. There is no more need for you or your friends to risk harm on our account."

"And your jefes?" I said.

Ernesto grinned. "We did not like our jefes very much. They are no loss. Tell Tavi not to bother searching for them."

"You will see their funeral pyres to the north and south of you," Horatio added. I am sure no law enforcement in your country or this one will do anything but bless their demise."

Ernesto slapped me on the back. "And now, since you have no coffee, we will leave you."

"You two. What . . ." I began.

Horatio took Ernesto's calloused hand in his delicately manicured own and looked with affection into his eyes.

"Ernesto and I found we have much in common. Amazingly, he is a fabulous hair stylist. As a boy, he would hide in his mother's salon to avoid abusive men she brought home. The women there loved him and taught them all their secrets."

Ernesto shuffled modestly. "They were fine teachers. Horatio and I have decided to set up a salon and spa in Fort Worth. Texas women spend a fortune on their hair."

Horatio hugged his partner and smiled. "I know Ernesto is a rough brute. But I like that in a man."

They left without another word. I watched them drive off, and then I called Tavi and Jesse.

Buendía's mansion was flaming much higher than Little Sammy's, probably because the old house was mostly wood, while Sammy's was largely made of glass and steel. Neither one would be more than scrap and ashes when the fires were finally put out. Whoever had set the blazes knew what they were doing. I was reminded of a quote by a very funny guy named Terry Pratchett, "Build a man a fire and he'll stay warm for a day. Set a man on fire and he'll be warm for the rest of his life." Sick, I know. But appropriate for these two gangsters.

By the time I caught up with Tavi and Jesse they'd already been to Buendía's house and were now at what was left of Sammy's. The three of us watched Sammy's conflagration with the hypnotic fascination most humans have in the presence of large fires. All Cancún's fire trucks had been deployed between the two cartel home fires. We rarely had this level of catastrophe, and dozens of TV and newspaper reporters were busy posing to dramatic effect with flames in the background. No cartel men were around either place. I told Jesse and Tavi about my visit from the cartel lieutenants.

"I think they may be right," I said, "about the serial killer. He didn't kill anybody, at least as far as we know, who wasn't a member of either Buendía's or Sammy's gang."

"Yes," Tavi agreed. "I would be surprised if he does not just disappear. That would be a good thing. I believe we can slow down our search. After all, the people he killed were not exactly worthy members of society."

I was a little surprised at his attitude. Tavi wasn't usually one to leave a job unfinished. "I don't agree, Tavi. We agreed to do our best to find the killer, and I'm going to do that. At least not give up. The maniac might keep killing. Next innocent civilians."

The chief looked slightly ashamed. "Yes, of course, JJ. You are right. We will do that."

"We have our reputations to consider, too." I pressed. "We don't want the public to think we're incompetent."

Jesse pointed behind us. "Here comes the media."

"I'll leave them to you, Tavi," I said. "Maybe you can come by the office after you get through here. Or I can come to yours."

"I'll come to you," he said. "My office phone will be besieged by media people after these fires."

"I'm going home to shower this smoke smell off me," said Jesse. "I'll meet you at the office after."

I was pinning the police photos of the posed victims of the serial killer on the corkboard in my office when Jayde knocked on my door. No, she didn't exactly knock. She just walked in.

"Decorating your office?" she chuckled.

She caught me. I thought I might as well come clean. "I was going to tell you sooner, but I was sort of sworn to secrecy."

"Secrecy about what? That you have a kinky thing for photos of . . ." She came to the board to get a better look. "What are these?" She frowned up at me. "Are these the victims of the serial killer? I think I saw a couple of these on the news."

"Yeah, they are. I was kind of hired to help find them."

"What!?" her jaw dropped. "Kind of? What does that mean?"

"It means I wasn't given a choice."

"How can you not be given a choice? Who hired you?"

"The cartels."

"The cartels? Which one?"

"Both of them."

She just stood there looking at me for a minute. I think she was reevaluating her opinion of me. "But I saw on the early news the cartels trying to move into Cancún were burnt out last night. Do you think the killer did that?"

I stuck a pin in the last photo and walked back to my desk. "No idea, really. Want coffee?"

"OK."

She sat while I poured her a cup. She reached into her bag and pulled out an envelope. "I've been authorized to give you this check."

I took it from her and opened it. "This is pretty generous considering I didn't get the painting back."

"I told my boss that you did get it back and were nearly killed trying to keep it."

"And he bought that?"

"Yes. In fact he said I could offer you the job of finding it again."

"Well, I . . ."

"Don't worry. I told him you were unavailable."

She moved the book Jesse had left on my desk to make room for her coffee. Then she picked it up for closer inspection. "Whoa! *Dante's Inferno*. Pretty classy reading for a private investigator."

I waved the compliment away. "That's Jesse's book, for his book club. He wants to improve himself so he can marry up."

She set the book back down, then picked it up again. "Did you find out why the serial killer targeted the people he did?"

"Not yet. So far, all the victims have been associated with the Río Seco or Luna Nueva gangs, and all were killed by fentanyl poisoning."

"So you could safely say all the victims were bad guys, right?" she asked.

"No doubt about that. What are you getting at?"

She walked back to the cork board and studied the photos again. “These are all the victims so far?”

“No. There are two more. I don’t have their photos yet, but I have them on my phone. Why?”

“Because I think we may have just stumbled on his pattern. It’s a big clue that may lead you where you don’t want to go.”

“I don’t understand what you—”

“There are nine circles of Hell in *Dante’s Inferno*. I think most of them match the way these victims were staged. I don’t know about . . . Who is this first victim? Is he a cartel guy?”

“He wasn’t a victim of the killer. He was a young man from a prominent Jewish family who died from an overdose, fentanyl. His body was stolen from the mortuary.”

“Look here,” she said turning to the pages of artwork in Jesse’s book. “The first circle of Hell. Limbo. For good people who were not baptized Christians.”

She moved to the next photo and I joined her.

“The rest are all cartel?”

I nodded. She turned to the artwork of the second circle of Hell.

“The next circle is Lust, for people who don’t control their sexual desires. See, this dead guy is fondling naked sex dolls.”

“Keep going,” I said.

“All this food and the fat man in the next scene. The third circle is Gluttony.”

I could see the pattern.

Jayde pointed to the fourth photo and showed me the picture in the book. “Greed is the fourth circle. This one with all the coins.” She pushed me back gently to move to the next scene. “Here in the fifth circle we have Anger. See how the killer illustrates the corpse in uncontrollable rage?”

I nodded and checked the picture in the book.

“The sixth circle is Heresy. The killer was particularly creative here. He puts the Bible in one of the corpse’s hands and a Santa Muerte doll, obviously a heresy for a Christian, in the other.”

"OK," I said. "I get it."

"Almost finished," she said. "The gun and the knife in this scene refer to those condemned to the seventh circle of Hell for their violence." She had come to the end of the photos. "You said you had two more on your phone."

She followed me to my desk, and I brought the photos of the last two killing scenes to the screen.

"The Eighth Circle is reserved for those who commit fraud. Notice the famous name *Ponzi* and the necklace of crypto coins." She tapped my phone's screen. "The ninth, and last, circle is Treachery. And there is Brutus stabbing his buddy Julius Caesar."

She sat down. I sat down. I was impressed.

"The good news is, the killer isn't going to kill any more, at least not using Dante's book. The Ninth Circle is the last in the Inferno."

"You're a smart woman," I said.

"I was a classical literature major in college," she laughed. "Sometimes we investigators just get lucky, right?"

She stood and extended her hand for me to shake. I did and she kissed me on the cheek.

"Well, J.J. Tabasco, I've got a plane to catch."

I walked her to her car without saying anything. I wanted to tell her I'd miss her, but I couldn't find the words. So I just blurted out, "I will miss you, Jayde. Very much."

"I'll call you when I get back," she said.

I watched her drive away. I wondered if she'd ever call me.

Jesse and Tavi showed up at my office at close to the same time. I looked out the window and saw Jesse hang back for the two or three minutes it took for Tavi to drive up.

They had a brief confab before they headed for my door. They were my two best friends, and I was hurt they'd kept such a major secret as staging the serial killer murders from me. To be honest, the eight victims didn't weigh heavily on my conscience. The narcos were very bad people.

Jesse knocked briefly and opened the door with a smile. "Good morning, JJ."

Tavi walked directly to the coffee maker and filled his cup. He glanced at the pinups of the serial victims on my corkboard and hesitated for a second before he approached them. "I see you have photos of the serial killer's handiwork arranged in order. Of course, there may be more."

I held up my phone. "I have the last two on my phone. There won't be any more."

Tavi shook his head. "We can't know that for sure."

I noticed that Jesse couldn't meet my gaze. I tossed him his book. "If there are more, you and Jesse will need another chapter."

Tavi started to lie, but he couldn't. We were friends, after all. "Jesse insisted we keep you ignorant of what we were doing, in case we were discovered. That way you would be held guiltless."

"We had to do something, Jefe," Jesse pleaded. "Damn narcos are ruining our country . . . and yours. Buendía and Little Sammy had to be stopped."

"We talked about doing vigilante justice," said Tavi. "After all, every one of the scumbags you have pinned on your board has the blood of hundreds on his hands, thousands if you count their contribution to fentanyl overdoses around the world."

"But Inez . . ." began Jesse.

"Inez!?" I broke in. "She was involved in this?"

"It was her idea," Jesse went on. "She is the smart one. It came to her during a book club meeting, when we were studying Dante."

"She told us a serial killer would strike fear in the hearts of the narcos, more than a simple murder," said Tavi. "And she was right. It worked beautifully." He went to the window and looked out. "Inez, like me and Jesse, was born and raised in Cancún.

Her family for generations is buried here. She could not bear to see it become another drug haven like Nuevo Laredo."

"Tavi had his contacts in the police forces around the country provide us with the bodies," said Jesse. "Inez helped with the creative work."

For what seemed like a long time, but probably wasn't, all three of us were silent.

Then I clapped my hands together and stood. "OK, now that I'm part of the conspiracy, how do we wrap this hoax up? We can't have more experts from the federales snooping around. We have to figure out a way to convince the media and Mexico City that the Cancún 'Nine Circles of Hell' serial killer is no more."

We decided the best way to dispose of the serial killer was to have him kill just one more time. We'd leave speculation about the actual number of killers to those who enjoyed speculating about such things.

Using latex gloves from the evidence kit in Tavi's patrol car, we cut out words and letters from newspapers and magazines I hadn't yet thrown out to build a suicide note that would keep authorities from spending much of their time or budget in pursuit of someone no longer a danger. We didn't know where Inez was or we would have asked her to be the author, although maybe it was good to have it a bit rough-hewn:

TO THE MAN WHO HUNTS ME, INSPECTOR GUSTAVO MAXIMILIANO HUERTA

I know that a man of your expertise would find me eventually. I saw when I had you in captivity that you could not be broken, and I do not wish to take the lives of the innocent. I have, I believe, fulfilled my mission, so I will allow us both to rest.

Those I have removed from this earth were evil men, well-illustrated in Dante's classic work. May their fate serve as a warning to others whose greed destroys lives. I will leave this mortal plane now and leave judgement for my actions to Him before whom we must all one day stand to be judged.

THE NINE CIRCLES OF HELL KILLER

We wrote the note in English because we felt the international press coverage would be quicker that way. Jesse slipped it under the Inspector's door that night. First thing next morning, the federale was at Tavi's office calling a press conference.

Jesse and I got there just as the first of the media were racing up. The inspector had changed from his tropical "undercover" attire to a conservative dark blue suit. He was already glowing from the attention he would be getting soon. He waved to us but remained seated when we entered. "Gentlemen," he said, flashing a self-satisfied smile. "I suppose you know the good news." He held up the note we'd pasted together. "Would you like to see a serial killer's suicide note?"

We bent down to read what we'd written.

"Why is it in English?" Jesse asked.

"Ah, my friend," he offered, "the mind of a serial killer is a mysterious thing. Perhaps he thought he would achieve more fame."

"It looks like he'd be no match for you, Inspector."

He closed his eyes and accepted the praise with false modesty. "Yes. That is true. He realized I would be hot on his trail. It obviously unnerved him."

Tavi's desk phone chirped. He picked it up and listened briefly. "Sí. Ya venimos."

"Gus, your press awaits."

The inspector shook our hands as he passed. "I know you gentlemen did your best to help. I would be pleased to buy you lunch after the press leaves me alone, if they ever do, ha ha. Perhaps, I can give you a few tips on tracking serial killers should the opportunity present itself again."

Jesse, Tavi, and I grinned to each other.

"We're always grateful to learn from experts," I said.

ACKNOWLEDGMENTS

I'm grateful to the team at the Stable Book Group, particularly Brooke Warner and Shannon Green, for championing this book. Thanks also to Celia Johnson, for her continuous support throughout the process and her many invaluable suggestions that improved the manuscript.

ABOUT THE AUTHOR

Carl Martin Johnson has worked in most Latin American countries. He was briefly arrested in Chile under suspicion of spying for Argentina and was a combat journalist for *Soldier of Fortune Magazine*. His fiction has been published in *Slice* magazine. A native Texan, Carl was accepted into the Australian National Institute of Dramatic Art Playwright Studio. While in Australia, he had a one-act play produced and wrote for a continuing dramatic series for the Australian Broadcasting Network. He graduated from the University of Texas at Austin and did graduate study at the University of Southern California. He currently lives in Allen, Texas.

Author photo © Trish Johnson

Looking for your next great read?

We can help!

Visit www.gosparkpress.com/next-read
or scan the QR code below for a list
of our recommended titles.

SparkPress is an independent boutique publisher delivering high-quality, entertaining, and engaging content that enhances readers' lives, with a special focus on commercial and genre fiction.